to save my child

BOOKS BY EMMA ROBINSON

His First Wife's Secret
My Husband's Daughter
The Forgotten Wife
My Silent Daughter
One Way Ticket to Paris
Happily Never After
The Undercover Mother

to save my child

emma robinson

bookouture

Published by Bookouture in 2021

An imprint of Storyfire Ltd.
Carmelite House
50 Victoria Embankment
London EC4Y 0DZ

www.bookouture.com

Paperback ISBN: 978-1-80019-898-2
eBook ISBN: 978-1-80019-897-5

For Isobel

Who makes my stories bigger, better and braver

ONE

Is there anyone in the world more full of joy than a six-year-old with a feather boa? Libby was strutting up and down the gift shop in her bright yellow boots, green bobble hat and – now – a cheap pink feather boa which she'd borrowed from a display of hen party paraphernalia. All she was missing was a catwalk and an audience.

Anna used her phone to take a couple of photos of her pirouetting daughter. Libby, never one to turn down an opportunity to pose, held her arms out and blew Anna a kiss, which made her laugh. 'Come on, you. We're supposed to be here for party invitations. Not fashion shows.'

Having reached a display of overpriced teddy bears holding heart-shaped messages, Libby spun on her heel and wiggled her hips before dancing back towards Anna. 'Please can I have it, Mummy? Please?'

When she looked at that face, Anna could understand how men made absolute fools of themselves for a pretty girl. Soft blonde curls, long eyelashes and a mouth that was quick to laugh. And pout. It was difficult to deny her anything.

Beyond an early display of Valentine's cards, she could see the young woman behind the cash register watching them with an expression of disapproval. Probably about to tell them they had to buy it now, anyway. 'How much is it?'

Libby screwed up her face as she tried to read the price tag. 'Twelve dot ninety-nine.'

Nearly thirteen pounds? For a bit of fluff? 'That's too much, Lib. We have to get the invites and the balloons yet. You want balloons, don't you?'

Reluctantly, Libby took the string of pink feathers from around her neck and passed it back to Anna. 'I just want to look pretty at my party.'

Anna glanced to see if the assistant was still watching them, then hooked the boa back onto the rail and bent down in front of her daughter. 'You don't need that thing to make you look pretty. You're the most beautifullest girl in the world.'

Libby grinned, old enough to know that wasn't a word, but still young enough to enjoy it. She placed her cold little hands onto Anna's cheeks. 'And you're the beautifullest momma in the world.'

Anna pressed her lips and nose into the softness of Libby's cheek. That was cold too. Outside, it was an icy January morning, but the heating was up so high in here that they'd both taken their coats off. 'Are you feeling okay, Lib?'

Ignoring the question, Libby grabbed Anna's hand and pulled her over to the carousel of party invitations. 'Come on, Mummy. Let's get my invitations. Can I have pink ones?'

For now, Anna didn't push her to answer. In the last couple of months, she'd taken her daughter to their new doctor three times and she got the impression that he thought she was wasting their time. Even her mum had gently suggested that Libby might just be getting used to her new school, new house, new life. 'Kids are very resilient,' she'd been quick to add. 'She'll be fine.'

Libby had been extra-tired the last couple of days though, and had complained of a bit of a stomach ache. But Anna had put that down to the excitement about her upcoming seventh birthday. This was the first time they'd have a party at home. Their new living room was small, so there were only four of her friends coming over, but Libby had barely been able to sleep with excitement when Anna had suggested it a couple of months ago.

'Really, Mummy? Really? Will we have cake and everything?'

Anna had smiled at her eagerness. 'Yes. And maybe some games and we could get some craft stuff and, well, whatever you want really.'

She'd paused at that. 'Will Daddy be coming?'

Anna hadn't been able to work out from Libby's face whether she was hoping that the answer would be yes or no. How much did she remember about the last time they'd seen Ryan? How much had she overheard? 'No, sweetheart. He won't be there.'

Was it even sadder that Libby didn't look surprised at the answer? 'But my friends can definitely come? You won't change your mind?'

Guilt tugged at the edges of Anna's mouth. A memory of Libby's birthday last year. In a different place. A ruined cake. Smashed plates. Hurried text messages to cancel friends before they left home. She forced herself to smile. 'I promise. You can give out the invitations this week if you want?'

Which was why they were here to choose them. Libby's face was a picture of concentration as she perused the carousel of invitations, pressing her finger onto each one as she gave it grave consideration. Last year, Anna had picked them out for her: pale blue with a clutch of balloons in the corner. Her friend Nicole had been with her that time, mocking her indecision and complaining about the minutes they were losing from the bottomless Prosecco lunch she'd booked for them both. Who was Nicole having lunch with these days? They'd barely spoken since Anna and Ryan broke up.

Libby was waving a packet of pearly pink cards in front of her eyes. 'Can I have these, Mummy? They're so pretty.'

Anna looked closer. There was a tiny stork carrying a baby in a bundle. It made her stomach twist. 'They're birth announcements for a new baby, sweetheart, not party invites. What about these ones with the little cats on? You like cats.'

Libby frowned. 'I want these ones. I like birds and babies, too.'

As much as she loved that face, the crease at the top of her nose looked just like Ryan's when he wouldn't back down. 'But they aren't for birthday parties.'

Libby clutched the invites to her chest. 'Please, Mummy. I really want these ones. Please.'

Anna could almost hear her mother's words. *Choose your battles, Anna. You don't want to squash the spirit out of her.* She held up her hands. 'Okay. If they are the ones you want.'

In the five minutes it took to pay for the invitations, Libby managed to tell the assistant – who was now smiling – that she would be seven in three weeks, that she was having a 'proper birthday party' and that the names of her best friends were Karis, Mary, Busola and Emily. She then quizzed her on whether she preferred chocolate or sponge cake.

The assistant laughed. 'I like all cake, to be honest.'

Libby was delighted with that response. 'My mummy is a chef. She makes the best cakes. She can make you one if you want. Can't you, Mummy?'

She looked up at Anna for confirmation. What was she going to say now? 'Well, I... I mean...'

The assistant winked at Anna. Maybe she'd misread the disapproval in her face earlier; she seemed perfectly friendly now. 'It's okay. I'm on a diet. I'm getting married in the summer.'

Libby's eyes widened. 'Are you? Have you got a bridesmaid?'

Anna needed to get her daughter out of the shop before she pitched for her lifelong dream of being a bridesmaid and offered Anna to cater the wedding and make this woman's wedding cake too. Her friendly nature had made the transition to her new school remarkably painless, but it got Anna into some sticky conversations at times. 'Come on, Libby. Let this poor lady serve some other customers.'

Before braving the frosty January air, Anna bent down to help Libby into her warm blue coat. Was she imagining it, or had her little girl's face paled in the last five minutes? 'Libby, are you sure you feel okay?'

Libby shuffled from one foot to the other. 'I feel a bit sleepy.'

It was only ten o'clock in the morning and she'd slept for twelve hours last night. She'd always been a good sleeper, right from when she was tiny. She shouldn't be tired.

'And how does your tummy feel?'

Libby paused as if to think about it. 'A bit funny. And my head is a bit fuzzy.'

It didn't matter what anyone said, Anna knew that something wasn't right and she needed to do something about it. 'Okay, baby girl. I think we need to go to—'

But, before she could finish, Libby collapsed into Anna's arms.

TWO

On the way to the hospital, Anna had to force herself to keep her eyes on the road and not in the rear-view mirror checking on Libby. *Please let her be okay. Please let her be okay.*

The friendly shop assistant had offered to call an ambulance, but Libby didn't seem to have actually lost consciousness and Anna knew it would be quicker to drive her straight to the Emergency Department herself. With every inch of her, she prayed that when they got there, someone would just check Libby over and tell her that everything was fine. Maybe she had a bug or had picked up a little infection? At this stage, Anna would have taken food poisoning or gastroenteritis – or anything that was easily and quickly remedied with a prescription from the hospital pharmacy and some bed rest.

From the back seat, Libby's voice was quiet and weak. 'I feel okay now, Mummy. I don't need to go to the hospital. I want to go home and write my invitations.'

Anna glanced back at her again. Head propped up in her car seat, she looked so pale, so small. 'That's great, Lib. But we just need to get you checked over before we go home.'

The Emergency Department was mercifully quiet and they were taken straight through after triage. After that, everything happened fast. Libby was given a full examination and then her blood and urine were tested. That was when it got even more scary.

The emergency doctor's face was professionally devoid of either positivity or concern. 'We need to take Libby to the renal centre. They'll be able to run some more specific tests there.'

Anna's mouth was dry. The renal centre? That was kidneys. Was this something serious? *Please, no.* 'What kind of tests?'

But the doctor was already being paged to see to another patient and backed away with a wave. 'They'll explain everything when you get up there.'

The renal centre was in another building and was 'all-singing, all-dancing' according to Danny, the cheerful orderly with a waist-length ponytail who pushed Libby there in a wheelchair. She would have been okay to walk, but – despite still feeling poorly – she had jumped at the chance when he'd offered her a ride. In the five minutes it took to get there, he kept her entertained with jokes which he must have learned from Christmas crackers. Anna was very grateful to him: she was so nervous she'd almost lost the ability to speak.

Within minutes of their arrival, they were seen by the consultant on call. Mr Harris had enough grey in his hair to look experienced; his lined face was both serious and kind. He smiled as he crouched down to Libby in the wheelchair. 'I can see that Danny here has been giving you our five-star service. Shall we ask him to take you to our VIP scanner suite so that I can have a look at what's going on inside your tummy?'

Libby looked up at Danny, who winked at her. 'Off we go again, then.'

As they wheeled away, Mr Harris held up a hand for Anna to wait. Once they were out of earshot, he spoke quietly. 'I've seen Libby's urine and blood test results and I want her to have an MRI scan straight away. I'll come over there with you now and we can go through some extra questions that I have.'

Anna followed him down the corridor like a small child. As

much as she was grateful for his personal attention, it surely wasn't normal to be seen this quickly. It must be serious.

They caught up with Danny and Libby before they entered the MRI suite. Mr Harris held the door open and they walked into a small antechamber where a technician sat in front of a screen. On the other side of the window before them, the MRI scanner looked monstrous. Anna reached for Libby's hand and squeezed it.

A smiling nurse took control of the wheelchair from Danny. 'I'll take you inside, Libby. Mummy will wait for you on the other side of the window.'

Anna didn't want to let go of her hand, but Libby smiled up at her. 'Don't worry, Mummy. I'll be back in a minute.'

It was all Anna could do not to sob as she watched the nurse wheel her little girl through and settle her onto the scanner bed. Only two days ago, Anna had remarked to Libby how grown up she looked, standing in the kitchen in her school uniform, able to reach the bottom shelf of the wall cupboard on her own. Now, watching through the window as she disappeared into that huge plastic tunnel, she looked so tiny. So vulnerable.

Behind Anna, Mr Harris was speaking quietly to the technician. Anna caught the words *immediate* and *urgent* before Mr Harris turned towards her with a smile which was clearly meant to be reassuring. 'I know that you have already been through this with my colleague, but can I check again how long Libby's been experiencing these symptoms?'

He wasn't trying to make her feel guilty; she was doing that to herself. 'We've been to the doctor several times in the last year with similar symptoms. Yesterday morning, she told me that she had a sore stomach. Then in the afternoon she said it was hurting when she went to the toilet. Normally I would take her to our doctor. She's had antibiotics for cystitis in the past and I thought it might be that, but they're not open on a Saturday and I was going to wait until Monday and then... then...'

If she had taken Libby to the emergency doctor yesterday, maybe she wouldn't have passed out in the gift shop. Mr Harris was frowning at the paperwork on his clipboard and, when he spoke, she wasn't sure if he was addressing her or the medical notes. 'It's not usual for a child this young to suffer with repeat cystitis. Her blood tests show some issues with her kidney function. We should have seen her earlier than now.' He raised his head and nodded towards the MRI scanner on the other side of the screen. 'As we explained, you are very welcome to stay here with her. That way you'll be able to reassure her over the microphone if she gets upset. Once we have the scan results, we can sit down in my office and discuss what happens next.'

As soon as the doctor left, the technician pushed a blue chair on wheels towards Anna and smiled. 'You're in good hands with Mr Harris. He's very experienced. And the centre here is the best in the country. Everything under one roof: diagnostics, dialysis, transplants. You couldn't be in a better place.'

Anna's legs wobbled as she sank down into the chair. He was trying to make her feel better, but those words hung in the air like threatening storm clouds. There was something wrong with Libby's kidneys? That's what the doctor had said. *We should have seen her earlier.* She wanted to throw up. Why hadn't she realised that her daughter was so poorly?

The nurse closed the door behind her and the technician clicked on his microphone. 'Okay, Libby, we're going to start the scan now, so if you can keep really still for me, it will all be over really quickly. Is that okay?'

'Yes, thank you.' Libby's voice was so small and hesitant, Anna had to clutch the hard plastic arms of the chair to prevent herself from running into the room and pulling Libby out of there. Instead, she fixed her eyes on the top of Libby's head, which was pointing towards the window. *Please let her be okay. Please let her be okay. Please let her be okay.*

Once the scan was over, the same nurse showed them to a play area where they could wait for the results. She introduced them to the playworker on duty, whose broad smile, bright floral shirt and upward lilt to her voice were a welcome splash of colour in the grey of the last few hours. 'Hi. I'm Corinne. Would you like to come and look at some of the games we have, Libby? You can stay here and play when Mum goes to see the doctor?'

Was it good or bad that Mr Harris didn't keep her waiting for long? As Anna entered his office, he motioned towards the chair opposite a large desk, empty except for a computer screen, a pen pot and a dark green folder. Judging by the look on his face, Anna wasn't ready for the news he was going to give her. As fear coursed through her, she wished she'd called her mother from the Emergency Department – she would have come straight to join them, and then Anna wouldn't have to hear this alone.

Mr Harris's voice was kind and gentle, but he cut straight to the point. 'As I suspected, there is a major problem with Libby's kidneys. We need to get her onto dialysis as a matter of some urgency. I'm going to admit her to the renal ward today.'

He paused, as if to let the news sink in. Anna could hear what he was saying, but it wasn't making sense. She just repeated it back to him. 'Dialysis?'

'I'm afraid so. The tests show that her kidneys are failing. The medical term is chronic kidney disease.'

The words felt like they were bouncing off Anna. She tried to focus, think about a question to ask, anything... But all she could process was that her little girl was ill. Really ill. Her little Libby, her only child. Her everything.

The doctor was still talking: 'Eventually and ideally, given her age, we would like to consider her for a transplant, but the immediate issue is improving her kidney function, hence the dialysis. Do you know what dialysis is?'

Anna was vaguely aware of it from watching TV dramas. 'I think so. Is it like cleaning the blood?'

'Yes, exactly. Basically, dialysis performs the functions of the kidney. When your kidneys are damaged by accident or, as in Libby's case, by kidney disease, they are no longer able to remove waste or fluids from your bloodstream. The dialysis takes the blood from the body, removes the waste, and then puts it back in again. It can be a very effective treatment for a long period of time, but the fact is that a transplant is better, and the need for that may become more urgent in due course. Transplants are particularly effective when the disease is found in someone as young as Libby.'

Again, all she could do was repeat the word that her brain was struggling to take in. 'Transplant?'

Mr Harris leaned forwards on his desk, his hands clasped. A pale blue shirt cuff peeped out from beneath his suit jacket. 'I know that this is a lot to absorb.'

Even now, Anna was desperately hoping that somehow, magically, he was going to say that this could all be avoided. 'You said that you should have seen her earlier. Is that why it's serious? Should I have brought her in before now? Is this worse for her because I didn't?'

Mr Harris didn't directly answer her question. 'With chronic kidney failure, there can be no rhyme or reason to it. For some patients, it's a gradual decline; for others, they can be fine for several years and then suddenly it's serious. Looking at Libby's results, we don't need to panic, though. We expect she can be treated effectively on dialysis for a long time, although it will obviously be quite intense for her to have to be in hospital three times a week. Especially at her age, and missing school. However, we're getting ahead of ourselves. Let's get her admitted and then we can discuss again.'

He pushed back his chair as if he was about to get up and leave. Anna's stomach lurched with the squeak of the chair wheels. Not knowing was more terrifying than hearing it all in one go. 'Admitted? I don't understand. Please. Can you tell me everything now? She has to have dialysis three times a week? How does that work? And you want her to have a transplant? How does that happen? What can I do?'

She knew how manic her voice must sound, but she wasn't going to make the same mistake of not knowing again. Mr Harris seemed to understand. He spread his hands out on top of Libby's file and paused before he spoke. 'Okay. Well, I can give you some general information, but we'll know more after we've started Libby on haemodialysis and seen how she responds. The good news is that this is one of the best centres for renal medicine in the country, and Libby will be able to come here for every stage of her treatment. The dialysis will happen three times a week and takes around four to five hours. Where possible, we will fit around her schooling. She will need a small procedure so that we can access her bloodstream for dialysis. There are a couple of options, but I believe that our best option for Libby is an arteriovenous graft. We'll connect an artery and a vein with synthetic tubing. We can do that tomorrow morning. I'd like her to be admitted for that procedure now.'

Anna's heart was beating so fast that it was difficult to breathe. 'Will that hurt? Will she be in pain?'

'It might be a little tender to begin with, and she'll need to wear loose clothing on that arm for a couple of weeks. But once it has healed, you'll just need to ensure that the site is kept clean and check that it is working. But we will teach you both about that before she goes home. All being well, she'll be back home on Tuesday evening with a schedule of her dialysis appointments.'

All being well. It didn't feel as if anything was going to be well, ever again. 'And the transplant?'

Mr Harris was calm and patient. 'Again, we can talk about this in a couple of days. But, yes, I would want to discuss transplant options with you. We can, of course, put Libby on the transplant list. However, a living donor is preferable to a donation from a deceased patient because there is likely to be a much greater life expectancy in the kidney. Libby is young and, although we can transplant another kidney further down the line, and even a third or fourth time, each subsequent transplant is more complicated and the kidney would have a reduced life expectancy.'

A living donor? That, then was something she could do. 'So, I can give her one of my kidneys?'

'We can certainly test you for compatibility if you are willing to be a donor. Yes.'

Was she *willing*? She would give both kidneys, her lungs, her liver, her life: whatever Libby needed to be well. 'I'm her mother, so it's likely I'll be a match, isn't it?'

Mr Harris held up his hands as if to physically stop her. 'Let's slow down. There are various possibilities. Paired donations. Altruistic donors. But the most common living donor is a family member, yes. And parents are often a good match.'

Parents. Mother or father. The doctor was obviously too polite to ask her if there was a father who might also be willing to be tested. And Anna would do almost anything if it meant not having to rely on Ryan to save their daughter.

THREE

The lounge in their two-bedroom house was small, but it was all theirs. When they'd moved in last summer, Libby had been the one to choose the dark pink paint – *If it's just girls in the house, we can have pink, Mummy* – and they'd painted the walls together; Anna cutting in the edges and Libby filling in the middle. Before they'd started, Libby had insisted they write their names in brushstrokes and then daubed a picture of the two of them holding hands. It was lopsided – and not particularly flattering in the hip department – but it had filled Anna with a rush of happiness and relief. They were going to be okay, weren't they? Fresh paint; fresh start. But now there was this to deal with.

As Mr Harris had predicted, Libby was discharged from the renal unit on Tuesday afternoon. Anna called her mother as soon as they got back from the hospital and could practically hear her putting on her coat to come over. Before realising that its biggest advantage was its proximity to the best renal unit in the country, Anna had chosen to live in Corringham because it was only ten minutes away from her mum and fifteen from her sister. Having them so close had felt like a safety net. And right now, she needed to be caught.

'How is she?'

Hearing the concern in her mum's voice almost made Anna cry

again. She'd spent the last forty-eight hours trying to keep her brave face pasted on. Sunday night, she had stayed over with Libby on the ward before her operation on Monday to put in the AV graft for dialysis. Mr Harris had been wonderful with Libby, explaining everything and letting her play with a section of the soft, pliable tubing that would graft the artery with a vein. Repeating the word *arteriovenous* tens of times – with actions – until Libby was satisfied that she'd got her tongue around the word.

'She was so amazing, Mum. So much braver than me. I couldn't believe how good she was.'

Once Libby had given in to her heavy eyelids, Anna had lain awake on the camp bed next to her, watching her breathing in and out, her small chest rising and falling. All evening she had surrounded her daughter with positivity and hope. Once she was asleep, the fear she had fought against crept over her once more. *Please let her be okay.*

As always, her mother's voice was proud. 'She's such a marvel, Anna. I was so relieved that the operation went well. And there have been no problems after?'

'No. All good. One of the dialysis nurses spent some time with her this morning, showing her the two thin needles which will be inserted into the graft for her dialysis and explaining to us about keeping the site clean and how to check that it is working. She has to put her palm on it at bedtime and in the morning to check she can feel a strong buzz.' Again, Anna had been astonished how easily Libby seemed to be taking everything in her stride. Despite admitting that her arm was feeling 'a bit poorly', she had kept up a pretty constant stream of questions the whole time, even asked if she would be able to put the needles in herself. The nurse had promised her that they'd teach her to get her dialysis trolley ready when she came in, and that had seemed to satisfy her.

Her mum breathed out a sigh. 'Well, that's a relief. And when have you got to go back?'

'We've got an appointment card for weekly dialysis sessions on a Tuesday, Thursday and Saturday.' It would mean Libby finishing school a little earlier on those days, and Anna was going to have to sort out her work, but it was the best schedule they could come up with.

'And what about you, my darling? How are you? I wanted to come up to the hospital and wait with you, but Catherine said I had to do as I was told.'

Anna couldn't help but smile. Her older sister, Catherine, had already sent a text saying that she'd had to talk their mother down from getting the bus to the hospital.

I've told Lynn you don't need her there, but I may have to actually sit on her until you get home.

It drove her mother crazy when they used her first name. So, of course, they did it all the more.

'I know, Mum. But they don't like too many people on the ward and we knew we'd only be a couple of days.'

Well, you can't stop me now that you're home. Catherine has promised to finish work early and pick me up, so we'll be with you soon. I can't wait to give Libby a squeeze.'

It was actually Anna who got the first squeeze from her mother when she arrived later. Libby was upstairs in her bedroom, so Anna could indulge herself in a little cry on her mum's shoulder while Catherine snuck what looked like a small sack of sweets up the stairs. 'Oh, Mum, I was so scared.'

Her mum stroked her hair as if she were a small child again. 'Of course you were, my darling. She's your baby. But we've got you. It's all going to be okay.'

Anna nodded as she took the tissue her mum gave her to wipe her eyes and blow her nose. 'Go up and see her. She's really drowsy, but she wanted to see you and show off the evidence of her bravery before she went to sleep.'

'Oh good. I picked something up for her this morning at TK

Maxx on the retail park.' Her mum rummaged inside her ever-present shopping bag and held up a bright yellow T-shirt with a smiling sun, a grumpy rain cloud and a rainbow. 'It's our Libby in a nutshell, isn't it?'

It absolutely was. 'She'll love it.'

Even in the midst of all this, her mum didn't miss an opportunity. 'I can pick some brighter things up for you the next time I'm there?'

Anna rolled her eyes. 'I'm fine as I am, Mum. Go and see Libby. I'll jump in the shower now you're here.'

After reading Libby a bedtime story and giving her the regulation ten-minute cuddle, her mother plonked herself down next to Anna on the small sofa she'd bought from the second-hand furniture shop in the town centre. 'So, then. We need to get our girl a new kidney. Well, they can test me. I have no idea what blood group I am, but she is welcome to any bit of me that is useful.'

Anna smiled. 'Thanks Mum. In terms of the donor, the doctor said that the younger the kidney is, the better. But I do appreciate you offering.'

'Well, I'll still be tested, obviously.'

While Anna had been in the shower, Catherine had found plates for the cakes she'd brought and made them all a cup of tea. 'So will I. And when I spoke to Vikram about it, he said he'd be tested too. I know he's not a blood relative but it's got to be worth a go. Both the boys said they'd do it too, bless them, but I explained they were too young.'

Tears blurred Anna's eyes before she blinked them away. They were so amazing, so generous. All that time she'd lived only an hour away, yet barely seen them. How selfish she had been. What a fool she had been back then.

Her mum reached over and squeezed her hand. 'Come on, love, don't get upset. Us Wallace women are made of strong stuff. We'll get through this, like we always do. Remember what your dad used to say? *When you three gang up on me, I've got no chance.*'

That had been a lifetime ago. Anna didn't remind her mother that she wasn't yet a Wallace again. Legally, she was still a Ferguson. Mrs Ryan Ferguson. And Mrs Ferguson had been a very different creature.

Catherine handed them a small plate each and helped herself to a chocolate eclair before taking the only other chair. 'So, what did the doctor say exactly?'

Anna rubbed either side of her eyes with her forefingers. It wasn't just the doctor's words which had worn her out. Trying to keep positive and upbeat as she'd explained it all to Libby had been exhausting. The doctor had suggested that there was no rush to spell it out to her just yet. Not until they knew for sure what they were going to do. But Anna had always sworn to be open with Libby. 'At the moment, the dialysis will keep her well. But he thinks the sooner she has a transplant, the better.'

He'd also explained that one of the problems with treating kidney disease was that it didn't necessarily progress at a steady pace. You could be okay for years, or you could need a kidney yesterday. It was the uncertainty that made it so difficult to make a decision on what was the best thing to do. She'd tried to explain to Libby that her body was a machine and one of the parts was faulty, so they were going to replace it. Her brave little girl had just nodded. 'Like the batteries in Baby Annabelle?'

'Yes, just like that.' If only she could order a kidney as easily as a packet of Duracell.

Her sister was already in process mode. 'So, we all get tested to see if we are a match and then, if not, they put her on a waiting list for a kidney from someone? Oh God,' Catherine put her hand to her mouth. 'That's a horrible thought, isn't it? Like you're waiting for someone to die.'

Her sister might be super-organised, but she wasn't known for her tact. 'I suppose so. Although you do apparently get living donors giving kidneys to strangers.'

Her mother's eyes widened. 'Really? Well, that's wonderful.

There are some amazingly generous people in the world, aren't there?'

It had been surprising when Mr Harris had told her about altruistic donors. Her own experience of the human race hadn't been quite so positive in the last couple of years. 'Apparently so. The doctor said that a living donor is preferable to a... not living one. Because the kidney is more likely to last longer. In fact, it could last for a long time.'

Mr Harris hadn't been more specific than that this afternoon and Anna hadn't asked. It was hard enough thinking about Libby having to go through this operation once.

This time, Catherine and Lynn glanced at each other before either of them spoke. They'd clearly had a conversation about this in the car on the way over and, whatever silent communication had just passed between them, Catherine had obviously been elected to voice their collective opinion. 'When are you going to call him? Ryan, I mean. When will you let him know about Libby?'

Even the sound of his name made anxiety prickle in Anna's chest. Those four letters floated on the air and she wanted to snatch them down and throw them out of her house.

'He hasn't called Libby in over six months. I'm not sure he would be remotely interested.' She avoided Catherine's eye by picking at the fruit bun on her plate. It was dry.

Catherine was about to use her solicitor voice, which was almost as irritating as her older sister voice. She had always been the clever one – *but Anna is so creative*, their mum used to tell people – and had spent most of their childhood rolling her eyes at Anna's lack of interest in doing her maths homework or learning her French verbs. It wasn't until Anna had found her passion for cooking that she had really come into her own. 'You have to tell Ryan what is happening when it's something this serious. Not doing so when you have shared parental responsibility is irresponsible at best, and illegal at worst.'

She had never *shared* anything with Ryan. He had taken everything and she had let him. Anna's shoulders were practically at her ears and she tried to let it go, this tightness, this fear. It wasn't Catherine's fault: she didn't know the half of it. And Anna had to remember how much she had to thank her sister for. Not only for representing Anna in her attempt to get Ryan to agree to a divorce, but also for pulling in favours from other legal friends to help her rent this little house for her and Libby. Without Catherine, and the money their mother had put towards the deposit, who knew where they would be living right now?

Still, when her sister used that voice, it made Anna feel like a stroppy teenager. 'But we don't share the parenting, do we? Because he doesn't see her, and won't speak to me about anything, not even a divorce.'

Catherine shook her head. 'You have to be reasonable, though. Anything you do – or fail to do – will be hurled back at you by his solicitor if she ever does get to the point of sitting down at her desk and doing anything.'

Their mother laid a hand on Catherine's arm like they were a tag team. Clearly it was her turn to make Anna see sense; tiptoeing towards the point she wanted to make like she was picking her way through verbal landmines. 'We know you're still angry with him, love – and goodness knows, he's not my favourite person after what he did – but he is Libby's father. You need to call him.'

What he did? They thought that she was angry because he'd cheated on her. Because she'd found him in bed with a random woman from work. If they knew what he'd put her through, how hard it had been to extricate herself from him, put herself back together, they might understand why she was so terrified to call him. But she couldn't tell them, because then she would need to tell them what she had done too.

She still couldn't look at them. 'Being a biological father is just an accident. Being an actual father means being there for your daughter. I know what a good father is because I had one.' Now she did look up at them, felt guilty for the flash of pain that crossed her mother's face. 'Libby doesn't have a father like that. Hers is living thirty miles away, sleeping with who knows how many women and pretending that his daughter doesn't even exist.'

Catherine sighed in that world-weary way of hers which signified that Anna – or whoever she was speaking to at the time – was being ridiculous and needed Catherine to spell out the truth to them. It might work well with her legal clients, but it went down sideways with Anna. 'That's the point, though, Anna. He is her biological father. Biological.'

Did she just like the sound of that word, or did she think that Anna was so stupid she needed to hear it twice? 'I know that, Catherine. I was there at the conception, remember?'

Lynn did her usual peacekeeping. 'Don't argue, girls. Anna. We're on your side here, love. Don't bite your sister's head off. She's just trying to help.'

Anna closed her eyes and opened them again. 'I know. I'm sorry. It's just all been a bit much the last couple of days.'

'I'm sorry, too.' Catherine nudged her with her foot. 'I've still got my work head on. But you are going to call him, aren't you? Not even for his benefit: for Libby's. He could be a good match.'

As ever, Catherine was right. Anna was going to call him. Even though every cell of her recoiled from the very idea of hearing his voice. His last words seared across her memory. *Stupid. Ugly. Bitch.*

But, of course, she was going to have to pick up that phone. Because what choice would she have if – God forbid – she turned out not to be a match for Libby? 'Let me get the results of my tests tomorrow and then I'll call him. I promise.'

Not for the first time that day, she sent out a plea to the universe that she would be able to give her daughter the kidney she needed. Because having to ask Ryan for help would give him an upper hand, one that he would be only too happy to slam down on their fragile new life.

FOUR

The Renal and Transplant Unit had only been officially open for a year. In the entrance foyer, there was a picture of Princess Anne unveiling a plaque, and all the furniture in the waiting room still had the smell of new plastic. When Mr Harris had visited Libby after her operation, he had explained to them both that it was rare to have the consultants, dialysis and surgery in one building. 'It should make everything a lot easier,' he'd told them. 'And it means we can move really quickly if we need to.' His words were both comforting and frightening: did he think Libby was about to go downhill fast?

Anna's initial tests to check her suitability to be a donor for Libby were just a medical questionnaire and blood tests. Mr Harris had agreed that there was no point in hanging around, so she'd had the tests while Libby was in surgery on Monday. Wednesday morning, she was back in Mr Harris's office to get the results and find out what came next.

On an ordinary Wednesday at 10 a.m., Libby would be in class and Anna would be in the school kitchen prepping lasagne and vegetarian meatballs. It had been a stroke of luck getting the Catering Manager job at Corringham Primary, Libby's new school. The money wasn't great, but it was so convenient dropping Libby off and then going straight into work. That was something else she was going to have to figure out. The Head had been understanding this week, but she couldn't be off indefinitely. If Libby had to leave school early to get to dialysis, what would she do about her job?

The hospital receptionist smiled as Anna approached the desk. 'Hi. I'm here to see Mr Harris. For test results.'

'Take a seat and I'll call you when he's free.'

The small waiting area was quiet and the air felt heavy with anxiety. Apart from Anna, there were only three other people: an older couple and a man of around forty who stared at the phone he was thumbing through. For something to keep her mind occupied, Anna took out her own phone. There was a message from her mum wishing her luck – she was at Anna's house watching Libby – and another from Tina at work, replying to Anna's message this morning. *All fine here. Not even an exploded jacket potato to report. Stop worrying about us and look after yourselves.*

Anna smiled. Tina had worked in the school kitchen since her own two were at the primary school. When Anna started as Catering Manager, she had thought Tina was going to be difficult to manage. As subtle as a meat tenderiser, she gave short shrift to anyone who didn't work hard. Within days, these became two of the many things Anna liked about her.

A door opened out onto the corridor and Mr Harris stepped outside and looked in her direction. 'Hi. Mrs Ferguson? Do you want to come through?'

She felt tainted by the fact she still had Ryan's name. 'Please, call me Anna.'

'Anna. Please take a seat. How's Libby?'

The office wasn't huge, but it was comfortable. A bookshelf of medical journals and a large desk were strangely reassuring. As were the thank you cards pinned to a noticeboard: grateful patients were a very positive sign.

She took the seat he was pointing to. 'She's great. She actually wants to go back to school already, but I've told her she needs to stay home for a few days. That's for the best, isn't it?'

Mr Harris sat on the other side of the desk. 'Not necessarily.

As long as she can keep the site clean, there's no reason for her not to go back if she wants to. I always think it's best to keep life as normal as possible as long as you can. Children are remarkably resilient, in my experience. Things that knock adults off their feet, they can often bounce back from. Be guided by her when you can.'

He couldn't possibly know how reassuring his words were. Her mum had already agreed to come and stay with Libby when Anna went to work on Monday. Maybe she could let her go back on Wednesday or Thursday. That would be better than a full week straight away. 'How long will she need to take off school when she has her transplant?' She would need to find out how long she would be likely to be off work then, too. Would having a kidney removed be more or less invasive than having one transplanted?

Mr Harris scratched behind his ear. 'We can cover that in more detail when we get to that point. In the meantime, I'm afraid that there's no easy way to say this: your initial tests have shown that you are highly incompatible as a donor.'

If it weren't for the grave expression on his face, Anna would have assumed she'd misheard him. 'Sorry? What does that mean?'

Mr Harris pulled a sheet of paper out from a green folder on his desk. 'We measure compatibility using these three numbers' He pointed with an expensive-looking pen to a row of digits. 'I'm afraid, yours are too high.'

Mr Harris was rattling off details about recipient blood cells attacking donor cells, but the facts bounced off Anna like hail on a tin roof. Of course, she'd known that it was *possible* that she wouldn't be a match, but had just assumed that it wouldn't be the case for them. It just didn't make sense. 'I'm her mother. I mean, she literally grew inside me. How can a mother and child be incompatible?'

It was more than stupid to question the basic biological knowledge of a leading medical specialist, but Mr Harris seemed to understand. 'It is confusing, I know. But it is not a given that a mother and child will have the same blood type. In some cases, it prevents a pregnancy from progressing altogether.'

Anna shuddered. She didn't want to think about that. And she wasn't ready to give up. 'But there must be something we can do? I mean, a way around it.'

Mr Harris nodded. 'Did you say there were other family members who have asked to be tested?'

She hadn't meant that. What she wanted was a way to do something to her kidney to make it suitable for Libby. It should be her, no one else. 'Well, there's my mother. But she is in her sixties and diabetic. Also my sister. And my brother-in-law. Although he is obviously not a blood relative.'

Mr Harris was making notes in the folder. 'That's great. As you can see, being a blood relative is not the be-all and end-all.' He stopped writing and looked up. 'Is there anyone else?'

Again, the anxiety crept up her back like a thousand tiny spiders. It wasn't as if Mr Harris knew anything about her situation. Families came in all shapes and sizes; of course, he wouldn't presume to ask about Libby's father unless she offered the information. 'There might be.'

Mr Harris didn't press her. Merely nodded. 'Well, this is all a lot to take in, I know. Libby is due for her first dialysis as an outpatient on' – he looked again at the green file – 'Thursday the 17th of January. That's tomorrow. Have you been given all the information: what time to arrive, how long you'll be here for and so on?'

Anna pulled her mind away from the dark avenue it was crawling down. Forced herself to remember the conversation she'd had with the doctor who had signed Libby's discharge paperwork. 'Yes. We're coming at two o'clock tomorrow afternoon. The nurse said it would only be an hour the first time?'

Did Mr Harris always look so intently at his patients, or was he concerned that she didn't understand? 'That's right. Then we'll gradually increase it each time. Once we're up to speed, it will take around four hours.'

Normally Anna would be at work until two-thirty, clearing away from lunch, loading dishwashers, prepping anything that needed doing for the next morning. Tina had told her not to worry about it. 'We can sort it out between us. It'll be fine. I'll tell old Jonesy we've got it covered.' She didn't have the energy to care right now whether Mr Jones – the headteacher – would allow her to leave early two days a week. Libby needed to be there for her dialysis and Anna had to be with her. If it meant leaving work and taking a job working nights stacking shelves in the big Tesco on the A13, she would do that.

Mr Harris was still going through the logistics. 'And did the dietitian come to see you while Libby was on the ward?'

'Yes. We talked about potassium and phosphates.' If she hadn't felt so numb, she would have smiled at Mr Harris's raised eyebrow. 'I'm a chef, so I know a lot about food and nutrition.'

'Ah. Well, that's good. Libby will be weighed before every dialysis session so that we can see how much fluid needs to be taken. But the nurses will explain all that to you both as you go along.' He paused and looked at her. Did her face look as terrified as she felt? 'It's going to be okay. We'll look after her. Soon all this will feel completely normal.'

In the car park, Anna sat with her hands on the wheel. She didn't want this to feel normal. She didn't want this to be Libby's life. Three times a week at the hospital. Dialysis. Weight charts. Blood tests. She wanted to make this better. To make it all go away.

She hit out at the steering wheel with the heels of both of her hands, again and again and again until it started to sting. Why hadn't she been a match? Why couldn't they take her kidney? Both of her kidneys? Why couldn't this be happening to her instead of Libby? She leaned her forehead onto the backs of her hands and started to cry. Short, hard sobs. It was so unfair. She would do anything to help Libby right now. Anything.

Her sister was right. There was nothing else for it. She was going to have to ask Ryan. As soon as Libby was in bed tonight, she'd call him.

Her stomach lurched at the thought.

FIVE

At bedtime, Libby had had a million questions about her dialysis the next day. After her AV graft the kind nurse had explained everything to her – to them both – in a clear, easy manner which was reassuring. Since then, they'd got used to checking the site of the AV graft by Libby lightly placing her palm on the top of the operation site and feeling it buzz. Tonight, the questions had been more about the ward to which she'd go as an outpatient. What would it look like? Who else would be there? Would there be another little girl for her to talk to? Could she take her iPad? Would she be able to play *Minecraft* while she was there?

Anna answered all of the questions that she could, but there were many she didn't know the answers to. She was just as apprehensive as Libby: not showing her fear was one of the hardest parts of parenting.

Finally, after three constantly interrupted chapters of *The 13-Storey Treehouse*, Libby's fair lashes fluttered closed and she gave in to sleep. For a few moments, Anna stayed beside her, watching her lips twitch as she slept, her blonde waves splayed across the white pillow. Had her skin always been that pale? Anna herself was slow to colour, so she'd never questioned it before. What else hadn't she noticed? How long had her baby been sick and she hadn't even realised? Before leaving the room, she bent down and pressed her lips to Libby's warm forehead. 'Night night, baby girl.'

Before calling Ryan, she'd make herself a coffee. The spoon was in the jar before she realised what a bad idea that was. It was going to be difficult enough to get to sleep tonight without putting caffeine in the mix. What she really wanted was a glass of wine, but the strongest thing she had in the house was the lemonade Libby had begged for as a treat from the hospital shop. Hardly a drink to settle her nerves. At least it would be easier to call Ryan now Libby wasn't in earshot. Although *easy* and *Ryan* were not two words that she usually put together.

Anna could cover the length of her lounge in five steps – and the width in three – so she lapped it several times in the ten minutes it took her to psych herself up for calling Ryan. Her stomach was in knots, her palms damp. As she walked, she rehearsed out loud what she wanted to say and, even more importantly, how she was going to say it. Calm, but not so laid back that he wouldn't realise the urgency of the situation. Cordial, but not so friendly that he'd think she wanted him back in her life.

For about the hundredth time, she stared at his name on her phone screen. There had been many occasions when she would have dearly loved to delete and block Ryan's number from her phone. But when you had a child in common, you didn't have that luxury. Not that they'd heard from him in over six months. A cold thought trickled into her mind. What if *he* had blocked *her* number? What if she couldn't get hold of him, and he was the only chance that Libby had for a kidney? Did he still even live in the same place?

Just do it. What was the worst he could say? Hadn't she heard it all before? It was just a phone call. It wasn't as if he would be actually *here*. She stopped pacing and pressed his number. It rang eight times and then clicked into voicemail. *Thank God.*

When Libby was small, Anna's mother had sent her a special version of the book *Guess How Much I Love You* with her own voice recorded into it. Whenever Libby opened the front page and activated the recording, Anna would feel herself slipping into sleep, her memory associating her mother's voice with her own childhood bedtime. Voices had the power to do that. Their cadence transporting you to a time or a place or a person you had loved. Unfortunately, the reverse was also true: Anna's stomach was in her throat at the sound of Ryan's recorded message, which was brief and bright and brutal. Just the sound of him – *Hi, this is Ryan. Leave a message and I'll call you back* – was enough to make her feel nauseous.

The initial relief that washed over her at not having to speak to him was short-lived: now she had to leave a message. She pressed her fingernails into the palm of her left hand. *Damn.* 'Hi Ryan. It's me. Anna. I need you to call me. It's about Libby. She's not well. It's serious. Her kidneys aren't working. She's going to need... actually, can you just call me? Thanks.'

She threw the phone onto the sofa. Of course he wouldn't pick up straight away. *I don't dance to your tune, Anna. You dance to mine.* Why hadn't she prepared a voicemail message? *Idiot.* Why had she sounded so hesitant and needy? *Pathetic.* Now he had that to throw back in her face. *You're such a doormat.*

Now she really needed a drink. There was a quarter of a bottle of Marsala wine in the cupboard from the tiramisu she'd made for Catherine's birthday. It'd have to do. But she had only made it as far as the kitchen when her phone started to ring. She leapt towards the sofa and snatched it up to see Ryan's name on the screen. Heat rose in her face. Her arms prickled. *This is for Libby.* She pressed the green 'accept' button. Swallowed down the anxiety wrapping itself around her throat. 'Hi Ryan, thanks for calling me back so quickly.'

There was a moment's pause before he replied. In that second, she could see him, composing himself, making her wait. 'Of course, Anna. I was so pleased to hear from you. You don't know how much I've hoped that you would call me like this.'

Wherever he was, he was using his 'audience' voice, which meant she was safe for now. It was just past eight o'clock, so he could conceivably still be at work with colleagues in the same room. Even so, she resisted the urge to reply that he could have easily called them. 'I need to talk to you about Libby.'

His voice was as smooth as caramel. He was giving her – or whoever else was listening – the full Ryan treatment. 'Of course, I can't believe she has a problem with her kidneys. Sounds awful. What happened?'

Anna hadn't realised that she'd started pacing again. She stopped at the sofa and perched on the arm. 'Nothing. Well, she felt ill, I took her into hospital and they ran some tests.'

This time his voice was a little sharper. 'And you hadn't picked up she was that ill? Before you took her in?'

She closed her eyes and pictured Libby's pale face on her pillow. 'Well, she had been a bit off for a few weeks, but the GP didn't think it was anything serious. Then she kind of, collapsed, so I took her straight to the hospital and they ran some tests.'

Audience voice was back. 'Well, you did the right thing eventually, anyway. What are they planning to do? Is she still in hospital?'

It was difficult not to bite back at his tone. Remind him of the times he'd accused her of overreacting. 'No. She's at home. She'll have dialysis as an outpatient. But the doctor has strongly recommended that we consider a transplant. Sooner rather than later.'

There was a pause at the other end, a muffled voice in the background, before he replied. 'Really? A transplant? Wow. That sounds major.'

'It is.'

'And this doctor knows what he's talking about?'

No, she wanted to scream, *he's a dentist covering for his doctor pal.* 'He's one of the top consultants in the country for paediatric renal disease. The centre here is new and there's everything Libby will need in one place. Plus it means everything will happen quicker than normal, like appointments and test results.'

Those had been the words of the nurse who had rubbed her arm and brought her a cup of tea when Libby was taken down to surgery. Every painful detail of those two days was etched into Anna's memory. The fear of what might happen. The guilt that she should have spotted the symptoms earlier. The gratefulness towards Mr Harris, who had been so kind and thorough and had made sure that she and Libby understood everything, giving them confidence that he would make sure she was okay.

His disdain dripped into her ear. 'Really? In *Essex*? Do you not think we should get a second opinion? Someone in London?'

The 'we' put her teeth on edge like the squeaking brake of an old car. 'No. But we do need to talk about it. The bottom line is, she needs a transplant and... I'm not a match. I don't even have the right blood group.'

How she hated having to tell him that she couldn't do it. It was still difficult to get her head around the fact that she had a different blood group to her daughter. How was that possible? Libby had grown inside her, been part of her. How could she be made of something different?

'So, you're asking me for a kidney? That's what this call is about?' Ryan's voice was louder now, but he didn't seem angry. Was there someone listening at the other end? Or was she just being paranoid?

'I'm letting you know what's going on.' She took a deep breath. *This was for Libby.* 'And, yes, I'm asking if you'll be tested to see if you're a match.'

She held her breath for his reaction, but it was totally unexpected. 'Of course! Of *course*, I'll be tested. To be honest, I don't even know what my blood group is. I've never been in hospital for anything. My doctor always jokes about how ridiculously healthy I am. Yes, yes. When do you want to meet up? I can come to you.'

Anna looked around her. Her walls, her sofa, her rug. No. She didn't want him here. 'I don't know that we need to—'

He cut her off. 'I tell you what. Why don't I take you out to lunch? Both of you? You and Libby. It'll be great.'

Once Ryan got his mind on a plan, he was like a steam train: unstoppable. But she didn't want to have lunch with him and she certainly didn't want him blowing in and out of Libby's life like an unpredictable whirlwind. That was the last thing she needed at the moment. 'Maybe you should hold off on seeing Libby just yet. Until we've talked it all through.'

His brittle laugh was short and abrupt. There was an edge to his voice now, a steel that she recognised of old. 'She's my daughter, Anna. You can't stop me from seeing her.'

She needed to tread very carefully. 'I'm not trying to stop you seeing her. She would love that. But she has a lot going on right now, like her first dialysis session tomorrow afternoon. And if you take her out for lunch, she'll get excited and think you're back in her life. And then if you...' She trailed off. Getting into an argument with him was the last thing she wanted to do. Almost as much as she didn't want to meet him for lunch. 'Look. Why don't I make an appointment with Mr Harris for you to go through everything with him? And then you and I can meet up after and talk.'

'Hold on a minute.' There was another scratchy muffled sound at the other end. Was he covering the microphone? She heard the words *yes* and *of course*. Then he was back. 'Send me Mr Harris's number. I'll make my own appointment.'

In spite of her reservations about calling him, it was a relief to let Ryan sort this out for himself. 'Okay. I'll text it to you.'

'Good. And' – this time his voice dropped to almost a whisper – 'I'm glad you've called, Anna. Really glad. I knew you would eventually.'

SIX

The day after her call with Ryan was Thursday: Dialysis Day.

Anna hadn't been able to eat anything that morning; her stomach felt as if it had been pushed into her throat. She would have given anything to be the one going for dialysis instead of Libby. How did you keep the corners of your mouth turned up when you felt as if the bottom was falling out of your world?

They arrived at the unit with half an hour to spare. Her mum had warned her how full the car park got at the hospital, but they'd been lucky to drive in just as someone else was leaving a spot close to the entrance. Not wanting to go in too early, they sat in the car and played 'I spy'.

It was Anna's turn to guess. 'Fire bucket? Flowers?'

'No! Come on, Mummy!' Libby wriggled in her seat; she loved this game. 'Think! Use the old grey matter!'

Anna laughed. That expression had come straight from her own mother's lips, usually when she was trying to do the *Times* crossword. 'Nope, I can't guess. I give in. What is it?'

'It's...' Libby dragged out the big reveal: 'Photo! Look over there. On the advert.'

She was so triumphant that Anna didn't have the heart to correct her. Instead, she hit her forehead with the heel of her hand in mock exasperation. 'Of course! Silly me!'

The advertisement Libby was pointing at so enthusiastically did indeed have a photograph. Two smiling women with oversized mugs, sitting at a table. Was she imagining the fact that one of them looked just like Nicole? What she would have given to be able to sit with her like that right now, spilling out her feelings. Nicole would have mopped them up and helped her wring them out.

'I win!' Full of her success, Libby practically bounced out of the car. But as soon as they entered the hospital, her steps slowed and her hand slipped into Anna's. Forcing a jolly tone, Anna tried to cover the echo of their steps in the long corridor with comments about the pictures on the wall, but Libby just shrugged.

When they got to the main reception of the Renal and Transplant unit, they were met by a smiling young woman in a crisp blue uniform. 'Hi. You must be Libby? I'm Rose, one of the nurses here. How are you today?'

It tore at Anna to see her bright, sparky girl looking so frightened. 'I'm okay, thank you.'

'Well, that's great. I'm going to explain everything to you as we go through it, but if you want to know anything you can stop me at any time and ask. We'll just take it slowly. How does that sound?'

Libby bit her lip and nodded. Her voice was barely above a whisper. 'Thank you.'

The room was smaller than Anna had expected. Of the ten reclinable chairs for dialysis patients around the edge, seven were taken by people older than Anna's mum. But, on the right, there was a boy not much bigger than Libby, holding a book which looked heavier than he was.

Rose pointed to a chair which was on the same corner as the boy. 'Okay, Libby, would you like to sit over here?'

Libby pressed herself into Anna's side and twisted the bottom of Anna's jacket between her fingers. Anna took a deep breath. 'Come on, honey, let's go and see how this is going to work.'

As they walked towards him, the boy looked up. A heavy fringe fell over one eye and his face broke into a smile at the sight of Libby. 'Hi! I'm Max. I'm nine.'

There was something about Max's grin, and the freckles across his nose, that made you want to smile back at him, but Libby couldn't have got any closer to Anna if she'd climbed inside her pocket. 'Hello.'

Rose smiled at Libby. 'Max is a professional at this business now, aren't you, Max? I bet he could tell you more about this than I could.'

Max clearly didn't need asking twice. Placing his bookmark carefully, he passed the weighty hardback to the woman sitting next to him, who had to be his mum. 'Okay, Rose is going to hook you up to the machine. It doesn't hurt, but you have to stay still otherwise Rose goes crazy.'

Rose laughed. 'You cheeky monkey. When have I ever told you off?'

Max winked at Libby. At least, it looked as if he was trying to wink. Half his face creased with the effort of getting it right. 'I'm only joking. Rose is very nice. It's Pat you want to watch out for.'

'Maxie, that's enough now. You're going to frighten the poor girl. She doesn't know that you're joking.' Max's mum smiled at Libby. 'Just ignore him. He wants to be a stand-up comedian when he grows up, so he thinks that everyone finds him funny.'

Anna put her hand on the top of Libby's head, then bent down to kiss it. 'That's okay. We like a joke, don't we, Libs?'

The woman rolled her eyes. 'You might regret saying that. I'm Julie. Max's personal assistant and mother.'

She could have guessed that from the colour of her hair: both Max and his mother had the same thick, fiery red hair, though hers was threaded with blonde highlights.

'I'm Anna. Libby's mum. This is our first time here.'

Rose tapped the arm of a blue seat with a tall back. 'Can you pop your coat off and sit here, Libby? And then I'll talk you through it all.'

Libby slipped off her jacket and handed it back to Anna. After the frosty morning outside, it felt really hot in here and Anna took off her own coat, draping them both over her arm as she watched

Rose explain the process to Libby, taking the time to show her all the equipment, making sure that none of it made her anxious or uncertain.

Max was leaning forward in his seat like a medical inspector, ensuring that Rose didn't forget anything.

Libby's voice was still small when she asked a question. 'How long does it take?'

'Usually, once you're all hooked up and ready to go, it'll be about four or five hours. Today we're just going to do an hour, though, and see how you feel.'

Libby frowned. Like most six-year-olds, she had no real concept of time. Anna leaned down to her. 'Five hours is less time than you would be at school, Libs.'

Julie, Max's mum, tapped him on the leg. 'Speaking of school, it's time for you to do some of the work they sent home for you, Max.'

Max groaned. 'It's boring.' He changed his voice and put a hand to his throat. 'I'm too poorly to do any literacy.'

Libby giggled at him and Max, clearly loving the attention, really put some dramatic effort into his lolling tongue and wheezing breaths.

Rose shook her head as she connected up the dialysis machine. 'You'll have your own comedy show here, Libby. All part of the service.'

Within ten minutes, Libby and Max were chatting away like firm friends, even arguing about the finer points of *Minecraft* castle building – whether pink or green was a more appropriate colour for the turrets – like brother and sister. Julie leaned forwards and spoke in a stage whisper: 'I don't think they need us. Shall I introduce you to the joys of the free coffee machine?'

Just outside the entrance doors to the ward was a coffee machine that looked like something from the space age. Anna had high hopes, but Julie quickly managed her expectations. 'It's hot and wet. That's as good as it gets, I'm afraid. In future, I'd recommend picking up a drink from the canteen before you come.'

She wasn't wrong. 'How does it manage to be both bitter and chalky at the same time?'

Julie shrugged. 'Beats me.'

There were a couple of couches and a small coffee table to the side of the machine. Julie nodded towards them. 'Sometimes I sit out here to get a break from in there. The kids will be fine with the nurses and it's a good place to have a chat without their eager ears eating up every word.'

Anna smiled. It would be good to talk to someone who was going through this too. 'Is it that obvious? That I'm finding this really hard?'

'If you weren't finding it hard, that would be more worrying. Come on, let's sit for five.'

The couches weren't particularly comfortable, but Anna felt real relief as she recounted to Julie the events of the last few days, ending with what Mr Harris had said about a transplant. And that she wasn't a suitable match.

Julie's face crumpled with sympathy. 'Oh, that's really tough. It was the same for me.'

With those six words, Anna felt as if this woman had reached out a hand and grabbed hold of her. 'Really?'

Julie nodded. 'I was devastated. It's what you do, as a mum, isn't it? Sacrifice? They get the best slice of cake, the extra Yorkshire pudding, the expensive school shoes while you go without. It's how we're programmed.'

Anna bit down hard on her lip. This was it. Exactly. 'So what are you going to do? For Max, I mean?'

Julie waved away her own experience. 'It's complicated with Max. I'll tell you about it another time. How are you feeling about all of this?'

Anna took a deep breath. 'Scared. To be honest. Really scared. Even the dialysis seems terrifying. And the thought of her having a major operation. Someone else's kidney? In one way, it seems good. I mean, if it all works out, she'll have a pretty normal life. But...'

Julie put her hand on Anna's arm and squeezed it. 'Don't think about the *but*. Let the doctors worry about that. I know it feels like a huge responsibility, making the decision. But we're not qualified doctors, are we? All we can do is take their advice, isn't it? Anyway, Mr Harris wouldn't steer you wrong.'

She was right. Anna had laid awake last night wondering if Ryan had been right about a second opinion. But she knew that Mr Harris was well respected. There wasn't really a decision to make. 'I'd just feel better if I could donate one of mine. I mean, at least I'd be doing something.'

'I completely get it. I spent days ranting about it to anyone who was unlucky enough to cross my path. Max is O positive. He can only take a kidney from O blood groups. Which rules me out because of my stupid blood.' She smiled at Anna, but her eyes showed the truth. 'Do you have anyone else who is going to be tested, or will you have to wait in the queue?'

'We do. My mum and sister have been tested. And my sister's husband. And I've also called Libby's father. We're not together and he hasn't really been on the scene for a while. But it was obviously the right thing to do.'

Julie sipped at her scalding black tea. 'And he's going to be tested too?'

'I hope so.' Even as she said the words, Anna wasn't sure if she meant them. Of course, she wanted Libby to have every chance of a healthy kidney, though even that wasn't a magic wand that would make her free of health issues. Mr Harris had taken pains to emphasise that a transplant was treatment, not a cure. But it would mean she wouldn't have to go through these dialysis sessions three times a week. She could carry on living a life that was normal for a six-year-old.

If only Anna could be the one to provide the kidney. She didn't want to ask her mum. Or her sister. Or any of the people she loved.

And she definitely didn't want Ryan flying in like some kind of superhero: he didn't deserve it.

'Does your ex have the same blood group as Libby? Or a compatible one? If he's O, you might be home and dry. They are the universal donor. Potentially, they can save anyone.'

And wouldn't that be exactly how he would phrase it. 'I don't know. Neither does he. Apparently, he's never needed to find out.'

Julie laughed, although there wasn't a lot of humour in it. 'Can you imagine being so fortunate that you don't even know your own blood group?'

Anna was just about to agree when her phone rang. Her stomach lurched when she saw Ryan's name. 'That's him now.'

Julie stood up. 'You speak to him and I'll let Libby know you'll be through in a few minutes.'

As soon as Julie had gone through the double doors into the dialysis suite, Anna pressed to accept Ryan's call. 'Hello?'

His voice sounded surprised. 'Oh. You are there. It rang so many times I thought you must have lost your phone.'

Panic rose up in her chest, which made her want to slap herself. *You don't answer to him any longer.* 'I'm in the hospital, Ryan. Didn't I tell you? Libby has her first dialysis. I can't really talk here. What can I do for you?'

He chuckled at the other end. 'Now there's a question. Actually, I'm here too.'

She frowned. Did he mean he was at the hospital? Surely, he hadn't got an appointment with Mr Harris already? 'What do you mean? Are you here for tests?'

He laughed again. 'No, of course not. But it's nice that you're concerned about me. No. I'm outside in the car park. I thought I'd come and see Libby.'

Anna's mouth was dry, and it wasn't the cheap hospital coffee. 'She's having her first dialysis, Ryan. You can't just come in here.'

She counted the five beats of his trademark pause. 'But you're there.'

Did she really have to go through this with him? 'I'm her mother. She needs me here.'

His response was quicker, and harder. 'And I'm her father.'

Anna didn't have the energy for this. Why did he have to make parenting into a point-scoring exercise? This was about Libby, not them. 'Look, there's another mum here who can keep an eye on Libby. I'll pop out and speak to you. I'll meet you at the entrance to the car park.'

As usual, he wouldn't acquiesce to any suggestion of hers. 'It's freezing out here. I've seen your car. Why don't you meet me there and then we can at least sit inside that if you won't let me come in and see my own daughter.'

Anna shut off her phone and closed her eyes. *And so it begins.*

SEVEN

To be fair, Ryan hadn't been exaggerating about the temperature. Anna pulled her coat around her, keeping her head down against the biting January wind. It wasn't the most flattering of looks, she knew. But that didn't warrant the insulting double take that Ryan performed as she walked towards him. Her face was the only part of her that was warm.

By the time she reached the car, her heart was thumping so hard she was sure he must be able to hear it. His absence for the last six months had done nothing to lessen his effect on her. If anything, it was worse. In her imagination he had become even more monstrous. She tried to avoid looking directly at him as she fished in her pocket for her car key and beeped to unlock it. 'I can't stay long.'

Ryan folded himself into the passenger side and then used the lever to slide the seat back as far as it would go. She'd need to remember to slide it forward again before Libby got in the back. 'This feels very clandestine.'

She stared forwards through the windscreen. 'It's easier than talking on the phone.' That wasn't true. She was here because she'd been worried that he would take it into his head to appear at the ward. She could imagine just how easily he might have charmed a nurse or receptionist to show him the way. 'I thought we'd agreed that you'd wait to see Libby? Today is difficult enough for her as it is. I don't understand why you'd just turn up.'

She forced her head to turn towards him at the same time as he shifted himself sideways to face her, unbuttoning the top of his suit jacket so that it didn't crease. It was no wonder he had suggested sitting in the car: his clothes were designed for style over warmth. 'I had a meeting not far from here. It finished early and I thought it would be nice to see Libby. To surprise her.'

It was so odd, being this close to him. Her Nissan Micra didn't leave much room between the two of them, so he was close enough that she could smell the familiar tang of his expensive aftershave. However she felt about him, she couldn't deny that he was a good-looking man. Chin tilted, pale blue eyes looking up at her from underneath eyelashes that she'd always argued were unfair to be wasted on a man. His shirt was taut across his chest, advertising the fact that he was still spending a fair amount of time in the gym.

She cleared her throat. 'What you see as a surprise might feel more like a shock to Libby. You haven't seen her in six months, Ryan. That's a long time in her life.'

He narrowed his eyes. 'A shock? Are you trying to imply that she wouldn't want to see me?'

'Of course not.' She knew full well that Libby would love to see her dad. For the first two months after that last horrendous visit, she had asked every weekend, 'Is Daddy coming?' Her disappointment every time twisted Anna's stomach with guilt and anger: guilt that she'd taken Libby away from her father; anger that he couldn't be bothered to drive less than an hour to visit his daughter. 'She would love to see you. But the nurse said the dialysis might take it out of her. She'll be sleepy and possibly grumpy by the time we get to the car. It's better to stick to the original plan of waiting.'

There was an edge to Ryan's voice. 'Your plan, you mean?'

Anna sighed. Libby wasn't the only one who was tired. 'Well, I'm the parent who has been looking after her. Possibly I know a little better what she can handle.'

'Well, that was your choice, Anna. I didn't ask you to leave.'

She'd have to tread carefully if she wasn't going to be sucked into a tennis match of blame. 'This isn't about you and me, Ryan. Libby is your daughter, whatever happens between the two of us. And how is your love life, by the way?'

Ryan adjusted his shirt collar as if it felt tight. 'Okay, Anna. You've made your point. Can't we put our differences behind us, for once? I just want to see my little girl. Surely, you wouldn't deny me that?'

How was this her fault? She had never told him to stay away. 'I'm not stopping you from seeing her. Just not right now.' Anna looked at her watch. 'She's going to be in there for about another thirty minutes. Then I'm going to need to get her home, fed and in bed. Tomorrow, I'll tell her that you want to see her and we'll make a plan. How does that sound?'

He looked at her as if he was trying to work out the catch, the trick. 'And when will you allow me to actually see her?'

'This weekend. Sunday is a good day. She has her dialysis on Saturday, so we've kept Sunday clear. We could meet you somewhere for lunch.' Something occurred to her. 'Just you.'

A smile played around the corner of his lips. 'I have no idea what you mean. Who could I possibly be thinking of bringing?'

He was clearly baiting her. *Say nothing.* 'Great. Well, Libby likes the local Harvester at the Five Bells so—'

'The Harvester?' he laughed. 'I think we can do a bit better than that.'

He was such an insufferable snob. 'It's what Libby likes.'

He held up his hands in submission. Clearly, he'd slid straight back into reasonable Ryan mode. 'Then Harvester it is. What time shall I pick you up?'

Although she'd been the one to suggest it, it felt as if he was taking the reins. 'I don't know. Let me see. Maybe it would be best to meet you there.' There was no way she wanted him inside her house. That she did know. 'I really need to go. Someone is watching Libby, but I don't want to leave her for too long. She might need me.'

Ryan nodded. 'Okay. I'll leave you to it.'

For a split second, it looked like he might be about to lean over and kiss her goodbye. Before he could, she fumbled with the handle on the door and almost fell out of it.

Again, that smile on the edges of his mouth as he climbed out and then pressed the door closed. 'Take care. And when you speak to Libby about me, will you tell her that I've missed her?'

For a moment, there was a fleeting vulnerability in his face that she hadn't seen before. He looked as if he genuinely meant it. She'd meant what she said, too. Whatever happened between them, he was still Libby's dad, and Libby loved him. 'Of course, I will.'

Back in the dialysis suite, Libby had barely noticed that Anna had been gone. She and Max were watching a YouTuber unboxing a huge carton of toys.

Julie shook her head at Anna. 'I have no idea how they can watch this rubbish. This is about the tenth one I've had to listen to.'

Anna reached over and squeezed Libby's knee. More to reassure herself than Libby. 'Me neither. Thanks for watching her.'

'No problem at all. Everything okay?'

'Yeah. I think so.' Actually, it had been. After the initial strangeness, it had been remarkably civil. Maybe Ryan did just want to see Libby. It wasn't as if they could just wipe out his absence of the last few months, but there was a bigger issue to deal with right now. Like it or not, they needed him.

Once the dialysis was finished and Libby had said a prolonged goodbye to Max – even though they were due to see each other again in two days – Anna bundled Libby into her warm coat and took her hand. 'Come on, Libs. Let's get you home.'

Libby rubbed at her nose. 'Can I have pizza?'

'Not tonight, bunny. But we have got leek and potato soup in the fridge at home.' Her mother's recipe had been a firm favourite with Libby since they'd moved back to Essex, and she'd dropped off a vat of it yesterday, 'Because you don't want to have to worry about cooking when you get back.'

'Nana soup? Brilliant!'

Anna smiled. Everyone thought their child was wonderful, but Libby really was. Such a happy, brave little girl. 'And if you finish your soup, I might be able to rustle up a custard tart.'

Libby grinned. 'I love custard tarts.'

Anna pushed open the heavy door to the car park, then bent down to kiss Libby on the top of her head. 'I know you do, poppet.'

She heard Libby's gasp before she looked up and saw what had caused it. Not five feet from her car, Ryan stood holding a teddy bear half the size of Libby.

Libby's voice trembled a little. 'Daddy?'

Ryan looked as if he'd been caught. 'Libby. Hey, baby girl.'

Anna had to hold tight to Libby's hand to stop her from running across the car park. Ryan walked towards them and held out the bear. 'This is for you.'

Ryan had always loved an extravagant gift. When they were first together, he used to find the most amazing things. At the beginning, he would listen, too. If Anna said that she was interested in something, he would search it out and get it for her. One Christmas, he had bought tickets for a Tennessee Williams play that she'd mentioned she'd studied for A level, then hidden them in a copy of the script which he'd wrapped and placed under the tree.

He crouched down in front of Libby in an empty car parking space. 'I can't believe how grown up you look. I've missed you so much.'

Libby had no problem forgiving him for his absence. She threw her arms around his neck. 'I missed you, too.'

Once she was cuddling the bear, Ryan stood up and looked at Anna. 'I was on my way home and then I remembered the teddy bear. I was just going to leave it on the bonnet of your car, honestly.'

Libby's face peeked over the top of the teddy bear she was struggling to keep her arms around. 'Can Daddy come home and have some Nana soup, Mummy? Can he? Please?'

Ryan held out his hands in a 'what can I do?' pose.

Which meant Anna had to be the bad guy. 'Not tonight, Libby. But Daddy is going to take us for lunch on Sunday.'

Ryan bent down to Libby. 'And I can't wait to be out with my two best girls again.'

He looked up at Anna and it was all she could do to keep her teeth clamped shut. Libby might be his daughter, but Anna was not 'his' anything. Not any longer.

EIGHT

Friday was pizza day at Corringham Primary. Strictly speaking, Anna didn't start work until nine thirty, but she usually came directly to the school kitchen after dropping Libby to her classroom door: there was no point going home only to head straight back. Although she wasn't bringing Libby today – she'd been so tired after dialysis, Libby had reluctantly agreed to Anna's proposal that she stay home with Nana until next week – Anna was still the first of the kitchen staff to arrive. The strip lights dinked as she switched them on.

Being in an empty kitchen made her feel calm. This was her environment: she knew what she was doing here. From a really young age, she'd loved to bake with her mum. Then she'd moved onto pancakes and omelettes. By the age of nine, she was making lasagne for the whole family. Catering college had been an obvious choice after her A levels.

Moving to a college in West London from her small town in Essex had been an epic adventure. Exciting and terrifying in equal measure. Days were spent learning her craft, evenings she nursed pints of snakebite and black in the college bar. Nicole, who was studying Hospitality and Hotel Management, had the room next to her in their shabby student house. Many a drunken night they had conjured up names, colour schemes and menus for the boutique hotel and restaurant they would open together one day.

Moving methodically around the kitchen, Anna switched on all the cookers and the steamers. Sometimes it felt like she was preparing a space shuttle, the number of switches and dials she had to press and turn.

Underneath a huge fur-lined hood, Tina shuffled in. 'Morning!'

Anna glanced at the large clock on the far wall. 'You're early.'

Tina pushed the hood off the back of her head and unzipped her coat. 'Yeah, there was a big argument at home about who had eaten the last of the Crunchy Nut, so I've come here for a bit of peace. I'll get the kettle on. Coffee?'

'Please.' Tina disappeared into the small office which doubled as a cloakroom. Her kids – who Anna assumed were the ones fighting over the breakfast cereal – were in their mid-teens. Anna had met them both at Tina's fortieth birthday party last November. Zak had disappeared in the direction of his Xbox pretty quickly, but her daughter Gracie had stayed to chat and she was just like her mum: short, soft featured, quick to laugh. Even though Tina had assured Anna the party was a 'small gathering', her house had been full of people. Anna had tried to hide in the kitchen, sneakily washing up glasses and plates until Tina caught her and pulled her into the loud melee.

When Tina reappeared from the office, she was clutching a packet of Jaffa Cakes. 'They were so busy rowing about their breakfast, they didn't notice me swipe these out of the cupboard.'

Anna smiled. Tina often arrived with some form of treat; she liked to say that she'd never met a cake she didn't like. 'Great. I could do with some biscuits this morning.'

Tina ripped open the box and slipped out the plastic wrapping. 'I thought you might. How's Libby?'

Libby had been more upset about staying home from school than she had been about having an operation. 'She's fine. She's at home with my mum. Dialysis was okay yesterday. But... Ryan turned up at the hospital.'

Tina stopped wrestling with the Jaffa Cakes wrapper. 'As in, your ex, Ryan?'

Anna took the packet of biscuits from her, tore it open and passed it back. 'Yep. He called me from the car park. He wanted to see Libby.'

Tina looked as if she'd just smelled stale milk. 'I hope you told him to get lost.'

If only she was as able to speak her mind as Tina did. 'How can I? If I'm not nice to him, he might change his mind about seeing Mr Harris, getting tested.' Many times, there had been a big difference between what Ryan said he'd do and what actually happened. Other times, he had followed through on a threat she hadn't believed. It was difficult to know which was worse.

Having just taken a large bite of Jaffa Cake, Tina had to chew quickly and swallow before she replied. 'What kind of father wouldn't get tested? So, what happened?'

Talking about Ryan had squashed Anna's appetite, so she shook her head at the proffered biscuits. 'I asked him to wait until Sunday to see her and he agreed. But when we came out, he was still there, huge teddy bear in his arms.'

'What?' Tina's sharp intake of breath started her on a coughing fit followed by two sneezes; she waved away Anna's concern. 'I'm okay. What was he thinking? He just completely ignored what you asked?'

'I don't know.' She still wasn't sure whether to believe Ryan's story that he had left and come back. His car had been parked close to hers the second time, but as it was a new car she'd never seen before, it could have been there the first time too, and she wouldn't have known it was his. 'Libby was so excited to see him.'

'I bet she was. How long has it been?'

'Six months.' Anna could remember that night like it was yesterday. On the doorstep, Ryan had told her to 'stop this divorce nonsense and come home.' Said he'd 'had enough of her games.'

When he'd realised that she wasn't going to give in like she had every time before, that had been when the real nastiness had started. The vile names. The intimidation. The threats. It still made her shudder at how close he had come to pushing her aside and telling Libby what she'd done.

Some of her memories must have clouded her face, because Tina was gentler when she next spoke. 'And no phone calls in that time? No letters? Birthday cards?'

Anna shook her head and stood up from where she'd been leaning against one of the large upright refrigerators. 'No. Although she hasn't had her birthday yet. It's in a couple of weeks' time.'

'Of course. So, did he come back to yours last night?'

'No. I managed to prise Libby off him and remind her that she needed to get some rest. I promised that we would see him this weekend. She wasn't happy, but Ryan made up some story about needing to get home. Said he had training to get to.'

She'd been surprised that he'd supported her. After his ill-judged reference to 'his favourite girls', Libby had held onto him tightly. 'Don't go, Daddy.'

And he had dealt with the situation surprisingly well. 'Your mum's right, Libby. We'll have much more fun on Sunday.' He had smiled up at Anna from where he was crouched in front of their daughter. She'd returned the smile before she'd realised what her mouth was doing.

Inside the little office, the kettle clicked off and Tina stepped back inside to make their coffee. 'Training for what?'

'He does triathlons.'

'Triathlons. Blimey.' Tina passed her a mug of coffee. 'Sure you won't have a Jaffa Cake?'

It felt good to laugh.

Just before nine thirty, the rest of the kitchen staff arrived and Anna handed out the day's jobs. At some point, she was going to have to see Mr Jones to ask about changing her hours on dialysis days. She couldn't afford to lose any money. Finances were already tight. Which reminded her. 'Tina?'

Tina turned from the dishwasher, which was already half full. 'Yes?'

'I meant to ask you to thank your John for me. For getting those leaflets printed for Anna's Kitchen. I was going to bring him round some beers, but then this week happened and I forgot all about it.'

Tina smiled. 'No need. He was happy to do it. Just remember us when you have any leftovers from the posh parties you'll be catering.'

Starting up a catering business felt quite daunting, even though Anna had worked in kitchens her whole life. After college, she'd worked in a hotel restaurant in Mayfair, mostly washing dishes and being a general dogsbody. It had been the hardest, most exhausting, most fabulous thing she'd ever done. You needed to have worked in a kitchen like that to understand the pressure, the atmosphere, the exhilaration. There were TV shows now which took the audience inside the lives of these kitchens, but they didn't come close to showing what it was like.

It was a strange twilight life, though. By the time they'd finished cooking and had cleaned down the surfaces, prepped any ingredients and marinades for the next day, they were leaving work at the same time as the rest of the city was tucked up in bed. Inevitably, the people she worked with became the people she went out with. Though they were exhausted, a busy night in the restaurant meant that their heads were too wired to go home and sleep. Being in the centre of London meant there was always somewhere to party, and they didn't need to be back in work until midday. By then, she and Nicole lived in a shared house in Hackney with a couple of Americans they'd known from college, but with their different shifts, they could go for almost a week at a time without seeing one another.

After six months at that hotel, Anna had moved to being a commis chef in a Michelin-starred restaurant in the West End. Pre-theatre and post-theatre meals made for long shifts. She lost touch with the Mayfair gang, but it was around that time that the Americans went home and they had to find new flatmates. Nicole had the perfect solution. Two friends she'd known since school were fed up of commuting to London from Hertfordshire and were looking for somewhere to live closer to their jobs in the city. One of them was Ryan.

'Baked beans are in the steamer, Anna. Shall I start prepping the pizzas?' Frankie was new, but already she felt like one of the team.

Anna glanced at the clock above the serving hatch. 'Can you call the office and see if the lunch registers are up yet? If not, you can start the bases, but don't put any toppings on until we know who's decided to go vegetarian this week.'

Frankie laughed. 'Is the sauce already done?'

'Yes, Tina made it yesterday, so it's in the back fridge.'

It was a source of pride how much of the food was made from scratch, now. That's how she and Tina had hit it off. Apparently, she had nagged the last catering manager for months to let her make the tomato sauce for the pizza and pasta, but he had wanted to stick with buying it in jars. When Anna had told the head-teacher she wanted to change to making it themselves, Tina had clapped her hands and rolled up her sleeves.

Once everyone knew what job they were on, the kitchen would run like a well-oiled machine all morning until it was time to prepare for the influx of hungry children at midday. At ten thirty, Anna was in the office planning a dry goods order, when Tina stuck her head around the door and winked dramatically. 'Mr Benham to see you.'

It was obvious what that wink meant. Anna wagged a warning finger at Tina and pushed her chair away from the desk. 'Don't start.'

Tina held up her hands in mock innocence as Anna walked out of the office and through the kitchen to the school hall, where Libby's teacher was waiting for her. 'Hi Paul, did you want to see me?'

In the classroom, Mr Benham was confident, funny and Libby adored him. When he spoke to Anna, however, he would shuffle from foot to foot, clicking a pen, rustling papers or flicking through the pages of a book. 'Hi. Yes. Sorry to interrupt you working, but I had some planning time and I wanted to speak to you about Libby. Mr Jones gave me an update on what's happened. Is she all right?'

It was getting tiring, explaining this to everyone. 'Yes. Well, we hope so. She's started dialysis and seems to be coping well with it. We are hoping she will be able to have a transplant, but there's no clear plan for that at the moment.'

His eyes widened. 'A transplant? That's a lot for her to take in. And for you.' He looked her in the eye. 'How are you coping?'

Despite herself, Anna couldn't help a nervous flutter in her stomach at the intensity of his expression. 'I'm okay. Just getting my head around it all. Libby will be back next week. She was desperate to come in now, but the dialysis takes it out of her. I want to give it a week for her to get used to it before she tries to do school and dialysis in the same day.'

'Of course. Of course. Well, I mainly wanted to say that I'm here to support her, whatever she needs.' He coughed. Lowered his voice. 'And whatever you need, too. We're colleagues. Friends. If you need anything, just shout.'

Anna's face grew warm. He was just being nice, she knew that. That's who he was: a nice guy. She only felt embarrassed because of Tina and her winks and comments which started after they'd sat and chatted at the staff Christmas do. She had tried to tell Tina there was nothing in it. 'Just because neither of us wanted to be up on the dance floor with you lot. Doesn't mean there was an ulterior motive.'

But Tina didn't believe her. 'What about all those stories you told me about you clubbing in London till 5 a.m. with that Nicole friend of yours? You can't tell me a bunch of teachers swinging their hips at the Old Regent Ballroom was too much for you. He fancies you. It's obvious.'

It wasn't obvious to Anna. And she wasn't the same person as that girl who had bounced around the dance floor with Nicole, fuelled on vodka and adrenaline. Life had changed her. Ryan had changed her. And, this Sunday lunchtime, she was going to have to sit opposite him and pretend that she wasn't absolutely hating every moment of it.

NINE

On Sunday morning, Anna woke with a tightness in her stomach which made it impossible to eat breakfast. Libby, on the other hand, had been ravenous since her second dialysis the day before and requested three pancakes: one with Nutella, one with lemon and one with honey. Normally, Anna would say that was way too much sugar for a little stomach, but she was letting Libby have whatever she wanted right now.

From the moment her eyes were open, Libby had also been chattering with excitement at the thought of meeting Ryan for lunch. Her enthusiasm was so welcome after her sleepy irritability yesterday evening that Anna was almost glad that they were meeting him. 'How long is it now, Mummy? How long till we meet Daddy?'

Anna glanced at the clock on the wall. 'Three more hours, yet, baby girl.'

'Does Daddy like restaurants? Did you go to restaurants when we lived with Daddy?'

Was it strange that Libby couldn't remember? 'Sometimes we did, yes.'

. . .

At weekends, after Ryan and Kevan had moved into the house in Hackney with her and Nicole, Anna would bring leftovers from the restaurant home with her and the four of them would sit up late eating gourmet scraps with their cheap red wine. If Nicole had an early shift at the hotel, she would slope off to bed first. It didn't take long for Kevan to deduce that three was a crowd.

Once they were a couple, Anna would slip into bed with Ryan after a late weekday shift at the restaurant, preferring his warmth to the heat of the clubs her colleagues were hitting. Nicole had been upset about it at first, making barbed comments about how they may as well rent out Anna's room, but she'd had a steady stream of boyfriends herself in those days. For over a year, it had been brilliant. Looking back at those days, Anna could only remember love and laughter, frantic nights out and passionate nights in. It wasn't until Kevan decided to move back home to his parents' to save up a deposit that Nicole announced that she wanted to move to Hammersmith to be nearer to her new hotel manager job. Ryan was rising through the ranks of Pricewater-houseCoopers by that time and he was fed up with renting. With help from his parents, he was able to put down a deposit on a one-bedroom flat in Hackney and asked Anna to move in. Maybe it was because it was his flat and not hers. Or maybe it was because it was now just the two of them. Either way, from the moment they'd moved in together, things had begun to change.

Eventually, midday rolled around and Anna strapped Libby into the back of the car to meet Ryan. A text had arrived an hour before offering to pick them up, but she had declined. Again. The restaurant was only ten minutes away from their house and Libby spent the whole time alternating between wondering whether Daddy would be there and asking Anna if they could invite Max to go to the Harvester soon. Anna knew which one of those two she would rather be sitting opposite this afternoon.

A chain restaurant like this was an odd choice for a chef, but it was an easy, child-friendly lunchtime venue. Before she'd moved back to Corringham, Anna had met her mum and dad here a few times when Libby was still small enough for a highchair. Ryan had never come. Today, it was particularly busy and the restaurant area was full of clattering plates, the sharp ring of cutlery and the bark of laughter and loud conversation. At the door, there was a dense queue of people waiting for a table, but she saw a waving hand in the near distance: Ryan was already there.

'You're here at last!' As soon as they approached the table, Ryan made a big show of wrapping his arms around Libby. Two old ladies on a nearby table smiled over at them. If only they knew he hadn't even contacted his daughter in the last six months. On the table was a sequinned pencil case from Smiggle, full of gel pens and novelty erasers and glittery pencils; Libby was ecstatic. 'Thank you, Daddy! Mummy said these were too much money!'

Ryan smiled. 'That's what daddies are for.' He picked up a glass of white wine and placed it in front of Anna. 'I ordered your usual.'

Anna bit the inside of her cheek. This was all feeling way too cosy. 'I don't drink white wine any longer.'

Libby laughed. 'Yes, you do, Mummy. Auntie Catherine brought a bottle to Nana's barbecue and you said you were going to stick a straw in the top and drink the lot.'

Ryan winked at her. 'Rumbled.'

One of the main reasons that Libby loved coming to the Harvester was the salad cart. She loved the independence of the salad servers and helping herself to what she wanted. Not that she took advantage of much of the selection. She returned to the table with a bowl of cucumber slices and small mountain of sweetcorn.

Ryan looked at her bowl and raised an eyebrow. 'Is that all you're having? What about some carrot or peppers? Or tomatoes?'

Libby pulled the face which signified the level of disgust she reserved for tooth brushing and tomatoes. 'I hate them.'

'But they are good for you.' He looked up at Anna. 'Don't you encourage her to eat healthily?'

Anna sighed. She could have predicted that this would be her fault. 'Cucumber is fine. When we're out, she can eat what she wants.'

As he well knew, there was a time she couldn't even get Libby to eat cucumber. She'd been such a tricky baby to wean. Anna had tried everything: homemade purees, shop-bought baby food, baby-led weaning: everything had been refused.

Ryan leaned in towards Libby as if he was about to confide a secret. 'I was the one who introduced you to cucumber, you know.'

Libby glanced at Anna for confirmation and she nodded. He had chopped the cucumber into all different shapes to interest her. Squares, triangles, even a star. 'It's true.'

'Your mum was out somewhere and it was just you and me. You sat in your high chair and looked at me suspiciously.'

He made the same face Libby made, even now, when she was curious about something. She giggled. All kids liked stories about when they were younger. 'Then what happened?'

'Well, I took one piece at a time and' – he picked up a slice of cucumber from her plate with his fork and held it in the air – 'I pretended I was going to give it to you and then I—'

Quick as a flash, he popped the whole thing into his mouth at once so that the edges pushed his cheek out like a hamster's. Libby squealed and wriggled on her seat. Even Anna had to laugh.

He held up a finger as he did an over-emphasised chew and a big swallow. Then he stuck his fork into another one and Libby squealed. 'No! That's my cucumber!'

He turned slowly to Anna and feigned surprise. 'Well, would you believe it? That's exactly what happened last time, wasn't it, Mummy?'

It was weird hearing him call her that. 'Yes, it was. And we couldn't stop you eating cucumber from that day to this.' She reached under the table to tickle Libby, but her daughter only had eyes for her dad.

Ryan grinned at her. 'I teased your mummy about it for ages.

She was the chef in the house, but she couldn't get you to eat anything she'd made. But if I gave it to you, you'd eat the lot!'

'Is that true, Mummy? Did I not eat your food?'

The two of them were laughing so much that she had to join in. But it hadn't been funny at the time: she'd felt a complete failure. 'Come on, you. Eat some of that cucumber; your macaroni cheese will be here in a minute.'

Libby was halfway through the bowl when she spied a friend of hers from school being shown to another table nearby. 'Karis is over there. Can I go and say hello? Please, Mummy?'

Anna looked in the direction that Libby was waving. Karis' mother smiled and nodded when Anna mimed Libby coming over to say hello. 'Okay. But just until our food arrives and then come back.'

Ryan watched her go. 'I can't believe how tall she is.'

'Yes, well, children have a habit of that. Growing.' Anna realised that this might sound judgemental and she needed to keep him on side. 'She's exactly the height and weight she should be at her age. That's why it was such a shock when Mr Harris said that her kidneys are failing her.'

Ryan nodded slowly and sipped at his mineral water. 'You hadn't noticed at all that she was getting sick?'

She had been running this over and over in her head for the last few days. 'Of course, I realised that she wasn't herself. She'd been tired and out of sorts. I took her to our new doctor a couple of times, but he put it down to Christmas and getting settled back into a school routine. She really didn't seem ill.'

Ryan pressed his lips together before he spoke. 'I only ask because she looks quite pale to me. And if she isn't eating properly...' He motioned towards the plate of cucumber.

It was ironic that in the past, whenever she had taken Libby to the doctor's, Ryan had told her she was overreacting. *You're being ridiculous. There's nothing wrong with her.* 'She does eat properly. But she's a kid, Ryan. You should see how picky some of the children at school are. They make Libby look like a restaurant critic.'

Ryan tipped his head back and a slow smile spread across his face. 'Oh yes. I'd forgotten you were a dinner lady now. How the mighty have fallen.'

Anna squeezed her fists under the table. She had never been 'mighty' about her job as a chef. And she hadn't so much fallen as been pushed. Once they had moved in together, and had started to get invited out by Ryan's colleagues – whose lives ran on a more conventional timetable – working in the restaurant had meant she missed out on a lot of the fun. Which was why, when Ryan had seen there was a new cafe opening near where they lived, Anna hadn't needed as much persuading as she once might have done.

At first, she'd been dismissive. 'A cafe? But I'm a chef. Not a sandwich maker.'

He had held her by the elbows of her folded arms, his face alive with enthusiasm. 'I had a chat to the owner as I was passing. Apparently, it's going to be more like a bistro or gastropub or whatever. Hot food. High end. It's got to be worth asking?'

She had still been unsure. At that time, she'd just started working under a chef who was a genius with Asian fusion. And he liked her. She was doing really well. 'But still. A cafe?'

Then Ryan had pulled her close to him and kissed her on the nose. 'But regular working hours. You'd be home in the evenings. We could actually go out to dinner like normal couples.'

She'd laughed then. That was what love could do to you. It clouded your judgement. And when she had spoken to the cafe owner, she *had* sounded ambitious and imaginative. So, much to Ryan's delight, Anna had made the move.

Which is why it rankled even more that he was mocking her now. 'I'm a school catering manager, actually.' She wished she hadn't bothered to rise to his dinner lady jibe when she saw the laughter in his eyes.

'Have you thought about researching a diet for her? I eat macrobiotic. Nicole has got me into it. For the triathlons. It's so energising. Maybe that would be good for Libby? I could ask her to put together some ideas for you? She gives me a meal plan a week in advance which fits around our training schedule.'

Our training schedule? It still hurt that Nicole had chosen Ryan's friendship over hers. It felt childish even thinking like that, but it was the truth. Of course, Nicole and Ryan had known each other since school. Of course, it was awkward for Nicole when he and Anna had split up. But Ryan had cheated on Anna, not the other way around. Didn't that earn her *some* loyalty? It definitely meant she deserved more of an explanation than Nicole leaving her calls and messages unanswered until she gave up trying. And now they were training for triathlons together? Anna swallowed a thousand sarcastic replies with a bite from a celery stick. 'I think we're okay, thanks.'

The Nicole she'd known drank like a fish and lived on crackerbread with bananas. In those days, she'd have laughed herself into a heap if Anna had suggested she plan out her meals in advance. Clearly, she had changed too.

Libby skipped back over to their table just as the waitress arrived with their plates of hot food. She slid a bowl of macaroni cheese in front of her. 'There you go, little one.'

Libby smiled up at her. Anna was always proud of her lovely manners. 'Thank you.'

Ryan was watching her, too. Last night, she'd chatted on the phone to her sister about this lunch, and Catherine had advised her to see Ryan as two people: her soon to be ex-husband and Libby's dad. 'Just because he was a bad husband, doesn't mean he is always going to be a bad father, too.' Maybe Catherine was right; maybe she should give him a chance to prove himself to Libby?

But then she realised that he wasn't looking at Libby, he was looking at Anna's plate. 'There's a lot of sauce on that chicken. You need to scrape some of that off. And the chips. Why didn't you get a jacket potato with it? Or salad?'

How dare he start this again? Anna's cheeks burned. She wanted to pick up the whole chicken breast and shove it in her mouth. Not trusting herself to reply, she turned to Libby. 'How is Karis today?'

Libby stopped inhaling her macaroni cheese and put down her fork. 'She's fine. And she's going to see a film with her mum and dad after lunch. Can we go, too?'

Anna sliced into her chicken. It was difficult to eat with the burn of Ryan's judgement on her. 'Not today, lovely. We have to go home. I need to do some jobs ready for next week.'

Libby frowned. 'But what about me? And Daddy? Can Daddy come home with us and play with me while you do the jobs?'

Anna gave Ryan a moment to answer, then, when he said nothing, she tried to explain. 'Not today, Libs. Daddy has to go home after lunch and so do we.'

Frowning at his watch, Ryan eventually joined in. 'Yes, you're right, I do need to get back after this. But I can come over in the week. How does Tuesday sound? I meant to tell you that I've already completed the health questionnaire and have booked my appointment to see Libby's consultant for then. I can come over and talk to you about it. And you can take me on a tour of your new house, Libby.'

He directed this last part to Libby, who started chattering instantly about all the things she wanted to show him when he came over. There was no way Anna wanted Ryan in her house, but this was the most animated and excited Libby had been since her diagnosis. How was she going to get out of it, without looking like the bad guy again?

When Libby wandered over to Karis to say goodbye, Anna tried to put him off. 'Tuesday will be Libby's first full four hours of dialysis. She'll probably be tired and irritable. Why don't we make it another time?'

But Ryan wasn't taking no for an answer. 'We need to talk about my appointment with Mr Harris and we can do that once Libby is in bed.'

If the thought of him being in her house wasn't bad enough, the idea that they would be alone together made her skin itch. Both her mother and sister had the same blood group as Anna, so they weren't going to be a match. Her brother-in-law, Vikram, had been tested and he was not a viable candidate. Which meant, if Ryan wasn't a match, they would probably only have the donor list to fall back on, and who knew how long that might take? Anna wanted to get this process moving as quickly as possible. If inviting Ryan into her house on Tuesday was what it took, she would do it.

TEN

Libby was overjoyed at the prospect of having her dad there on Tuesday evening. When they pulled up at home after dialysis, she shook off her sleepiness the minute she saw that he was waiting outside in his car. 'Come on, Mummy. Let's hurry up and get out. Daddy is waiting for us.'

Ryan met them at the front door and Libby's excitement to see her dad brought out resentful feelings that Anna wasn't particularly proud of. For the last six months – actually, longer than that – she had been the only parent to look after Libby. Admittedly, Ryan's money had gone into her bank account each month, and they wouldn't have been able to keep up the rent on the house if it hadn't. But even before the hospital appointments of the last ten days, she had been the one keeping everything together: the dinners, the laundry, the school runs, the bedtime tussles. Yet Ryan, who had done none of this, who had walked away from her after slinging mud at her on her own doorstep and then ignored them for the last six months, had been allowed to just walk back into Libby's life. This evening, Libby didn't miss a beat before slipping her hand into his and taking him straight through the house and out to the pocket handkerchief of a garden to show him the tomato plants which they'd planted. It just wasn't fair.

It was alien to have him here in their new house. Even before the hiatus of the last six months, he had never come inside when he collected Libby for the day. Anna had always made sure that Libby was packed and ready to go. It wasn't difficult: Libby would be at the window waiting for him, making a path to the front door as soon as his car pulled up outside.

Which is what had made it hard when he had started to be late. Using work as an excuse, or merely alluding to the fact that he had 'plans' that he couldn't get out of. That was when Anna had started to get really angry with him. It was one thing to let her down. For her to find out that he had slept with someone else. She could handle that. But to upset Libby? That was something else altogether.

She'd tried to explain it to him. How Libby would stand at the window twenty minutes before he was due to come and then refuse to come away when he was thirty, forty minutes or an hour late, terrified she would miss him.

However much he let her down, Libby was never cross with him. It was Anna she would take it out on. Anna who would have to field the tantrums and the tears when he started to not turn up at all.

'She's a child. She'll get over it,' had been the sum total of his explanation. And then: 'You were the one who chose to move so far away. If you lived nearer, it would be easier for me to see her.'

And then there had been the big argument. The one where he had told her – on the doorstep – to stop being so stupid and just come home. Where he'd tried to push his way in through the front door and she had had to close it on him, heart racing, listening as he kicked the door and swore at her from the other side. 'I'll tell her what you did. I'll tell her what kind of a woman her mother is.'

After he finally left, they hadn't heard from him again.

For a month afterwards, Libby would refuse to go anywhere on a Sunday, sure that her daddy was going to turn up and see her. It had torn Anna apart to watch her: the hope when she saw a car of the same colour drive past, the disappointment when it turned out not to be him.

Libby had been angry too. Angry at Anna for moving them here. Angry at Ryan's job that meant he was busy. But never angry with Ryan. Never with him.

Looking at them together now, as they came in from the garden laughing, it was difficult to believe that they had been apart so long. Anna had another tub of her mum's leek and potato soup – which she was making in industrial proportions at the moment – in the fridge, and she warmed some up for Libby. Normally she would have eaten too, but Ryan's presence had stolen her appetite and she wasn't about to offer him anything to eat. It might encourage him to stay longer.

Half an hour later, Libby's face was almost white and she was starting to sway on her feet. Anna stood behind her and kissed the top of her head. 'Come on, Libby, you're shattered. Time for bed.'

'No.' Libby took a step towards Ryan and held onto his arm. It was as if she was scared to let him out of her sight in case he never appeared again.

Ryan bent down to her. 'Come on, Libs. Let Mummy put you to bed and then I'll come up and read you one of my special stories. How about that?'

Libby's face lit up with the glow of memory. Ryan used to create his own stories from the pictures in Libby's story books. She loved the nonsensical characters and ridiculous situations that he could make up on the spot. They were far more exciting that the actual written story which Anna had read to her a hundred times.

Anna couldn't settle while he was upstairs. It was like having a splinter that you wanted to work out of your hand: she could feel him in the house. Emptying the dishwasher, tidying away Libby's colouring pens, even straightening the black and white photos of Libby on the wall: anything to keep busy. As soon as he was downstairs, she'd get this conversation over with so that he could go home and she could relax.

When he finally walked back into the lounge, he had a big smile on his face. 'I've missed that. I forgot how funny I am.'

He was joking, but Anna wasn't planning on being his audience. 'So, how was your meeting with Mr Harris?'

'Oh, I see. We're getting straight to it? It was good. He explained everything clearly. About the tests. I can go in for the first blood tests as soon as I like. He suggested next Tuesday. Isn't that when Libby has her next dialysis?'

Had it been Mr Harris who'd suggested the same day as Libby and Anna would be there? 'That's great.'

'Yes. I was surprised it was so soon, what with it being the NHS. I'd thought it would be a few weeks at least.'

Anna felt nervous. He sounded okay with it, but she'd fallen for that in the past. 'Is it a problem that it's so soon? I mean, we just need to know if you are a match or not.'

Ryan waved away her concern. 'Of course not. Like you say, I may not even be a match. I was just surprised he could see me so soon, that's all.'

She was just about to explain that Mr Harris wanted to get things in place for the transplant in case Libby's condition worsened quickly, when they were interrupted by the sound of the doorbell. That was strange. Who would call round unannounced in the evening?

She opened the front door to Paul, Libby's teacher, standing on the doorstep. 'Hi. Sorry to call around unannounced. I was driving past on my way to see a friend and I wanted to pop in the cards that the kids have made for Libby.' He held out a handful of handmade cards with almost discernible pictures on the front. He smiled. 'I did manage to persuade them not to draw any blood on the front, but I can't vouch for how flattering the pictures of Libby lying in bed are. I think there might also be a couple of you making her dinner.'

His smile was infectious. Of course, she was a dinner lady to them. What else would she do at home other than cook dinner for Libby? 'That's really kind, thank you.'

'Not at all. I know you were hoping she'd be back soon so I wanted to get them to you before then. Is that still the plan?' He had said that he was on his way to meet a friend, but he didn't seem in any rush to get there. It felt rude not to invite him in, but with Ryan on the other side of the wall, she couldn't risk it.

'At the moment, we're thinking that she'll be back at school at the start of next week, maybe even the end of this one. I'm going to wait and see how she is tomorrow. If there's any work you want her to do, I'm sure she'll be happy to do it.'

Paul pulled at his ear lobe. 'I can send you work if she wants to do something, but there's no urgent need. She's a bright girl, she'll soon catch up.'

As he finished speaking, Paul's eyes moved over her shoulder and she turned in the direction of his gaze to see that Ryan had stepped into the hallway. For some reason, she felt herself blush as she introduced them. 'Oh Ryan, this is Paul. Mr Benham. Libby's teacher.'

Ryan stepped forward and held out his hand. 'I'm Libby's father. Pleased to meet you.'

Paul quickly stifled the flash of surprise on his face. 'Oh, I see. Pleased to meet you. I was just dropping off some cards for Libby, but I won't keep you both from your evening.'

Anna wanted to explain to Paul that this was not what it seemed, but how could she say anything without it looking like she was making a point of telling him she was single. Her face burned. 'Thanks again, then. I'll see you at school.'

Ryan waited for her to close the door before he asked the inevitable question. 'What's going on there, then?'

It was always best to play it cool in these situations. At least, it had been in the past. 'I don't know what you mean. He's Libby's teacher.'

He tilted his head, jutting his chin in her direction. 'So why were you flirting with him? What's with the "*see you at school*"?'

She took a step back, conscious of the closed door at her back. 'I wasn't flirting. I will see him at school. I work there.'

Without stepping forwards, he still seemed to get closer. 'Yes, but you're just kitchen staff. I assume you don't go and sit in the classroom with the teachers?'

Sweat was gathering on her top lip. The hallway was narrow, two people would struggle to stand next to each other shoulder to shoulder, but she wasn't about to let him trap her here like a frightened mouse. When he leaned to the right, she saw her chance and ducked around the other side of him. She tried to keep her voice steady and unconcerned. 'Anyway, I need to get some ironing done, so shall we leave it there for tonight?'

He followed her slowly, as if he was considering something. 'I wanted to talk to you about Libby's school actually.'

Her nerves were on edge; she had no idea what he would suggest next. 'Really? What about it?'

'Well, I've been thinking. You've been making a lot of decisions about Libby. Where she lives, what school she goes to, which hospital she's going to be treated by. I think it's time I had some input. There's a very nice private school near me. It would be much easier if she was there. I could see her after school then, rather than having to wait for the weekend.'

Anna's heart thumped in her chest. 'But she's happy at the school she's at now. There's no reason to move her.' As soon as he was gone, she would call Catherine. He couldn't make her change Libby's school, could he?

But then he shrugged as if it wasn't even important. As if he'd just wanted to throw that at her, rattle her cage. Why did she let him get to her? He plucked up his coat from the arm of the sofa. 'Just something we can talk about. We'll have plenty of time together over the next few weeks to discuss these kinds of arrangements, won't we?'

ELEVEN

After Ryan left, Anna felt too drained to go through the legalities of Libby's education with her sister over the phone; she'd call her tomorrow. Instead, she made herself a cup of tea. Then sat in the lounge and watched it grow cold.

There had been something in the way Ryan spoke which had chilled her in the same way. Libby changing school? Where had that come from? In the week since her meeting with Mr Harris, she had been through a whole spectrum of emotions. Panic, fear, anxiety. Now there was a new one to add. Dread.

Had calling Ryan been a really bad idea?

Not to Libby, of course. She had been so excited to see her dad. When Anna had tucked her in, Libby had whispered to her how her friend Karis had thought she didn't have a daddy, but now she had seen him, she could see that Libby wasn't making him up. *Don't get too close*, Anna wanted to warn her. *Don't give him too much of your heart.*

There was no point drinking this tea now. She might as well get an early night herself. Their small kitchen was directly off the lounge and, after she'd tipped the tea down the sink and washed it away, she stood and looked out of the kitchen window into the dark of their tiny back garden.

The garden at their old house had been four times the size of this. Big enough that Libby learned to ride her bike up and down the path. Ryan had helped her then, holding the back seat and running alongside until she was ready for him to let go. Seeing him with Libby tonight had brought moments like this back to her. Happy memories. Times when he was funny and caring and full of love for them both. Why couldn't he have always been like that?

She rubbed the memory from her eyes. The clock on the cooker blinked 9.15 p.m., but she needed to go to bed.

The bathroom was at the top of the stairs. Ryan had been up here just before he left and now she saw it through his eyes. Clean, but shabby. It didn't matter how hard she scrubbed, she couldn't make it look any better. She could imagine the comparison he must have made in his head with the dark tiled wet room and state-of-the-art shower at their old house. Not for the first time, she wondered if she should have stayed there and asked him to move out. Not that he would have gone.

And how could she have kept sleeping in that bedroom? Knowing that that was where she found him. Him and his young assistant: it was such a cliché. She'd wondered since where she and Libby would be if she hadn't come back from her mum's to pick up Libby's elephant that she couldn't go to sleep without. If she hadn't found the two of them half-undressed in her bed. Would she have continued to put up with the way Ryan treated her? Would they still be there?

No. However small and shabby this house was, it was safe and it was hers. She'd made the right decision in coming back home to Essex, too. Having her mum close was an absolute godsend. It was going to be difficult enough holding down her job with Libby's treatment to consider, but it would be impossible without her mum here to provide childcare on the days Libby couldn't go to school.

She stood at the doorway to Libby's room and looked in at her sleeping. So insistent about how grown up she was at six, *nearly seven*, she'd hate to hear Anna's thoughts of how much she looked like a baby sleeping there, her blonde hair spread across the pillow.

She was so tiny, so vulnerable: it frightened Anna when she thought of the road ahead.

The first operation to put in the AV graft had been bad enough. She had paced the floor of the hospital waiting room like a caged tiger, unable to settle for a moment. A kind nurse had urged her to sit, calm down, drink the coffee she'd brought her. But as soon as she sat down, she wanted to get up again, walk, run, do *something*.

That was one of the hardest parts of all this. This feeling of helplessness. A mother was supposed to protect her child from hurt. Anna felt useless. Like she'd failed Libby.

The night before the operation, once Libby was asleep, she'd crept outside the ward, called her mum and cried. 'Why can't it be me, Mum? Why can't it be my kidney that doesn't work? Why does it have to be her? I'm her mum; I'm supposed to protect her and I can't do anything to help.'

And her mum had cried on the other end of the phone. 'I know, honey. I really do. I wish I could take this away from both of you.'

Watching her in bed, Libby's body looked too small to cope with a kidney transplant. When she was a baby, Anna had marvelled at the fact that her tiny six-pound body contained a heart, lungs, kidneys, stomach. How did it all fit in?

Of course, they hadn't known then that her kidneys were going to cause her so much trouble. At the time, Anna had been so thankful that she was okay. The pregnancy had been pretty difficult; she had been sick and tired a lot of the time. Ryan had had a lot on at work so she had often been alone. Nicole had been brilliant. When her shifts allowed, she would take Anna out to lunch or – when Anna was too exhausted to even put her shoes on her swollen feet – she would come over to the house and just watch TV with her. She would regale Anna with stories from the hotel or disastrous Tinder dates she'd been on. When Ryan came home, he'd join them. Often, they'd get a takeaway and Anna would snooze on the sofa as the other two argued about what to watch on

TV. It had been just like the old days back in their house in Hackney.

As she watched her, Libby's eyes fluttered open. 'Mummy?'

She stepped into the small bedroom and knelt down by the side of the bed. 'I'm here, baby.'

'I'm thirsty. Can I have some water?'

'Of course. Let me go and get it.'

She was back at the bedside in less than a minute and she helped Libby sit up to drink it. 'Just sip it.'

'It's cold.'

'That's because you're all snuggly and warm.'

She pulled a few sticky strands of hair from Libby's face and kissed her cheek gently. Her eyes were already half closed again and the glass needed to be rescued from her hand. Anna envied her ability to go straight back to sleep and not lie awake worrying through everything that was going to, or could, or might happen.

Head back on the pillow, Libby's eyelids started to close. 'Did Daddy read my story or was that a dream?'

Anna smiled. 'He really did read it, baby. It wasn't a dream.' It had been good to hear Libby's laughter spill down the stairs from her bedroom. Ryan was great entertainment: she had to give him that.

Libby smiled; her voice was just a murmur. 'I've missed Daddy.'

Anna's heart ached at that. When she'd left Ryan, it had been for her own sake. He had always been good with Libby. The guilt of that first week at her mum's when Libby had cried for her old bedroom, her old school, her daddy. But she'd had to do it. She couldn't have lived in that house with him any longer.

And now Ryan was back in their lives. Smiling, joking, making Libby happy. That was a good thing, wasn't it? If they could keep it like this – if Anna could bite her tongue when he waxed lyrical about his life or questioned whether Anna was doing all she could to make Libby well – then maybe they could make this work.

Whatever happened, she needed Ryan to find out if he was a

match for Libby, whether he would be able to donate his kidney to her. And if he was? Then Anna would do whatever she had to, if it kept him happy and on side and willing to help. Because all that mattered right now was that Libby got what she needed to be a happy, healthy child. Everything else, she would think about afterwards.

The first step was his appointment on Tuesday.

TWELVE

Less than twenty-four hours later, Ryan called Anna to ask if she would go with him to his first appointment at the renal unit the following afternoon.

Initially, she was confused. 'But it's just a blood test. You don't need me there.'

He loved to know more than she did. 'Actually, it's not. I've told the hospital how difficult it is for me to get to them, so they are going to do the X-ray and ECG tomorrow, too. I thought you were going to be there anyway? Isn't Thursday one of Libby's dialysis days?'

His self-important tone made her toes curl. 'Exactly. I'll be with Libby.'

'Well, that's perfect. You can come and meet me for my appointment and then we can both go back to Libby together.'

Did he think that dialysis was like some kind of day care? Anna sighed, remembered her resolution to hold her tongue. Stay positive. 'I want to stay with her, Ryan. This is still all very new for her.'

He'd sounded irritated. 'Can't a nurse watch her for a while? I am driving all the way over for this appointment. I'm having to take the whole afternoon off work.'

He clearly wasn't going to give in. It would be easier to just do it. Maybe she could ask Max's mum, Julie, to keep an eye on Libby again. 'Okay. Call me when you get to the hospital and I'll come down.'

But when they got to the dialysis ward on Thursday, Max's mum wasn't there. Judging by the slightly protruding ears which were exactly like Max's, it was his dad who was sitting next to him, watching him complete what looked like some kind of school work, whilst surreptitiously scrolling on his phone. Anna made him jump when she said hello.

'Oh, hi. Anna, isn't it? And Libby? Max has been telling me all about you. I'm Tim, Max's dad.'

While the nurse was hooking Libby up, he stood to give them some room.

It was awkward standing next to each other and not making conversation, so Anna stated the obvious. 'No Julie today?'

He ran a hand through his hair; scratched the back of his head. 'No. She is absolutely knackered. Our little girl has been poorly this week and she's been up in the night. Julie's had hardly any sleep. So, I took the day off work today so she could get some rest.'

Envy twisted at the edges of Anna. How nice it must be to have someone else to share the burden of all this. 'I hope your little girl feels better soon. Poor Julie. And there was me about to ask her if she could keep an eye on Libby while I see Mr Harris. I had no idea she was having a rough week.'

He shrugged. 'I can keep an eye on Libby for you. It's not as if the two of them can go anywhere, is it? And judging by the last couple of minutes, I'll be a spare part anyway.' They both turned to look at the two children, who were chatting away like an old married couple on Southend seafront.

Damn Ryan for forcing her into this position. She didn't know Tim, but he was Max's dad. And the nurses were all here. Hopefully she wouldn't need to stay with Ryan for long, anyway. 'Thank you.'

. . .

It was strange to see Ryan looking nervous when she found him in the waiting room. Rather than sit on one of the plastic chairs along the wall, he was standing reading the noticeboard behind them, tapping his foot. With his well-cut suit and expensive shirt, he looked more like a visiting consultant than someone here for a blood test.

In the midst of worrying about Libby, dreading the prospect of calling Ryan and now stressing about whether he would be a match, Anna had forgotten how much he disliked hospitals. Even visiting his mother when she had been in for treatment had made him twitchy and irritable. He hated the dentist and the optician, too. Not that he needed either of those very often: both his eyesight and teeth were perfect.

Maybe it was the relief of her appearance that made him do it, but she was surprised when he leaned in and kissed her cheek. 'Thanks for coming down. You know how much I hate these places.'

'No problem. You're quite early, though. I didn't expect you for a while.'

'The traffic wasn't as bad as I'd anticipated. I probably left earlier than I needed to. As usual.'

He smiled at her and she couldn't help returning it. When they were together, he would always build in plenty of time to arrive somewhere, whereas she was always leaving at the last available minute and dashing in by the skin of her teeth. They used to drive each other crazy about it.

She pointed at the chairs, which were becoming as familiar to her as her own lounge. 'Shall we sit?'

He held out a stiff paper bag with rope handles. 'Actually, I have something for you.'

She took it and sat down and peeked inside the bag. 'What's this?'

He held up his hands. 'I know it seems a bit random, but I was in a store this morning picking up something and they had this crazy sale on. I saw a Karen Millen section and I remembered how much you used to like her stuff, so I picked it up for you.'

She pulled the dress from the bag. It was beautiful. Her favourite shade of dark blue, elbow-length sleeves, scooped neck. The half of her wanting to try it on right now was fighting with the half that wanted to give it straight back. 'You shouldn't have.'

Just then, a young nurse she didn't recognise walked past. 'That's gorgeous. Lucky you.' The way she flicked her eyes from the dress to Ryan, Anna wasn't sure which she was referring to.

She'd got used to the attention he got from women when they were going out. Mostly it was just the odd glance, although she had been in nightclubs with him when women passed him their numbers. It wasn't just that he was good looking, he had that something else. Her mum would call it charisma, although that always made Anna think of Frank Sinatra. Charm, maybe? What she hadn't enjoyed so much were the looks she'd got which seemed to say: *You? He's with you?*

'It's just a dress, Anna. I used to buy you things like that all the time.'

She didn't like the way he kept referring to their past life: for her it was a country she didn't want to revisit. 'Yes, but that was when we were married.'

He held out his hands, raised an eyebrow. 'What's with the past tense? We still are. You're still my wife.'

Before she could begin to get into that subject, Mr Harris opened his office door and strolled out to shake Ryan's hand. 'Ah, you're here. And Anna is with you. Good. Good. Well, as you are here as a potential donor, you won't be seeing me today. Although I can still talk to you about Libby as her parent, as a donor, you'll have your own doctor from this point on. Everything is kept separate. As you know, we're able to move quite quickly here, so one of the nurses will look after you today and then Dr Wells will meet with you within the next couple of weeks to go through the results. All being well, Dr Wells, myself and the rest of the transplant team will meet to discuss the next steps.' He turned to Anna. 'How has Libby been?'

'Good, yes. She's fine. She actually went into school for a couple of hours this morning.'

'That's great news. Like I said before, the more normal her life can be, the better. And she'll be missing school in due course for the transplant, as and when that happens. Let her see her friends while she can.'

Anna knew he was right. And it helped that she was in the same building as Libby if she was needed. But since the diagnosis, she just wanted to wrap Libby up and keep her safe.

Ryan's mobile rang out in his pocket and he frowned at the screen. 'Sorry, I need to take this.'

'And I need to go.' Mr Harris raised a hand in farewell and headed for the exit.

Ryan stepped away from Anna to take his call, and he turned his body away from her and lowered his voice, but the corridor was silent and she could still hear everything he said.

'No, Nic, I won't be here that long tonight... No, I'm on my own in the waiting room...'

Nic? As in Nicole? They were clearly closer than she'd realised. And why was he lying about being alone?

'No, She's not here... Of course, not...'

She? They must be talking about her. Nicole wanted to know if she was there, did she?

'Yes, that would be great... Yes, you too.'

You too? Wasn't there only one kind of question he would answer like that? What had she said? I miss you? I love you? Were they *together?* A horrible, sickening feeling crept over Anna. It wasn't just that Nicole had chosen Ryan's friendship over hers. That had been hard enough to take. But this? Ryan and Nicole were a couple. How had she not seen it? How had she been so stupid?

Ryan still had his back to her as he wrapped up the call. 'Okay,

Ryan tilted his head to the side. 'Unless you want me to cancel and put it off for another time?'

What she wanted was to slap his face and walk away. But she knew he would turn and leave. Instead, she picked up the bag with the dress in it and followed him into the nurse's room. She would stand there with him if it got Libby a kidney. But she wasn't about to hold his hand. And, as soon as this was all over, she was going to make damn sure that she was no longer his wife.

THIRTEEN

Anna had barely slept the night before, replaying the last few times she had seen or spoken to Nicole in her head.

After discovering Ryan's affair with the girl from work, Anna had stayed with her mum for a few days, ignoring his barrage of text messages and voicemails. In the end, she had only returned to the house when he had promised her that he would move out for a few days to give her some space. Later, she found out that he had gone to Nicole's.

Even though Anna regarded Nicole as her best friend, Nicole had known Ryan for longer. And in the end, that had won out. She'd gone from not wanting to take sides, to trying to encourage Anna to see him, to telling Anna that she was being unreasonable in refusing to give him another chance. *He knows he made a terrible mistake.* That was what she'd said. As if that made everything okay. Anna had been so hurt that she'd wanted to pull Libby in close and ignore the rest of the world. To begin with, it had been her who had been too angry to speak to Nicole. Then, the tables had turned.

After many unanswered calls, she had tried to speak to Nicole one more time. The day they'd moved into their new house she had called her to say that she had a new address. That final call had gone straight to voicemail and was never returned.

In the school kitchen on Friday afternoon, Tina listened with an open mouth as Anna told her about Ryan's phone conversation the day before. Then she had enough colourful names for Ryan and Nicole that she could have painted a rainbow. 'So, let me get this straight. For making you go and hold his hand while he had a two-minute blood test, he gave you a sodding *dress*?'

Anna nodded and passed Tina a cup of coffee. Everyone else had gone home for the day and they were having a quick drink before Anna had to collect Libby. She'd had her mum on standby all day in case Libby got tired and needed to go home, waiting at the house because it was walking distance to the school. Anna could imagine that the bathroom and kitchen would have been cleaned within an inch of their lives by now and there would probably be a lasagne or a casserole in the oven. Any thanks would be waved away with both hands. *It's nice to be needed.*

But Libby hadn't needed to be collected from school. Tired or not, she hadn't asked to go home. Towards the end of the morning, before the children started to queue for their lunch, Anna had even allowed herself to pop out of the kitchen and take a peek in at her daughter's classroom. Mr Benham had caught her eye and given her a thumbs up, nodding over to the corner of the classroom where Libby had her head down, focused on some artwork, her friends on either side of her, sharing the pots of paint and showing each other their work.

One of Libby's friends saw her spying on them, nudged Libby and pointed in her direction. She saw them mouth, 'It's your mum.' When Libby first raised her head, her expression was blank and dreamy, her mind still on the picture in front of her. God, she was beautiful, her flushed cheeks, bright eyes, perfect mouth. Then her expression changed as she saw Anna, her whole face lifted in a smile and she stuck out her hand and waved, then picked up her painting to show her.

How much longer would she have this? That her mere presence made her daughter happy? That she wanted to show her everything she did? When would teenage years pull her away from

Anna and towards her friends, maybe boyfriends? How far away would she go?

It was difficult to take her to dialysis three times a week now. How much harder would it be as she got older? When she wanted to be out with her friends? When she wouldn't want to miss school because she was studying for tests? When – like all teenagers – she just wanted to be like everyone else? A regular kid. Not different. Not special. Not ill. However much she hated him right now, Ryan was potentially the best option for Libby's future.

'What kind of dress was it?' Tina fished her sweeteners out of her bag and pressed the plastic dispenser twice. 'Like a sexy dress?'

After the swearing and sympathy, Anna knew that Tina was now trying to make her laugh, lighten her mood. 'No. It was a Karen Millen. He knows I like her dresses, or I did, when I could afford them.'

'How much would it have been, then?'

Anna shrugged. 'I don't know. They're usually around £200, but he said it was on sale.'

'On sale? And happened to be your favourite colour and size? Do you believe him?'

It had actually been too small for her. Had that been on purpose, a jibe at the fact she wasn't as slim as she'd once been? Or was she being oversensitive, suspicious of everything that Ryan did? 'I don't know. I tried to get him to take it back, but he wouldn't hear of it. And it felt like I was making too much of it.'

'Don't knock it. If you like it, I'd accept it.' Tina's laugh was as dirty as her tabard was clean. 'I can't imagine in a million years John buying me a dress as a surprise. Wouldn't even occur to him. And goodness only knows where he'd get it from or what it would be like. Closest thing to that I've ever had from him was a pair of thermal gloves from Camping and General on Canvey. He said I could wear them to take the bins out.'

It did sound like an odd gift, but Ryan had often bought clothes for her when they were together. He travelled to other cities for client meetings and, if he saw something in a shop window that he thought she'd like, he'd get it for her. 'To be fair to him, he does have a good sense of style. He picked out half my wardrobe.'

'Really? I wouldn't trust John to pick out a bobble hat. Even though we've known each other for twenty years, I don't think he could even tell you my favourite colour. Must have been nice to have someone buy you good clothes.'

Was it nice? In the beginning, she had thought so. It was lovely to have the surprise of a shirt, or a pair of shoes, or even a coat. But gradually she'd begun to realise that Ryan bought her the clothes he liked – straight skirts, shoes with a heel – rather than her preference for more floaty things, which he dismissed as 'hippy chic'.

'I'm not actually sure I'll get any wear out of the dress, actually. It's very fitted. I don't go anywhere to wear those kinds of clothes these days. It's probably a bit much for the supermarket.'

Tina tapped the side of her nose, like a bookmaker at a race-track. 'Depends what time of day you go. Apparently, late night shopping is a great time to meet someone.'

Anna shook her head. 'Don't start that again.'

A voice called out across the kitchen. 'Anna? Are you there?'

Tina reached out and took Anna's mug. 'It's Mr Benham. Quick, straighten your hair. There's lipstick in my bag if you want it.'

Anna flushed. 'Stop it. He'll hear you!' She hurried out of the office so that she could shut the door on Tina's laughter. 'Hello! I'm just coming.'

They almost bumped into each other, but Paul managed to stop just in time. 'Hi. The class are having a story on the carpet with Jenny. I just wondered if you wanted to collect Libby after the story, rather than having her queue at the door with the other children.'

Anna's stomach clenched. 'Why? Is she okay? Is something wrong?'

Paul looked alarmed. 'No. Not at all. Sorry. I didn't mean to worry you. I just thought it might be easier.'

It wasn't strange that he'd left Jenny – the class support

assistant – in charge of reading to the class. For a start, she had a beautiful Welsh lilt that meant she could take the register and make it sound good. But normally teachers took that time to sit behind a pile of marking, not pop out to talk to a parent. Even one that worked in the same building.

'I'll wait outside for her, then. She likes to come out with the others.' Libby, too, craved normality. She'd already made it clear that she didn't want special treatment, or for her friends to treat her differently because she was sick. When Anna had the urge to wrap her up in cotton wool, she had to remember that.

'Okay, that's easy then. She can leave with everyone else.' Still, Paul didn't make a move to return to his classroom. 'Anyway, I, er, wanted to ask how you were?'

Anna frowned. 'Me?'

'Yes. It can't be easy. Worrying about Libby.'

She was so used to people asking about Libby that it made her mute for a moment. How was she? Scared? Exhausted? Confused? 'I'm fine. But thank you.'

'Good. I wondered, seeing Libby's dad at yours. Is everything...'

He tailed off, obviously unsure what to say. At the staff Christmas do, when they'd both had too much to drink, they had ended up talking about separations and divorces. He had just been through one; she was about to.

Talking frankly about your relationships when you'd had too much of Tina's Christmas punch was one thing. Standing in a school kitchen was another. 'He was just visiting. We're hoping he might be able to be a donor for Libby.'

Paul's eyes widened. 'Wow. That's amazing.'

Anna twisted the dishcloth she hadn't realised that she'd picked up. 'Yeah, well, we have to wait and see. I haven't said anything to Libby yet. I don't want her worrying about something that may or may not happen.'

'Of course. I completely understand.' He mimed zipping his lips, then looked at the large clock on the wall. 'I'd best get back to class and start the coats and bags quest before home time.' He walked away two steps and then turned back. 'No worries if you've got too much on now, but I wondered if you were still free next Wednesday night? It's a while since we arranged it.'

Anna's stomach lurched. When had she agreed to go out with him? Had it been when she was drunk at the party? There was no way she was in a place to even think about a date right now. But how was she going to let him down without making it obvious that she had no recollection of it? 'Wednesday night?'

He nodded. 'Yes, the PTA thing. You suggested bringing some canapés and finger food. To get the word out about your business?'

Anna felt herself flush red hot. What an idiot. He wasn't trying to make some clumsy move on her. As if he'd fancy her anyway. Why had she let Ryan's suspicions into her mind? 'Of course, yes, sorry. I'll be there.'

FOURTEEN

Anna waited on the playground for Libby's class to come tripping out of the classroom. Libby was one of the last ones out: bundled into her thick navy coat, rucksack dangling from one shoulder, her short ponytail pulled slightly left of centre. Anna waved and Libby grinned before skipping over.

Anna held out her arms and folded her in, breathed in the top of her hair and kissed her forehead. 'Hey, baby girl. How was your day?'

Libby slipped her hand into Anna's and they followed the rest of the parents off the playground. 'It was good. We stayed in at playtime and played Connect Four from the games cupboard.'

Anna took the rucksack before it fell off Libby's arm onto the ground and swung it onto her own shoulder as they walked. 'But it wasn't wet today. How come you stayed in?'

They were outside the school gates by now, but Libby glanced around her to check no one was listening. 'I told Mr Benham that I didn't feel well, so he let me stay inside. And he said I could choose two friends, so I chose Karis and Mary.'

'But you didn't feel poorly?'

'No. But it was really cold outside so I might have got poorly if I went out to the playground.'

'Libby Ferguson. I am shocked. You told Mr Benham a fib?' It wasn't a terrible crime, but Anna was still surprised at her.

Libby just shrugged it off. 'Will Nana be at home when we get there?'

'Yes. And I'm worn out, so I'm hoping she's made dinner.'

When Anna opened their front door, she could hear her mother speaking to someone. Libby kicked off her shoes and made it to the lounge before she did. Anna heard her squeal. 'Daddy!'

Ryan was here?

Sure enough, once she'd wrestled her heels out of her comfortable work shoes and made it through to the lounge herself, there was Ryan sitting on her sofa, holding one of her mugs in his hand, talking to her mother.

She pulled off her scarf. 'What are you doing here? I didn't see your car outside?'

'No, there's a battered old Micra out there. I couldn't get anywhere near.'

He knew her car. Was he joking or being mean? Hard to tell. 'The battered old Micra is mine. I don't need it to drive to school.'

'Well, that would explain the dents.' She still wasn't sure.

Anna's mother stood up. 'Good day at work, love? Ryan came to give you some news. I'll go and make you a tea.'

Libby sat so close to Ryan on the sofa that she was almost in his pocket, gazing up at him as if he was a god. Irritation scratched at Anna. She didn't sit down. 'What's the news?'

'I got my blood test results.'

Anna's stomach flipped and her face flushed. 'But you only had the test yesterday. How can you have your results already?'

Ryan raised an eyebrow. 'It's surprising what you can get when you ask. I don't have all of them. But I called Dr Wells' office this morning and told his receptionist that you were really anxious about the results. I suggested that it would really help if I could at least know my blood group. Then they agreed that I could collect the result from them if I came in.'

Anna could just imagine him charming his way around the

receptionist. And the way he'd described her to this new doctor. Right now, however, she had more important things to focus on. 'And?'

But now Ryan had shifted his attention to Libby. 'I brought you something, Libs. Do you want it now or after dinner?'

Libby bounced up and down on the sofa. 'Now. Now. Now.'

Ryan put his hand in his pocket. 'Are you sure? Are you sure you want it now?'

This was unbearable. 'Ryan. What were the results? Is it good news?'

Ryan didn't even look at her when he spoke. 'Stop being a killjoy. I've got a surprise for Libby.' He turned to his daughter. 'Do you want to wait for your surprise until Mummy has spoken to me?'

'No! Mummy, don't spoil it! I want my surprise.'

Anna's heart was pounding in her chest. Surely, he wouldn't be dragging it out like this if it was bad news? Even Ryan wouldn't be that cruel. 'I'm just going to check on Nana in the kitchen. You have your surprise.'

But he wasn't letting her get away that easily. 'No, she wants you to watch her open it, don't you, Libby?'

He took his hand out of his pocket and then reached under the coffee table, where he had stashed a gift-wrapped box which was far too big to have fitted into his pocket. 'Here you go.'

Libby squealed with excitement and began to carefully pick at the tape at one end. Ryan reached over and tore a whole strip across the top. 'You don't need to do it slowly. We're not going to use the paper again, you know.'

It was a Nintendo Switch. Libby recognised the red and blue of the games console because Max had one that he brought with him to dialysis. And because Libby had been asking for one for months. And because Anna had been saving to buy her one for her birthday. They cost over £300.

Libby's face looked like three Christmases had come at once.

'A Switch! For me? Thank you, Daddy. Thank you.' She threw her arms around him and he grinned at Anna over her shoulder.

'I think your mum is about to tell me off for buying you such an expensive present. But I'm sure I can win her over.'

Anna could hear the tightness in her own voice. 'Libby, why don't you go and get changed out of your uniform and then you can come back down and play with it?'

'Okay. I can't wait to show Max!' She took the box with her up to her room; her footsteps thumped up the stairs.

Anna pushed the lounge door closed and stood with her back to it. If Ryan's answer wasn't what she hoped for, she might need its support. 'What was the result of the blood tests?'

Still he evaded her, like a slippery eel. 'Really? You're not going to tell me off for buying her a present out of the blue?'

Anna wanted to scream at him. Of course, she was annoyed about the Switch. He hadn't even asked if she already had one. But, right now, she had more important things to worry about. 'Ryan. Please. Just tell me what the results were.'

A lazy smile spread over his face. 'As you've asked so nicely. They were good. My blood group is O. so I could potentially donate to any blood type. There's a good chance I could be a match for Libby.'

Relief nearly knocked Anna over. On shaky legs, she moved to the chair opposite him. 'That's great news. When are the next tests?'

The kitchen door opened and her mother walked in with two mugs of tea. 'I made you a fresh one too, Ryan. Are you staying for dinner?'

Hope was beginning to bubble inside Anna. Even her fingers tingled with it. 'We were just discussing the tests, Mum. It's looking good.'

Her mum's smile matched Anna's own. 'Well, that's great news. Maybe we should have something stronger than tea in these mugs.'

Ryan accepted his tea from her, then swapped it with the

empty one on the coaster in front of him. 'It's too early for that. The next tests will be more important, I think.'

Anna turned back to him. She was so elated, she could have hugged him. 'So, when can you have them?'

'They said they could get me back in as soon as possible. So, it kind of depends on you. When are you free?'

Her smile faltered. What did he mean? 'I don't need to be there, though. They know that I am not a match.'

'To come with me, I mean. I'd appreciate your support.'

This again. Why did he need her there? 'Can't you take Nicole with you?'

Ryan's smile disappeared. 'I hardly think that would be appropriate in the circumstances, do you? To be honest, as my *good friend*, Nicole is quite concerned about me putting myself at risk in this way. I don't want to make her feel worse by asking her to come to the appointments. Anyway, we can schedule it for when you're at the centre. Libby's dialysis.'

As if she'd heard her name, Libby came bounding in with the Nintendo console in her hands. At times like this, it was hard to believe how sick she was. The day after dialysis she had so much more energy than usual. Her cheeks were flushed with excitement. 'Do you want to play with me, Daddy?'

Anna opened her mouth to say that Ryan was probably going to need to get going, when she felt her mother's hand on her arm. 'Can you come and look at this chicken in the kitchen for me? I just want to make sure it's properly cooked.'

Leaving the two of them unpacking the console and charger from the box, Anna followed her mother into the kitchen, where she closed the door behind them.

Her mother didn't beat around the bush. 'Maybe you *should* go with him.'

Anna had been about to actually check the chicken when she realised that had just been a ruse to get her out there. She dropped the oven gloves back onto the counter. 'What? He's a grown man; he doesn't need me to hold his hand. He's just trying to be difficult.'

Her mum nodded slowly. 'I know that. Even so. You want him to have the test as quickly as possible, don't you? Is it really worth making a fuss about? It'll only be a couple of hours and then you'll be done. Think of the bigger picture.'

Her mother was right, of course she was. But she couldn't bear for Ryan to get his own way. 'Why can't he just want to do this for Libby? Why is he making out like he's doing me some huge favour?'

'I'm not sure that's what it is. I think' – her mother paused, as if to test the air – 'I think he's missed you. He was here for about twenty minutes before you got here and he was talking about you a lot. Not Libby. You.'

Anna laughed. 'Don't be fooled, Mum.'

'Don't worry, love, I'm nobody's fool. But you mustn't let your feelings for him and what happened cloud your judgement. I know things ended badly between the two of you and, believe me, I haven't forgiven him for it. But maybe this will give him an opportunity to do the right thing. Now that he is doing this for Libby, the two of you can put that behind you and have a more amicable relationship. You do still share a daughter.'

Though her words pretty much echoed her sister's sentiments, Anna had the urge to shake her mother. How could she be siding with him like this? She had absolutely no idea what he was like. If only she knew what he used to say about her and Anna's sister. How he would talk dismissively about them being from Essex and talk about how he 'saved' her from turning out like them. How he never wanted to visit and then made it difficult for her to go. How he had said, so many times, that Catherine was a lot closer to their mother than Anna was, that she had started to believe it.

But, of course, she had never told her mother those things because it would only have upset her. Every time he hadn't come with her to visit, she had made excuses about his work. When he had booked holidays which coincided with family celebrations, she had lied and said that he'd made a mistake, couldn't get a refund.

When he'd returned the dress her mother had bought her without telling her, because he said the material was cheap, she had gone out and bought an identical one to wear to her mother's birthday, which he had not attended.

So, if her family didn't understand just how difficult her life had been with him, was it their fault or hers?

'Okay, Mum. I'll try. You're right. I need to keep him on side until we get Libby what she needs.'

Her mum reached over and kissed her on the cheek. 'That's my girl.'

She put her hand over that of her mother's, which was still on her shoulder. 'Thanks for being here today.'

'I'm always here, you know that. Whatever you need.'

That reminded her. 'Actually, on that note, can I be cheeky and ask you to babysit next Wednesday night? There's a PTA meeting and I forgot that I'd promised to bring some canapés. I'm hoping to start getting the word out about Anna's Kitchen.'

'I saw those leaflets on the side there. They look great.'

'Yes. Tina's John did them for me at his work a couple of weeks ago, but with everything going on right now, I haven't had a chance to do anything with them.'

Her mother's face creased with concern. 'You're not taking too much on, are you? With Libby and your job and everything?'

'To be honest, it's giving me something else to think about rather than worrying about Libby on a loop. And we could do with the money now I've had to drop those hours for her dialysis.' Tina had insisted that she and Frankie could cover her work between them so that they didn't even need to tell the headteacher about it, but Mr Jones wasn't one to bend the rules for anyone and Anna didn't want to risk getting found out.

Her mum looked even more worried. 'Well, babysitting is never a problem. But please don't take too much on yourself, Anna. If you need money—'

Anna shook her head. 'No, Mum. You've given us enough. You need to spend your money on yourself. We'll be fine.'

Back in the lounge, Ryan and Libby sat on the sofa, their heads together looking at the Nintendo screen. They were so alike that it took Anna's breath away. It was a strange feeling when the person you loved most in the world reminded you of the one you most hated.

Anna's mother picked up her handbag from the floor and took out her diary. 'Before I forget, what time do you need me to be here next Wednesday when you go to the PTA?'

Anna blinked as she pulled herself away from staring at the pair of them. 'I think it starts at 7 p.m., so could you come at six thirty?'

Ryan looked up from the screen. 'What are you doing Wednesday?'

At the same time as Anna said, 'It's nothing, just the PTA,' her mother said, 'My clever daughter is launching her catering business at the school PTA meeting. She's going to wow them with her amazing canapés.'

Damn. Now he knew, she waited for the mockery to begin. But his reaction was actually worse. 'Really? At the school? That sounds like something I should come to. Good to show support for my daughter's new school, don't you think?'

Before Anna could think of an excuse, her mother had smiled at him. 'What a good idea. You can come here and help her carry all the boxes to and from the car.'

Anna loved her mother but, right then, she could have cheerfully taped up her mouth. 'I'll be fine, honestly. It's just a PTA meeting.'

'Nonsense.' Ryan winked at Anna. 'It's a date.'

FIFTEEN

There was a circle of maybe twenty blue plastic chairs in the middle of the school hall. This was where the children ate lunch, but it seemed different in the evening. For a start, fifteen adults made a lot less noise than sixty children. The women who ran the PTA seemed perfectly nice and friendly, and they did a lot of good for the school, but – in the five months that Libby had been there – Anna had never attended one of their meetings.

Paul Benham spotted her and came across the hall to take the plastic containers from her hands. 'This looks great, Anna. I've set you up some tables along the side here.' He was just about to turn when he saw Ryan behind her. 'Oh. Hello again. Good to see you.'

Ryan merely nodded. Anna's stomach tightened. *Please don't be rude.* 'I'll just pop out to the car and get the rest.'

She had her head in the back of the car, pulling the last box towards her, when Ryan appeared. 'Your boyfriend is getting some plates out. Give me the rest of those.'

'Ryan, please don't embarrass me in there. He's Libby's teacher.'

Ryan held up his hands. 'It was a joke, Anna. What happened to your sense of humour?'

Aside from Paul Benham, Ryan was the only man in the room.

Why was it that meetings like this were only attended by mums and not dads? It wasn't as if the dads didn't care. At the school Christmas Fayre, all the partners of the PTA women were there: putting up tables, ferrying stuff around, even manning the stalls. But they never came to the meetings.

However, Ryan never minded being the only man in a room; he thrived on female attention. Before Anna knew it, he was standing at the tea urn, chatting to a couple of mums she didn't recognise. It suited her, though. She could lay out the canapés without his helpful suggestions.

'Hi. Can I give you a hand?' She looked up into the smiling face of Felicity Martin, new chair of the PTA. 'Mr Benham told us you're a great chef, but these look incredible. Definitely worth breaking the diet for.'

Felicity's reference to Paul made Anna smile. Half the school mums would joke at the gate about having a crush on him. 'Thank you. Yes, I was just going to take the foil off the platters and then take them around. If you don't mind helping, that would be great. Unless you have to get set up?'

Felicity had the figure and face of a model, but such a kind and warm personality that you couldn't resent her for it. 'Nothing to set up. We like to give everyone fifteen minutes to have a drink and a chat. It gives people some extra time to arrive. You know what it's like when you're trying to get out the door and the kids just keep finding reasons to call you back.' She nodded in Ryan's direction. 'Did you two manage to get a babysitter?'

'No. I mean, yes, my mum is with her. Libby, I mean. My mum is with Libby. But we're not... I mean, Ryan and me. We're not together. He's Libby's dad, but we're not... together.'

If her verbal vomit hadn't been excruciating enough, Anna pressed her two forefingers together as if to indicate to Felicity what the word *together* meant. What an absolute idiot. She never used to be this nervous about talking to people for the first time. It was Ryan being here; he put her on edge.

Felicity peeled the foil from the plate of blinis. 'I see. Well, these look amazing. Can I steal one before I start handing them around?'

Anna smiled in relief. 'Of course.'

There was something about watching someone enjoy food she'd prepared that never got old. In her more romantic moments, she wondered if this was the same feeling that a novelist had catching someone reading their book, or a composer playing their song for an audience. Giving someone pleasure with something she'd created gave her such pleasure.

And Felicity was very complimentary. She held her fingers up to her mouth and kissed them. 'They are amazing. They taste even better than they smell.' She turned to a small group standing near the circle of chairs. 'Ladies, you have got to come and try some of these.'

For a few minutes, Anna forgot her awkwardness as she answered questions on ingredients, menus and her plans for Anna's Kitchen. Everyone was so kind and enthusiastic and a couple of them even asked for one of her new leaflets for parties they were planning in the next few months. At one point, Paul Benham caught her eye and gave her a subtle thumbs up. She returned his gentle smile. This was just the start she needed and she had him to thank for persuading her to do it in the first place.

She'd moved on to handing out the salmon puffs when Ryan reached over to take one. He popped it in his mouth whole and closed his eyes. 'I'd forgotten how good you are, Anna.'

Anna flushed at the unexpected compliment. 'Thanks.'

'She was a top chef, you know.' He spoke to the women around her as if he was her agent. Or pimp. 'In London. Top restaurants.'

Anna squirmed; this was uncomfortable. The women murmured their interest, but she couldn't help feeling like a kid with a pushy parent. 'Well, it was a long time ago and I think "top chef" is a bit generous.'

She laughed to deflect the attention, but Ryan wasn't taking the hint. 'Not at all. You were brilliant. And she gave it all up to look after our daughter.'

Felicity Martin turned back to Anna. 'How is little Libby? I saw she was back in school this week.'

And, just like that, Anna was back to being the mum with the sick kid. In the last few days, every conversation in the playground had started like this, with a head on one side and a sympathetic expression. She knew that people were only being kind, but that didn't make it any easier. If only they could go back to being just Libby and Anna; not the kid with a kidney disease and her mum. 'She's doing okay, thanks. Pleased to be back with her friends.'

'And once the kidney transplant has been done, she won't have to keep having time off for dialysis.' Ryan folded his arms.

All eyes were on Anna to back this up. Felicity held her hands together as if in prayer. 'Libby is having a transplant?'

Anna could have kicked Ryan. She didn't want this going around the school like wildfire. As soon as the parents started to talk about something, it wouldn't be long before the children overheard, and she didn't want Libby to have to deal with any difficult questions from her schoolmates. She tried to play it down. 'Nothing is certain yet. The doctors are exploring—'

Ryan cut her off. 'What Anna is trying to say, is that we are waiting for me to have some tests to confirm that I can donate one of my kidneys. A living donor is so much better for a child of Libby's age. She is going to need that kidney for a long time, after all.'

There were several sharp intakes of breath at the same time. 'Wow. You're going to donate a kidney?' One of the younger mums was looking at Ryan as if he was some sort of supernatural being. 'That's incredible.'

Ryan merely shrugged. 'It's what any parent would do for their child, surely?'

There were murmurs of agreement. Everyone there would give their own child whatever they needed. Anna knew that. What they probably wouldn't do was find an opportunity to boast about it to a roomful of strangers.

Thankfully, Felicity glanced behind her at the clock on the

wall and clapped her hands together. 'Crikey, look at the time! We need to get started.'

Anna took her place in the circle of chairs, but didn't contribute anything to the discussions about forthcoming fundraisers, except to offer a cake for an online raffle that someone was organising. Ryan, on the other hand, seemed to be enjoying himself interjecting with bright ideas to make their plans even better. More than once, Anna wanted to tell them to ignore him. He talked a good game, but he wouldn't be the one standing in the cold selling hot chocolate, or sticking a sponge in a bucket to clean someone's car. In the end, she just let it all wash over her.

After the meeting, it didn't take long for Anna to thrust her empty platters into the shopping bags she'd brought. Paul stepped towards her to help, but Ryan got there first. 'Thanks, we've got it covered.'

She just wanted to get home, away from here, away from Ryan.

On the way home in the car, he was really mean about the women he'd been speaking to. 'That lot haven't got a clue. The events they want to do will cost more to set up than they'll make.'

She was used to this. He always did think that he knew better than anyone else in the room. 'I don't suppose that matters. As long as the kids are having a good time.'

'It's that kind of small thinking that holds you back, Anna. Your leaflets, for example. That layout is so amateur.'

She didn't reply to that. When he pulled up outside the house a couple of minutes later, Anna had her hand on the door handle before he'd even stopped. 'Okay. Thanks for taking me.'

'No problem. Oh, I forgot to tell you. My appointment with Dr Wells is going to be next Tuesday. Three p.m.. Shall I meet you in the waiting room?'

Anna sighed and turned to him. 'Look, do you really need me to be there? I don't think it's a good idea, Ryan. I don't like leaving Libby while she's having dialysis. The nurses are great, but I worry that she might feel funny and not want to bother them.'

well I'll call you as soon as I'm about to leave... You may want to go on your run before I get back; I might not be up to it.'

Of course, they were both triathletes now. She could just imagine the pair of them in their designer Lycra.

'I've got to go, darling... Yes, see you soon.'

The kiss he blew into the phone made Anna want to throw up. He clearly thought he'd puckered up quietly enough for her not to hear, because he gave her a different story when he turned back to her. 'Sorry about that. A business call. Had to take it.'

What an absolute liar. 'You and Nicole are together?'

She had to give it to him: he was convincing. 'Where did that come from?'

'That was her, on the phone. I heard you.' She threw the bag with the dress at his feet. 'You should be giving that to her, not me.'

'Calm down, Anna. You know that Nicole and I are friends.' A smile played at the edges of his mouth. 'Very good friends.'

She felt sick. Was it the betrayal, or the humiliation of being the last one to know? Had they laughed at her behind her back? 'How long has it been going on?'

Ryan raised his eyebrows in mock innocence. 'I have no idea what you are talking about, Anna.'

There were so many thoughts wrestling with one another to be the first out of her mouth that she was speechless. Had Nicole stopped speaking to her because she and Ryan had got together? Or had that happened after? Were they serious? And, if they were together, why was he making it so difficult to get divorced?

Before she could articulate any of those thoughts, she was interrupted by a door opening. Anna recognised the tall black-haired man with an Irish accent as the same nurse who had taken her blood samples. 'Mr Ferguson? Do you want to come through?'

Ryan smoothed down his jacket and nodded at the nurse. 'I'm all yours.' Then he turned to Anna. 'Are you ready to hold my hand?'

She stared at him. Did he really expect her to meekly follow him in after that bombshell?

For just a moment, she thought he was going to let her off the hook. He smiled. 'I understand. I'll call and cancel. We'll make it another time when you can attend.'

He held her eyes until she looked away, pushing open the car door. 'All right. Don't cancel. I'll see you there.'

SIXTEEN

Anna's stomach was a churning sea of emotion. It wasn't just that she was apprehensive about the test results, although the outcome could be life-changing for Libby. There was something else. Was it... jealousy? Because it shouldn't be Ryan doing this. It should be her. She should be the one giving Libby a part of herself. Libby had come from her body. She was made from her body. Giving her a kidney, or any part of her body that she needed, was instinctive. It was desperately unfair that she wasn't able to do it.

Ryan's doctor stood as they came into his office. 'Good to meet you, Mr Ferguson. I'm Dr Wells.'

'Ryan, please.' Ryan leaned across the desk to shake the doctor's hand. 'And this is Mrs Ferguson. Anna.'

Why was he introducing her as if they were still together? She took the doctor's hand. 'We're separated.'

The doctor frowned at the form in front of him and made a note. 'Okay. Understood.'

Ryan's face darkened. Maybe she should have let it go.

If only it was Mr Harris here. She didn't know Dr Wells at all. Although apparently, that was the point. Ryan's doctor would look after him, while Mr Harris focused on Libby.

'Well, then, Ryan. The first thing we need to do is go through your medical questionnaire. Before we start, are there any questions that you'd like to ask me?'

Ryan was dressed as if he was going to a client meeting, and he had the assured air of someone who was chairing the discussion. 'No, let's just get cracking.'

Anna glanced at her watch. 'Do you know roughly how long the appointment is likely to be? It's just that Libby is up in the dialysis suite and I don't like to leave her too long.'

Dr Wells frowned again. She could imagine that she wasn't painting a particularly supportive picture. 'It's important that we take our time and cover everything properly. You don't necessarily need to be here. It's Ryan that I need to speak to.'

She glanced at Ryan, but he was looking at the doctor. 'I'd like Anna to stay. I'm sure Libby will be fine with the nurses.'

'As you wish.'

Most of the questions were pretty straightforward. Apparently, Ryan was the picture of health. Dr Wells even commented on the positive results from the ECG. 'You have a very strong heart.'

'I'm a runner. Well, more than that, actually. I enter triathlons.'

With his girlfriend. Anna wanted to say. *My ex-best friend.* She wasn't the bad guy in this room.

'That's fantastic. The fitter you are before the operation, the quicker the recovery will be.'

They already knew that the blood tests had come back showing that their blood groups were compatible, but the doctor went through everything again meticulously. Anna resisted the urge to look at her watch again; she didn't want the doctor to think she was unsympathetic. And she didn't want to risk annoying Ryan either. As they talked though, her mind was on Libby. She hated leaving her up there alone. As soon as she was out of sight, she couldn't help but imagine some emergency might happen. Anna slipped her hand in her pocket and held her mobile like a talisman: they would call her if Libby needed her.

The word 'cancer' caught her attention. This time Ryan's face had paled rather than darkened. 'You have to test me for cancer?'

The doctor nodded. 'It's standard procedure. If tests indicate cancer, we would obviously not be able to use your kidney, but we would be able to look after you and ensure that you got the treatment you needed.'

Ryan swallowed. Coughed. 'I see.'

'I've read on your form that there is a history of cancer in your immediate family. Your mother.'

Ryan cleared his throat again. 'Yes. Breast cancer. She died seven years ago.'

Anna had been pregnant with Libby when Ryan's mother died. It had been awful for him. They had been close. She'd brought Ryan and his brother up on her own. Anna didn't want to speak ill of the dead, but Ryan's mother had been a tricky woman to deal with. For a start, her darling son could do no wrong in her eyes. Anna, on the other hand, seemed to do plenty.

He looked so sad, she was almost tempted to reach over and hold his hand. No one deserved to lose their mother when they were still in their twenties. She knew how hard it had been for him.

Dr Wells could obviously see that it still affected Ryan. 'I'm sorry for your loss. There's no reason to think that you will have anything, but it's a good opportunity to know for sure. That's the questionnaire dealt with, anyway. Before we move on, is there anything arising from those questions that you'd like to ask or discuss?'

Ryan coughed to clear his throat. 'Just how long it will be before the operation, really.'

'Of course. Usually, if all is straightforward, it's around three months from this stage to the operation. But you are very fit and well, the recipient is your daughter, and we have the benefit of having all the facilities at this centre at our disposal, so – further tests permitting – we may be able to move things along a little more quickly than that. However' – Dr Wells placed his elbows on the table and made a temple from his fingers – 'we need to ensure that you have enough time to process all of this. And I have to emphasise that you can pull out of this at any time along the way. This is a big decision and you need to be certain that it is the right one for you.'

'Are you trying to put me off?' Ryan laughed, but there was a nervous edge to him. 'What are you not telling me?'

'Not at all. But your health is just as important to us as Libby's. Before your final tests you will need to see an independent assessor from the Human Tissue Authority. They will want to ensure that you're not being coerced in any way.'

Dr Wells glanced at Anna. She almost laughed. *Her coerce him?*

Ryan was back to his usual overconfident self. 'I'm fine, doctor. Whatever Libby needs, I am here for her.'

Now she wanted to throw up. The perfect father routine. The doctor smiled. 'That's good to hear. I'd like to do a quick examination now if you don't mind. Mrs – er – Anna, would you mind waiting outside?'

In the waiting area, Anna deliberated whether she had time to go and check on Libby and come back. Instead, she called the ward. Libby was fine. She and Max were watching cartoons. Max's dad was sitting with them again.

When Ryan came out of the doctor's consulting room, the two of them were laughing like old friends. She had to give it to him, he could charm a roomful of vipers.

He strolled over to where she was sitting and perched on the chair next to her. 'I've booked an appointment to see the independent assessor next week. After that, I can book my final scans and tests. Apparently, they even have to do a scan to make sure I've actually got two kidneys.'

'Really?'

'Yes. Occasionally someone only has one and they don't know it because it doesn't cause them any problems. Although I obviously won't be able to donate if I've only got one.'

He laughed, as if it was unthinkable that he would have anything less than a perfect set, but for Anna, this was just another entry on her mental list of things to worry about. 'Okay, well, let's hope that it's all okay. I'm going to have to shoot off now and see Libby.'

Ryan stood at the same time she did. 'Why don't I come with you?'

Anna had already stepped away, but she turned back. 'What?'

'I'd like to come with you and see Libby. If I'm doing this, I need to be involved with all of it, Anna.'

If? She didn't like that word. 'Okay. There's not much room up there for lots of people, but I'm sure the nurses won't mind if you come and say hello.'

She started to walk and Ryan followed. 'I don't care if they do mind. I'm her father and I've got a right to be there.'

In the event, the nurse on duty didn't mind at all, especially when everyone could see Libby's excitement. 'Daddy!'

'Hey, Libby. How are you doing?' Ryan strolled towards her like a movie star on a charity visit.

'I'm okay. This is Max.' Libby looked as if she might burst with pride in showing off her friend.

'Hi, Max. I'm Libby's dad.' Ryan held out his hand.

Max looked startled, but he reached out and shook it. 'Do you have a sports car? Libby said you have a sports car.'

Ryan chuckled. 'I do. Would you like to see a picture of it?' He pulled out his mobile and found a photo to show a very impressed Max. Who had a picture of their car on their mobile?

Anna took the opportunity to speak to Tim, Max's dad. 'Thanks so much for keeping an eye on Libby again.'

'No problem at all. They've been on their Nintendos and haven't needed me. Apart from to settle a disagreement about which *Animal Crossing* character is the cutest. I said Stitches. Obviously.'

Anna grinned. 'Obviously.'

Ryan stood up, his body angled towards Anna. 'What's *Animal Crossing*?'

Max's dad laughed. 'It's just a game they play on these things. I'm embarrassed I actually know the names of the characters.'

Anna smiled: that was the difference between a father who was in his child's life and one who wasn't.

Ryan ignored him and crouched down in front of Libby. 'Okay, Libs. How about we go to the cafe and get something to eat?'

There was an awkward silence. Max's father pretended to be looking for something in the bag he'd brought. Anna kept her voice low. 'She can't leave now, Ryan. She's in the middle of her dialysis.'

'And she can't move? Can't wheel it with her to the canteen? Or stop it and come back?'

Thankfully, Libby was forgiving: she giggled. 'Of course not, Daddy. I have to stay here until it's done.'

Max's father sat back up. 'But if you two want to go and grab something to eat, go ahead. All is fine here.'

Anna started to politely decline but Ryan interrupted. 'That would be great, mate. Thanks.'

And then Libby sealed the deal by requesting cake. 'Can you get me a chocolate muffin for later, please? And a blueberry one for Max.'

'Two lemon muffins it is.' Ryan winked at Libby as she squealed at him for getting it wrong.

The hospital cafe was quiet and it didn't take long for them to buy sandwiches and find a corner table. Anna wasn't usually a fan of pre-packaged sandwiches, but she tore open the box as soon as she sat down: the quicker she started, the quicker she could be on her way back to Libby.

Ryan had been quiet in the queue, other than insisting he pay for the sandwiches, muffins and coffee. Sitting opposite her, he pulled the plastic lid from his coffee and took a sip, wincing at the temperature. 'How long does she have to stay there, then? How long does it take?'

'The dialysis? About four hours.'

'And she has to come here for it? They can't rig up a machine at home?'

'There are two types of dialysis. Her kind has to be done here.'

Sometimes, Anna was so consumed by all the information relating to Libby's condition and treatment, that she forgot that people in the real world didn't know how this all worked. Although a father should.

Ryan frowned into his coffee. 'Wow. And that's three times a week? Does it hurt?'

'No. Sometimes she can feel a bit weird. And she gets really tired after. But the next day she feels good. We just have to get our routine right.'

Saying it like that made it sound so simple. But it wasn't. Already, Anna was realising what a massive impact this was going to have on their lives. Spontaneity was out of the window: anything they wanted to do had to be planned around appointments and dialysis, peaks and troughs of energy. During one tearful phone call to her mother, Anna had wondered whether they would ever be able to go on holiday again.

If she was feeling charitable, it wasn't necessarily Ryan's fault that none of this had occurred to him before now. 'Wow.'

'Yeah. Which is why the transplant will be so life-changing. Apart from managing the medication, she'll have the life of a regular kid.'

Ryan looked up. Were those tears in his eyes? 'I'm glad I can do this for her, Anna. Really, I am.'

There was something in the honesty of his expression which tugged on her from the inside. 'I am too.'

He stared at his coffee again. 'I know that I haven't been there these last few months. And I don't want to start up that argument again, but I will be around more.'

Again, this seemed like genuine remorse. Maybe her mum was right about him. Maybe the past was in the past. Libby was clearly overjoyed to have Ryan back in her life, and if he was willing to undergo major surgery for her, that had to be a sign that he loved his daughter. Maybe Anna needed to hold out an olive branch, too. 'Look, I'm having a little party for Libby on Sunday. For her birthday. Just a handful of friends. I'm not sure it'll be your kind of thing, but I'm sure she'd love it if you were there.'

A smile spread across Ryan's face. 'I'd love to come. Thank you. What time?'

'It starts at two.'

'I'll be there. I'll bring Nicole.'

SEVENTEEN

So much of Libby's new life wasn't normal. The time in hospital, missing hours from school, having to cancel their planned week in a caravan in Suffolk in February half-term because she would have to be back for dialysis. That was why today – her birthday party – felt so precious. For a few hours, they got to pretend that she was just a regular kid without a kidney disease that had turned her life upside down.

Because she had a bigger lounge and garden, Anna's mum had offered her house for the party, but it had felt important to Anna to have the party at their own home. Ryan had never wanted them to have a kids' party at their old house. He hated the idea of the noise and the mess and, the one time she had tried, they had had an almighty row the night before. In a fit of temper, he had destroyed the food, the decorations, even Libby's cake. The next morning, she had had to call the parents of Libby's friends to cancel, claiming a family emergency.

Last night, as soon as Libby was in bed, Anna had decorated the house with paper decorations and balloons. Then she'd done all the prep she could for the party food: homemade nuggets, cupcakes, cocktail sausages. The birthday cake had been made the weekend before and was hidden at her mum's house, ready to be brought over the next day. By the time she'd fallen into bed, she was exhausted.

Libby's excitement this morning made it all worthwhile. They had their traditional birthday breakfast – pancakes with chocolate spread – and Libby opened her gifts. The jigsaws, books and Lego seemed tame after Ryan's Nintendo extravagance, so Anna had also bought her a game for the console, which was ridiculous money, but made Libby jump up and down. '*Animal Crossing: New Horizons!* Max has this one! We can play in the same world together now!'

Even working in a school, Anna was always shocked by how much noise seven-year-old girls could make. It had seemed straightforward when Libby had said she wanted to play traditional party games, but that had been before Anna knew how much squealing was involved in musical chairs and pin the tail on the donkey. Thankfully, her mum had brought bags of craft materials, and the girls quietened down while they kneeled at the coffee table, sticking sequins and feathers onto card. Then it was time for food, so all five of them were squeezed together on the couch balancing paper plates and precarious cups of juice when Ryan and Nicole arrived.

Anna's mother let them in and, as soon as Libby saw Ryan, she jumped up in excitement.

'Daddy!'

She ran towards him and he folded her into a hug. 'Happy birthday, baby! You remember Daddy's friend, Nicole?'

Of course, Libby knew Nicole. At least, she'd known the old Nicole, the one who would play games with her on the floor of the lounge and sneak her glasses of fizzy drink from the kitchen. This Nicole made no attempt to hold out her arms to spin Libby around in the way that the old one would have done. 'Hi, Libby. Happy birthday.'

Libby held up a hand in an uncertain wave. 'Hello.'

Nicole looked very different from the last time Anna had seen her, too. For a start, she was a lot thinner, which must be a result of the triathlons. Her clothes looked more expensive too, compared to the jeans and shirts she'd worn most of the time Anna had been friends with her. Maybe Ryan was continuing his generous streak.

Libby was much more interested in Ryan than Nicole, anyway. She grabbed his hand and pulled him in the direction of the noisy lounge. 'Come on, Daddy. Come and play with us.'

To be fair to Ryan, he did a great job at the party. Getting involved with the kids' games and even buying a piece of 'art' from each of the girls. Libby was ecstatic to be able to show off her daddy to her friends. Nicole, on the other hand, sat in a chair in the corner of the room, sipping on a glass of water, looking as if she was avoiding touching anything.

Anna had her head inside the cupboard next to the fridge, looking for the extra paper cups she knew were in there somewhere, when the kitchen door opened and closed.

'What's going on, Anna?'

Anna pulled her head out and looked up to see Nicole, standing with her arms crossed. 'What do you mean?'

Apart from her thick, glossy dark hair, Nicole had never been someone you would describe as beautiful, but she'd always had such an animated face, quick to smile or laugh, that she had never been short of admirers. Now, though, that face was thin and pinched with anger. 'Don't treat me like an idiot. Between you and Ryan.'

Anna shuffled backwards and stood up. There was no way she was going to let Nicole look down on her. 'I have no idea what you are talking about.'

Nicole practically sneered. 'Don't try and act innocent. I know how much time you've spent together over the last few weeks.'

Anna laughed. 'You're being paranoid. Ryan is going to donate a kidney to his daughter. To help her have a better quality of life. I'm not sure that constitutes something *going on*. Unlike what is going on between the two of you.'

Nicole started, opened and closed her mouth. Anna hadn't been able to resist that final comment. She had to be nice to

Ryan, but that didn't mean she had to let Nicole speak to her like this.

'Nothing is going on between us,' Nicole's face was like stone. 'We're just friends.'

Her statement was so obviously a lie that Anna laughed. 'How could you do it, Nicole? You and I were friends. Really good friends. I told you everything. How Ryan was... How he was behaving. How unhappy I was. Do you know how much it hurt me when you stopped returning my calls?'

Nicole folded her arms, her face flushed. 'So that's why you're spending so much time with him? You're trying to get your revenge on me?'

How the hell were some people so self-centred? 'You have got to be kidding me. You think I would use my own daughter for something so petty?'

Nicole shrugged. 'You were worse than petty a few months ago. When you told Ryan that he couldn't see Libby anymore. And even before that, when you took her away from her home and dragged her all the way out here.'

It was all Anna could do not to snatch up the tea canister from the kitchen counter and hurl it at her. 'I *never* said he couldn't see her. And as for when we left London, what would you expect me to have done? I found him in bed, wrapped around the twenty-two-year-old he was working with. Was I supposed to just carry on as if nothing had happened?'

Nicole shuffled to her other foot. Even she couldn't defend his behaviour. Or so Anna thought. 'I'm not saying he was right to do that, but you kind of drove him to it.'

Anna put her hand to her mouth in shock. 'I *drove* him to it? What the hell does that mean?'

'He told me what it was like. That he had to work longer hours so that you could give up work and then, when he was home, you just wanted to be with Libby all the time. Or visiting your parents. He said you were over here all the time. I don't think you realise how upset he was at being taken for granted like that. He felt abandoned. What you described to me as jealousy was really him being desperate to spend time with you. I felt sorry for him.'

Heat rose from the very depths of Anna. 'I was looking after our daughter. And I spent a lot of time with my parents because my dad was *dying*. You make it sound like I was lying on a beach somewhere. And he wanted me to give up work. I cannot believe you are making out that I abandoned him.'

She wasn't surprised, though, that Ryan had described it that way. After all the support she'd given him when he'd lost his mother, none of it had been returned when her father was diagnosed with stage four pancreatic cancer. Her dad's decline had been quick and she'd had no idea how much longer they would have him: the quiet, strong, backbone of their family. If she could have camped at the foot of her parents' double bed, she would have done.

The pain of watching her dad slip away a little more each time she saw him was etched on her mind forever. But so were the vicious, cruel arguments she and Ryan had had about her staying overnight as he neared the end. The words *selfish* and *lazy* and *pathetic* had been thrown at her like emotional grenades. Then she'd had to turn up at her parents' and pull on a brave face, or pretend that she was grey-faced because of her worry about her dad. All that time she hadn't wanted them to think badly of Ryan. What a fool she'd been.

And Nicole was a fool for believing his version of events. That was what Anna couldn't believe. Nicole had been her friend. She had gradually begun to trust her with the truth of her relationship with Ryan. Bit by bit, she had opened up to Nicole about his need to know where she was at all times, his judgemental attitude towards the clothes she wore, his cruel barbs if he thought she'd put on weight or her hair needed to be cut. How had Nicole listened to all of this and yet still ended up in a relationship with him herself?

Nicole must have realised that she wasn't going to get anywhere with this line of attack, and so she changed back to her original focus. 'I'm not here to talk about the past. I'm here to talk about now. I know that he's been here a lot longer than it takes for a hospital appointment, and that he has been here for several evenings when Libby is probably in bed. Just tell me the truth. Are you trying to get back with him?'

If she wasn't so angry, this would be comical. 'No, Nicole. I am not. He is all yours.'

'If that's true, why won't you just give him a divorce?'

That one did surprise Anna. She'd tried so hard to push through the divorce. For a start, she was desperate to get the finances sorted out and, secondly, she didn't want to be connected to him anymore. It was Ryan who had held everything up. Ryan who refused to admit that he had committed adultery. And, like Catherine had explained, they had no proof. Although Anna hated it, it was easier just to wait out the time until she could divorce him without his agreement.

But he clearly hadn't told Nicole that. 'I would gift wrap a divorce and deliver it personally if Ryan would agree to it. In fact, now that you two are together, I can petition for adultery. It'll all happen more quickly.'

Nicole's face hardened. 'That's not going to happen. Ryan told me that you'd be looking for that. You and your sister. So that you can make sure you get complete custody of Libby. Handy that, isn't it? Your sister being your lawyer. Are the two of you enjoying making things difficult?'

How could Nicole be so blind? When had Ryan shown any interest in getting custody of Libby? Or, in fact, of even seeing Libby in the last six months? 'That isn't how it works anymore,' Anna said. 'It doesn't matter how or why a marriage ends. It's just about what's best for the child. But anyway, why would I want to do anything to slow down the divorce? How does that suit me at all?'

'Because you still want to be with him.'

There was so much she wanted to say in response to this that Anna couldn't get the words out. Then she was prevented from answering by Ryan opening the kitchen door.

'I was looking for you, Nic. What are you doing in here?'

Nicole's face changed into a smile. 'Just catching up with Anna. I think we're done. Actually, I've got a bit of a headache. Would you mind if we went home soon?'

Ryan looked from one of them to the other. Then nodded. 'Okay. Let's go now. Thanks for having us, Anna. I'll call you about the next appointment.'

She could see Nicole stiffen beside him. Maybe that was why she couldn't resist making her voice so warm when she replied, 'That would be great, Ryan. And thank you so much for being here. Libby has loved it.'

After they left, the party started to wind down and parents began to turn up to collect the children. It wasn't until that evening, once an over-tired Libby had been persuaded to finally close her eyes and go to sleep, that Anna thought about Nicole's words.

Despite her obvious lies, Nicole and Ryan were clearly now a couple. So why did Ryan not want to get a divorce? It couldn't be a custody issue, because he knew Anna well enough to know that she would never prevent him from seeing their daughter: for Libby's sake, not his. So was Nicole just hitting out because of her own jealousy, or was Ryan making the divorce difficult because he still had feelings for Anna?

And unpicking her feelings about *that* was like trying to work out the ingredients she could taste in a new dish: just when she thought she'd isolated the herbs involved, another flavour hit her to complicate it.

EIGHTEEN

For the first hour of dialysis on the following Tuesday, all Libby talked to Max about was her party.

Max had been invited to the party, but when he found out that all the other guests were going to be girls, he'd flatly refused to come. Having experienced the whole two hours with the pack of them, Anna thought he'd probably made a wise choice.

Large parts of Libby's party anecdotes included Ryan. How funny he was. How her friends liked him. Every time she brought him back into the conversation, Nicole's face flashed up in Anna's mind and she had to shake it away.

Julie, Max's mum, was quieter than usual. Anna tilted her head in her direction. 'Trip to the coffee machine?'

Julie followed her out, but Anna had to ask her three times if she wanted her usual black coffee. 'Is everything okay, Julie? I mean, Max is okay?'

Julie sighed. 'Sorry, I didn't get much sleep last night and sometimes... oh, sometimes it all just feels overwhelming. I want to shout at someone how it's just not fair.'

Anna understood. Of course, she did. How many times since the diagnosis had she cried in the quiet of the night that Libby had to go through all of this? 'Don't apologise. I totally get it.'

Julie swirled the coffee around the paper cup, staring into it. 'A letter came home from the school, yesterday. A residential trip. A week. Loads of activities. Canoeing, abseiling, you know the kind of thing. In Wales. A five-hour coach trip. You can imagine Max's reaction when I had to explain he couldn't go.'

'Oh, Julie.' The other gift of thrice-weekly dialysis: you couldn't go away for more than the day or two between sessions. Last August, Anna's mum had taken them away for a week to a caravan near Felixstowe. Libby had loved being able to paddle in the sea and they'd booked immediately to go away again this summer. A kidney transplant before then would mean that they might actually be able to go. They wouldn't be trapped by a dialysis schedule.

Julie nodded her head and pulled on a smile. 'That's enough wallowing. It sounds like Libby had a great birthday. She seems really happy to have her dad around more?'

Anna pushed the button for a mint tea and a second paper cup rattled into place. The machine hummed as the boiling water filled it up. 'Yes. She is.'

'And everything is proceeding well with the transplant?'

'Yes. So far, so good. There are still a lot of tests to go, but we're getting there.'

Julie blew on her coffee: it was always scalding hot. 'I remember how that felt. It's nerve-wracking, isn't it?'

'It really is.'

That was a surprise. Julie had never spoken to Anna before about Max and a transplant. And it had always seemed too intrusive, and tactless, to ask. But now Julie had been the one to bring it up, Anna could. 'Did you start the process for Max, then?'

Julie didn't answer straight away, and Anna worried that she shouldn't have asked. Then she looked up. 'Max has had a transplant. Christmas before last. Tim was his donor.'

Now Anna was completely confused. 'I don't understand.'

'It didn't work. His body rejected the kidney. That's why he's been back on dialysis for the last year.'

. . .

Anna bought them some chocolate from the vending machine and, after checking that the two kids were still happily creating a world in *Minecraft*, they sat in the small waiting area outside the ward.

'I didn't want to talk to you about it before now because we didn't have a good outcome, but I wish I had been more realistic, going in. It's a bit like childbirth – no one tells you the horror stories, so you go into it thinking a bit of breathing and a positive mental attitude will make it a walk in the park.'

The hospital armchairs were designed for functionality rather than comfort, and the vinyl seat felt particularly hard. Anna leaned on one of the thin wooden arms and tried to find a comfortable position. 'I see.'

'Both Tim and I were tested as a match, of course. Max has O positive blood, so we thought that meant he could have anyone's kidney. Unfortunately, it doesn't work that way around. He can only have a kidney from someone who is also O. And I am B positive.'

It was a painful irony that Anna had almost the exact opposite problem. Mr Harris had explained very carefully that Libby – who was also B positive – could only receive a kidney from someone with a B blood group or, like Ryan, an O blood group: the universal donor. 'Oh, Julie.'

'I know I should have been grateful that Tim could do it, but I really struggled. The doctors told me it was common that parents can't donate, but I felt awful. I mean, I'm his mum. I'm supposed to be the one who makes everything better, right?'

Anna reached out and squeezed Julie's arm. She knew exactly how that felt. The agony of seeing your own child in pain, and not being able to do a thing about it. 'I feel the same. It's so bloody unfair.'

Julie nodded. 'But I was glad that Tim is plain old O positive, so we could be hopeful. Tissue matching was good. His kidney function was good. We really thought it was going to go swimmingly.'

She broke off a piece of chocolate and took a tiny bite. Anna noticed her hand was trembling. 'You don't need to tell me about this if you don't want to.'

'I do want to. But only if you're sure you want to hear it?'

Anna did want to hear it. A strange prickling sensation on the back of her neck told her that she might not like it, but it was better to know what they were going into. 'I do.'

'There isn't that much to tell, really. The day of the operation, I was terrified. Nothing had prepared me for how I was going to feel with both my husband and son going into surgery on the same day. It felt like playing with fate, somehow. But they were both so brave. Tim seemed more worried about me than he was for himself. And Max gave me one of his *Star Wars* figures to hold onto while he was in for the operation.' A tear spilled from the corner of her eye and she wiped it away.

'He's such a lovely boy.'

Julie smiled at that. 'He really is. Everything he's been through, and he is still such a sunny, happy kid. I am so grateful he's ours.'

Anna felt the same about Libby. Life wasn't easy right now with the upheaval of dialysis and treatment. But she wouldn't be without her gorgeous girl for anything.

A nurse walked past who they didn't recognise. Maybe it was the uniform, or the sensible shoes, but Anna always felt more at ease when there was a nurse around: they were so capable, so kind. On the days it all got too much, one of the renal nurses was always there for her with a reassuring word, a kind smile – even a hug on occasion. They should be paid ten times what they were and it still wouldn't be enough.

Once the door to the ward had closed behind the nurse, Julie continued. 'The operation went well. They both recovered quickly and we had a couple of months of living like a normal family. Not having to be here for dialysis three times a week felt like getting out of prison. For the first couple of weeks, I would have a sudden panic that it was Tuesday or Thursday and we should be here. Then I'd remember that we didn't have to come, and relief would wash over me like a warm shower.'

'I can imagine.'

'We had even booked a holiday. A proper *abroad* holiday. Portugal. Something to look forward to once we got the final okay. Max was so excited to go on an aeroplane for the first time. He had a calendar in his room and he was ticking off the weeks.' Her voice caught and she stopped, taking another sip from her coffee. 'Sorry, it still gets to me.'

'Don't apologise, please.'

'Well, about two months after the operation, Max's temperature spiked and his hands and feet looked swollen. Obviously, we had been watching him like hawks, so we brought him straight in. But it didn't make any difference. The hospital tried everything they could with medication, and even considered a bone marrow transplant from Tim, but arteriosclerosis caused his body to reject the kidney.'

'Oh, Julie. I'm so sorry.'

'Yeah, it was pretty awful. Seeing him physically sick was bad enough. But the disappointment was worse. I'd never seen him so down.'

Anna couldn't imagine Max being sad. He had been such a light for Libby. Such a wonderful friend. She wanted to cry for him herself. 'Poor Max.'

Julie wiped another tear, took a deep breath. 'And now we're back here again. In some ways, it feels even more cruel now he's had a taste of life without dialysis. But when I think of the alternative...'

She didn't need to finish that statement.

Anna leaned in a little closer. 'Will he be able to have another transplant?'

'There's no reason why not, but I think we've all been a little frightened by the whole thing. He's on the list, but the doctors want to wait for an almost perfect match. I'm not sure how long it's going to take.' Julie sat up straighter; Anna could almost see her slipping her mask back on. 'Which is why it's really great that Libby's dad is a match for her. I don't want our experience to stop you from realising how great that is. It's why I haven't said anything up until now. I'm not even sure if I should have said anything. It's just been a tiring week, and—'

Anna held up a hand to stop her. 'I'm really glad you did. Thank you.'

She *was* glad. But she was also scared. She'd been so focused on whether or not Ryan would be a match, she had barely thought about the operation itself. The thought of putting Libby through all of that, and then it not working? She shuddered.

Back on the ward, Max was showing Libby how to craft with tools on *Minecraft*. The concentration on their two faces was so endearing that both she and Julie took out their phones and snapped a picture of them. Knowing more about Max's experiences made Anna feel even more grateful to him for the way in which he had taken Libby under his wing. She didn't know how the two of them would have navigated these early days of dialysis without him. She turned to Julie. 'You must be so proud of him.'

Julie smiled, not taking her eyes off her boy. 'I really, really am.'

Anna's phone was still in her hand when it buzzed with a call. Ryan.

'Hi.'

'Hey. Just reminding you that I'm meeting with the independent assessor tomorrow.'

As if she'd forgotten. 'What time are you meeting with them?'

'Well, that's the thing. The appointment is early in the morning. So, I was wondering, to save me having to leave ridiculously early to beat the traffic, can I come and stay over at yours tonight? I'm happy to take the sofa.'

Anna's fingers started to tingle and she squeezed the phone tightly. Ryan staying overnight? Being in her house when she was in bed? But how could she say no? 'Yes. That's fine. Will you need some dinner?'

His voice sounded very upbeat when he replied. 'Dinner cooked by my favourite chef? How can I refuse?'

It was only after she'd put down the phone that it occurred to her that he could easily afford to have booked the hotel a stone's throw from the hospital. Why had she not thought of that, rather than agreeing to him sleeping on her couch? *Damn.*

NINETEEN

'So, he stayed over? How was that?'

The following morning, Anna and Tina were the only ones in early so, as quickly as she could, Anna filled her in on Ryan's call and the fact he'd stayed the night.

It had been very strange to begin with. Ryan had turned up looking as if he was about to go on a date: shirt, smart trousers, expensive aftershave. Anna's stomach had actually flipped at the sight of him, but it was nerves, not attraction. He always dressed well. It meant nothing.

Libby had been over the moon about Daddy coming for a 'sleepover'. Because it hadn't felt right letting Ryan sleep on the sofa the night before his meeting with the independent assessor, Libby was going to give up her bed and sleep in with Anna. Libby had taken care to make sure her room was ready – even picking out a teddy bear to keep him company. When he arrived, Ryan took his bag straight up and then came down to join them for dinner.

Libby's appetite was hit and miss after dialysis. Sometimes she would be ravenous, others she would be so tired that she'd just pick at her food. When she'd started to push her peas around the plate half-heartedly, Ryan had taken her fork from her and rearranged her vegetables into a funny face that made her giggle. Then she had eaten every last one.

It made Anna sad. This was how it could have been. The three of them. She'd loved this side of Ryan. His jokes, his memory for small details, his thoughtfulness. How much would Libby have loved that, too? The three of them living in the same house. But it wasn't possible. It wouldn't have been like this all the time. *It's not your fault.*

Libby had also kept up a constant chatter. 'Are you scared about your tests, Daddy? Because I can come and hold your hand if you want me to?'

Ryan reached out and patted her arm. 'That's so sweet of you, Lib. But I'll be fine. Unless I can persuade your mother to take a morning off work?'

He raised an eyebrow at Anna and she shook her head. 'I can't. It's too short notice. And I feel like I'm pushing my luck at the moment anyway.'

He shrugged and leaned in to stage whisper at Libby: 'It was worth a try.'

'What are they going to do tomorrow? Do you have to have any injections? Because they can give you magic cream to make sure that it doesn't hurt. But you're an adult, so you might have to ask for it.'

It made Anna's heart squeeze, listening to her caring girl explain all the medical details. At the same time, it made her sad that she knew so much about how a hospital worked.

'No, no injections. I'm going to have a scan to make sure that I've actually got two kidneys.'

It was irrational for Anna to worry about this. They would have to be extremely unlucky to discover that Ryan didn't have a spare kidney for Libby. The number of people born with only one kidney was around 1 in every 1000 – she'd looked it up on the internet – but it *was* more common in males. 'Don't joke about it.'

Ryan smiled. 'Who knows. Maybe I've got three?'

Libby giggled. 'And maybe you've got two hearts too!'

'That would be handy, wouldn't it? I'd have one for you and one for—'

'Mummy!'

This was a game they used to play when Libby was small. Anna was amazed that she remembered it. Ryan would bring home two of something – chocolate bars, bunches of flowers, milkshakes – and he would make a big show of having two gifts. He would say exactly what he'd just said, and Libby would finish his sentence in the same way.

Now, though, it made Anna feel uncomfortable. 'Has everyone finished? Shall I clear the plates?'

Ryan stood up. 'Let me do that. You have a sit on the sofa. I'll put these in the dishwasher.'

She didn't want him making himself at home in her kitchen. 'We don't have one of those. The kitchen isn't big enough.'

That didn't put him off. 'Okay, then. Want to come and help me wash up, Lib?'

Libby – the girl who normally had to be asked three times to take an empty cup out to the kitchen – jumped off her seat as if he was taking her to the park.

As Anna could have predicted, twenty minutes after they had washed up and then returned to the lounge to join her, the after effects of the dialysis kicked in and Libby was yawning. 'Come on, baby girl. Time for bed.'

She must have been exhausted because she didn't even argue. 'Can Daddy do my story?'

It was a reasonable request, but Libby was sleeping in Anna's room. It was unthinkable that she would let him in there. 'Daddy needs to rest to get ready for tomorrow, Libby.'

But Ryan was already on his feet. 'I'd love to.'

Libby clapped her hands. 'Can you do one of your special stories?'

How could she say no, now? *Buy some time.* 'Let's go and do teeth and PJs, Lib, and then Daddy can come up in a minute.'

Leaving Libby in the bathroom to finish cleaning her teeth, Anna darted around her small bedroom, clearing her bed of yesterday's clothes, making sure all her drawers were firmly closed, even plucking the book from her bedside table: she wanted to leave nothing for his eyes or – worse – touch. If she'd had time, she would have stripped the whole bed of the beautiful silver-grey bedding that had been a moving-in gift from her sister. In a few minutes, Ryan would be sitting on those sheets to read to Libby and, later tonight, she'd have to lay down next to Libby on the very same spot. Would he leave the imprint of his body, the smell of his aftershave? She grabbed one of the pillows and stuffed it into her wardrobe with the rest of the things she'd collected. It was best not to think about it.

Half an hour later, stories had been performed and it was just the two of them in the small lounge.

Ryan seemed different this evening. More relaxed. 'Thanks for letting me stay tonight. It was really nice to be able to put her to bed.'

Being alone with him felt strange. How long had it been since they'd sat together in their much bigger lounge back at the old house, just the two of them, Libby tucked up in bed? 'Well, maybe you can have her over to stay at yours once this is all over. Everything will be easier once she's had the transplant.'

Ryan picked up the tea she'd made him. 'I miss this.'

Something prickled in Anna. She didn't want to ask what he meant, because she didn't want to hear the answer. She just kept sipping her own drink.

He didn't seem to notice the tension. 'You, me and Libby. We had good times, didn't we?'

Yes, they had had good times. But there had also been a lot of times which weren't so good. Anna tried to play it safe. 'She loves seeing you.'

He turned on the sofa so that he faced towards her. 'And what about you? Do you like seeing me?'

Anna could feel her face heat up. What could she say that wasn't going to start an argument? 'I'm glad that you're doing this for Libby. I'm grateful.'

He frowned at that; she could feel the tide turning. 'Grateful? I'm her father, Anna. Did you think I wouldn't do this?'

She needed to get things back on an even keel. 'I didn't mean it like that. I meant it's a relief. It's good. Having you here to share the burden of all this. It helps.'

This seemed to please him. His face cleared. 'Well, I want to help. I want to be there for her. For both of you. We made a mistake, Anna, but it's easy to make everything better.'

He reached out and took her hand. Her skin itched at his touch, but she left her hand there for a few seconds before slipping it out of his grasp and pretending she needed to cover her cough.

He felt too close; it was claustrophobic. She stood up. 'Well, tomorrow is going to be a big day for you. Shall I get you a glass of water to take up with you?'

'I'm not ready for bed yet. Well, not ready for sleep.' He laughed as if it was a light-hearted joke, but it made her flesh crawl.

'Well, I need to go up. I've got an early start tomorrow.'

'Just sit down a minute. You're always on the go. I need to talk to you.'

She sat down in the chair in the corner, willing him not to go where she thought he might.

'One of us has to say it, Anna, and I'm happy to start. I think we should give it another go. You and Libby come back to the house. Start again.'

Her throat was dry. 'And what about Nicole?'

He shrugged. 'She's not you, Anna. It's always been you for me. Tell me you don't feel the same?'

Years ago, she'd loved it when he'd made these sweeping proclamations of his feelings. Used to feel so fortunate to have a husband who wasn't afraid to show her – and the world – how passionately he loved her. Holding her hand when they walked anywhere. Surprising her with flower deliveries. Leaving notes and cards for her to find which told her how beautiful she was, how much he adored her.

But now she knew the flipside of this. And it wasn't worth the trade.

She sat up straight and looked him in the eye. 'No, Ryan. I don't feel the same.'

His face reddened; it was like a switch had been flicked. 'It's him, isn't it? That wet teacher at Libby's school. Are you screwing him?'

His coarse language made her flinch, especially connected with Paul Benham. She felt ashamed, even though she hadn't done anything. 'I'm not seeing *anybody*. For a start, when would I have the time, for goodness' sake?'

The expression on Ryan's face was the ugly sneer that she had seen so many times before. 'I don't believe you. Well, I hope you'll be very happy with him in your tiny little house with your pathetic little job.'

Anna closed her eyes. She felt so tired. 'Ryan, please.'

When she opened them again, he was standing. 'Don't even bother. I'm going to bed. One of us is going to put our daughter before their own selfish desires.'

As Anna recounted all this, Tina listened with a thin, tight mouth, lips pressed together as if she was trying to stop herself from interrupting. Eventually, she couldn't help herself. 'Oh, Anna. That's awful. Did you have any idea that he was still in love with you?'

'I don't think he is.' She knew Ryan. This wasn't about love. This was about ownership. She had been the one to leave him, and he couldn't handle it. He wanted to show her that she needed him.

The outside door clanged open and they heard the chatter of people arriving. Tina gave her arm a squeeze. 'We'll talk about this later.'

The day flew by because there were deliveries, and they were also a person down because Frankie had the flu. When Ryan had left that morning, he'd been stiff, but he had said he would call Anna when the tests were over. By midday, she'd heard nothing. Between then and 2 p.m., she checked her phone every ten minutes. Still nothing.

At two thirty, she sent him a text:

Everything okay?

When she and Libby got home at three thirty, she left a voicemail.

When she went to bed at 10 p.m., she still hadn't heard from him.

TWENTY

By Friday evening, two days after he should have had his meeting with the independent assessor, Ryan still hadn't called Anna. She'd done her best to keep busy since she'd got in that afternoon from work. Tomorrow she had her first booking for the catering company, and she would have been nervous even without all this going on. Now, she felt positively frantic.

So many different scenarios were running through her head. Had the assessor been concerned about Ryan's sudden reappearance in Libby's life? Had he found something in Ryan's test results that Dr Wells had missed? Had they told Ryan something that had concerned him, and he wasn't sure he wanted to go through with the donation? Was he so angry at Anna's refusal of his advances on Wednesday night that he hadn't turned up at all?

This morning, Anna had even contemplated trying to contact his doctor to find out if everything had gone well. But after the way Dr Wells had looked at her when she'd met him – the way he'd emphasised that Ryan should not feel coerced – she didn't think that contacting him was a good idea. And there would be no point calling Mr Harris, either. Even if he did know anything, patient confidentiality would prevent him from telling her.

At least she could take out her frustration on the meat for the sausage rolls. With Libby staying overnight at her mum's, she could make as much noise as she needed to in the kitchen, and work as late as she wanted, without fear of disturbing her. She'd chopped up apricots and was squeezing them into the meat with her hands.

Surely Ryan wouldn't just change his mind about the kidney because she'd turned him away? His pride might have taken a dent, and she knew of old how he hated to look foolish, but he hadn't said anything to her about changing his mind in the morning before he'd set off for the hospital. And if he had changed his mind, not saying anything wouldn't be his style. If he didn't want to do something, he would have definitely told her to her face. He'd have wanted to see her reaction, if nothing else.

And Libby was his daughter, too. The last few weeks he'd been so good with her. Making her laugh, buying her gifts, even coming to her birthday party. However angry he might be with Anna, he wouldn't let Libby down when her health – maybe her life – was on the line. Would he?

If she continued squeezing the sausage meat this hard, it'd end up as puree. She'd prepared the pastry earlier, so all she needed to do now was roll it out and fill it. Holding her hands under the hot water, she looked at her reflection in the kitchen window. Nicole had looked so fit and healthy at the party; why would Ryan even be interested in someone who looked as tired and old as Anna did at the moment?

Rolling pastry was usually one of her favourite things to do. There was something soothing about rotating the rolling pin, backwards and forwards. Tonight though, a big part of her wanted to not bother with all this. To call the woman who had booked her and explain that, she was sorry, but there'd been a family emergency: she wouldn't be able to cater for her husband's fiftieth birthday. It wasn't as if it was a huge celebration. It had been a last-minute booking when the customer had almost fallen out with her grown-up daughter over sandwich fillings and they'd decided to 'get in a professional' in the name of family harmony.

But Anna's Kitchen was the start of a financially better life for her and Libby. She'd even begun to fantasise about squirrelling any of her profits away so that, once Libby had recovered from her transplant, she could afford to take the two of them on a holiday abroad. Maybe even take her mum with them to thank her for her support.

If Libby had her transplant.

It wasn't until she'd filled out the sausage rolls and cut them that she remembered she hadn't bought any eggs to glaze them with. She wouldn't need to do that until the morning, but she had planned on making an egg mayonnaise tonight to fill the vol-au-vents, which had been specially requested as the birthday boy's favourite. She grabbed her jacket and keys – there was a twenty-four-hour supermarket ten minutes from here.

The supermarket was a strange place in the late evening. The aisles were so quiet. Other than a few shoppers, the only people there were the shelf stackers, pushing their tall cages of food along the aisles.

Normally, Anna loved food shopping. Particularly for fresh ingredients. Before she'd had Libby, one of her favourite things to do had been to visit the food markets in the city. Borough Market, Brockley Market, Maltby Street. The vibrant colours, the rich scents.

Tesco Extra wasn't quite the same experience, but since they'd started to stock a wider range of foods from around the world, she often liked to see if she could pick up an unusual ingredient and make something with it. Tonight, though, her mind was too busy to enjoy browsing the shelves. She knew where the eggs were, and she made a beeline for them.

She was almost at the checkout when she heard her name being called. 'Anna? Anna? Hi.'

She turned and almost bumped into Paul Benham. 'Oh, hi.'

It was the first time she'd seen him not wearing a jacket and tie. Jeans and an open-necked shirt suited him. 'You obviously do your shopping at the same random hours of the night as I do.'

'Not usually. Normally I'm home with Libby in the evenings. But she's at my mum's, and I'm catering a party tomorrow night and I realised that I'd run out of eggs.'

'A party. That's great. You're getting Anna's Kitchen off the ground, then?'

It was sweet that he'd remembered the name. 'Yes. Well, this is my first proper booking, so I want to do a good job.'

'I'm sure you will. I mean, you're really talented. Those canapés you made for the PTA event were fantastic.'

Anna felt her face redden. 'Oh, well, they weren't really difficult.'

'You say that, but to someone who can burn baked beans, they were amazing.'

She should have laughed, made a joke in return, picked up the eggs and left. Instead, she hovered, awkward and uncomfortable. 'Well, I'd better get back to my sausage rolls.'

Paul stepped back as if he had been barring her way. 'Of course, good luck with it.'

As soon as she got back home, Anna checked her phone again. Still no messages. It was ten o'clock. She wouldn't normally call someone at this time of night, but she couldn't go to bed again not knowing. If she woke him up, that might work in her favour. He might pick up the phone before he even realised that it was her on the other end.

The phone rang five times and then someone did pick up, but it wasn't Ryan.

The voice on the other end was practically a hiss. 'Anna. Will you just stop calling?'

'Nicole? Is that you?'

'Yes, it is. Ryan is in bed. So was I, until I heard his phone ring. You need to stop hassling him like this.'

Evidence – if she'd needed it – that the 'not being together' was a complete and utter lie, but right now she didn't care about that.

She had to fight an urge to burst into tears. She didn't want to hassle him. If he had just kept his promise and called her after his hospital appointment on Wednesday, she wouldn't be calling him at all. 'Please, Nicole. I just need to know. Did he have the scan? And the kidney function test? What happened?'

Nicole sighed dramatically on the other end of the phone. 'That's not for me to say. You need to speak to Ryan about—'

'I've been *trying* to talk to him!' Anna realised she was shouting at Nicole and paused, took a breath. 'I'm sorry. I've been trying to talk to him for the last two days but he won't take my calls or answer my texts. Please, Nicole. Tell me something. Or tell him to call me.'

She could tell by the change in Nicole's tone that she'd irritated her. 'I'm not going to *tell* him anything. And neither are you. You're not going to get anywhere like this, Anna. This is your problem. You go on and on at him and then wonder why he doesn't want to speak to you. You need to back off and leave him alone. I don't know what you said to him on Wednesday morning, but he is pretty angry with you right now.'

It wasn't what she'd said on Wednesday morning that had made him angry. Anna wanted so much to tell Nicole exactly what had gone on between them on Tuesday night. Or what she had stopped going on between them. But causing problems between the two of them wasn't going to help Libby's situation in the slightest. Plus, Anna didn't feel like she owed Nicole any favours in that department. 'It's not me that's important. It's Libby.'

Nicole's voice softened a little. 'What you're asking him to do – it's huge. It's not like you're asking for money for a school trip. This is a major operation.'

Now Anna really did want to cry. She wouldn't be asking Ryan to pay towards a school trip, for the simple reason that Libby couldn't go on a trip away with the school because of her need to get back for dialysis. A fact that would continue to be true if she couldn't have this damn transplant.

But there was absolutely no point in arguing with Nicole about this. She tried to keep her voice calm. 'Can you please just tell me if he had the tests?'

There was silence on the other end of the phone for a few moments, then Nicole spoke. 'Yes. He did. But I'm not discussing it any further with you. He will contact you when he's ready. Goodbye.'

Nicole hung up before Anna could echo her goodbye. She rested against the counter. At least she knew he had had the tests; that was an improvement on twenty minutes ago. But she still had no idea what the results were and, as Nicole said, she was just going to have to wait until Ryan was ready to tell her. Whatever his agenda was in making her wait – payback, power, petulance – she had no choice but to let him sit in the driver's seat.

She wrapped the raw sausage rolls in baking paper and put them into the fridge next to the plastic containers of samosas and bhajis she had prepared earlier. When she closed the fridge door, she leaned forwards and rested her forehead on it, closing her eyes. Her lips moved as if in prayer. 'Please don't do this, Ryan. Please don't let my baby down.'

TWENTY-ONE

The next day, Anna immersed herself in a production line of sandwiches, vol-au-vents and cocktail sausages. All she could think about was Ryan and when he was going to call. Even so, when she heard a knock on the door, she was surprised.

'Ryan. I wasn't expecting you.'

Under normal circumstances, she wouldn't want him turning up without warning. Today, she couldn't hide her relief, and his smile showed that he knew that. 'Really? After you've been calling my number relentlessly for the last two days? You can't do that, Anna.'

She swallowed down the rising anger and stood back to let him in. 'Do you want to come through?'

He looked around him as he entered the lounge. 'Where's Libby?'

'It's Saturday. She's at dialysis. My mum is with her.'

Ryan turned and raised an eyebrow. 'Really? So you aren't the one taking her three times a week, giving up work to look after her, being a martyr? Your mum does it?'

This was the first time that Anna wouldn't be at the hospital with Libby, and it had been hard to let her mum take her place. She had tried to work out the timings so that she could be at the hospital with Libby and still get the food to the fiftieth birthday party on time. Maybe once she'd done this a few times, it might be possible. But this first go, she couldn't afford for anything to go wrong. And her mum had offered. 'I had work to do. Libby was excited for my mum to be with her. It was a novelty.'

She emphasised the word *novelty*. But why was she attempting to justify herself to him? She *did* go to all of Libby's appointments with her. She *had* sacrificed her career for Libby, and a lot more besides. Not that she resented it for a minute. If there was one thing in her life she was proud of, it was her girl.

Ryan noticed the boxes of food on the sideboard. 'More PTA meetings with your boyfriend?'

Don't rise to it. 'I have a job. A catering job. A *paid* catering job.'

'You're actually doing that Anna's Sandwiches thing? Interesting.'

What was she expecting? That he would congratulate her? Say 'well done' for trying to carve out a career that would fit around Libby's education and health, while supporting them both? She should have known better. She'd had enough of the small talk. 'How did your appointment go at the hospital? The scan? The kidney function test? Was everything okay?'

He scratched the top of his head. 'Can I sit down before you start grilling me?'

Right now, she wanted to grill him on top of a large fire, but she settled for squeezing her hands tightly into fists and taking a deep breath. 'Of course.'

He unbuttoned the front of his jacket and flicked out the back of it before taking a seat: heaven forbid he should crease it. 'Aren't you going to offer me a drink?'

He was playing with her; she knew this treatment of old. Torturing her by making her wait. She shouldn't have to play his games anymore. 'Look, I'm really sorry, Ryan, but I have to finish preparing this food for later. Mum and Libby will be back from the hospital soon and I want to get as much done as I can before then.'

'I see. Well, actually, that kind of feeds into what I wanted to talk to you about.' He laughed. 'If you'll pardon the pun.'

Now she was completely confused. What did her catering booking tonight have to do with his kidney tests? 'Sorry?'

'The thing is. I don't think you've been very straight with me about the implications of this operation.'

A cold trickle started at the top of Anna's spine. 'I don't understand, Ryan. What implications?'

'How incapacitated I'm going to be, for one. I'll need weeks of time off work.'

Anna's legs felt wobbly. She sank down onto the sofa opposite Ryan's chair. 'But you will get sick leave, right? And you spoke to the doctor yourself. He explained everything. I was there.'

He shook his head slightly, as if there was an annoying insect nearby. 'Yes, well. I don't think I took it all in. Foolishly, I trusted you when you said that it was safe. Maybe that's why I was less than focused on the doctor.'

Anna didn't want her voice to tremble as she spoke, didn't want him to see that she was afraid. 'But it is safe. The risks to the donor are incredibly low.'

He held up a finger. God, she hated it when he did that. It always used to signal a profound declaration about why he was right and she was wrong. 'Low. But not non-existent. And I'm not even referring to the risks. I'm talking about convalescence. The amount of time I'll be laid up after the operation. After I've had a whole one of my kidneys removed.'

Anna pressed her lips to stop them from trembling. He was watching her. Was he enjoying this? 'It's only a few weeks.'

He mimicked her voice. 'It's only a few weeks.' His face returned to the stern expression he'd been wearing. 'That's all very well when you're just a dinner lady. It's slightly more important when you've got clients who need you.'

She really wanted to make a comment on whether it was more important to feed children or the bank accounts of the rich and privileged, but she kept quiet. Waited for him to continue.

Ryan leaned towards her and it was all she could do not to flinch. 'This thing is, Anna. I could lose a lot of money over those *few weeks*, as you nonchalantly refer to them. And I could even lose clients to other execs. It's not something I can consider lightly.'

With every ounce of her being, Anna hoped that he was just doing this in an attempt to mess with her head. That, any minute now, he would sigh dramatically and tell her that of course he would do it. What did she have to do to get to that point as quickly as possible? Compliment his sacrifice? Massage his huge ego? 'I understand that, Ryan.'

He shook his head at her. 'Do you? Because I don't think you do. You've never really had a lot of staying power with a job. The restaurants. Then the cafe. Now you're at a school.'

Anna pushed her hands under her thighs. It was all she could do not to leap at him. It was *him* who had wanted her to change jobs. 'What do you want me to say, Ryan?'

'At the moment, it is all one way. I'm the one going through a major operation. I'm the one who is going to suffer financially. We need a logical solution. A fair solution.'

Did he want her to pay? 'I can't help you out with money, Ryan. I don't have anything. That's why I'm trying to do this.' She swept an arm to indicate the boxes of wraps and sandwiches and sausage rolls.

Ryan put his hands on his knees and nodded his head. 'Exactly.'

Again, he was making no sense. She was tired of this cat and mouse conversation. 'Please, Ryan. Just tell me what you want.'

'Since my last appointment, I've been thinking about this in detail. And I can only see one solution. I need to stop the maintenance payments. For the foreseeable future.'

Anna felt as if he had punched her in the stomach. His maintenance payments for Libby – while probably only a fraction of his huge salary – covered a large part of their rent and bills for this house. Even with that, and the money she earned from her job at school, they were only just keeping their heads above water. If that suddenly stopped... She shuddered. 'But you can't. We agreed.'

Even so, she knew that the agreement was informal rather than legal. Catherine had explained to her that, until Ryan actually agreed to the divorce, they couldn't start the negotiations for a formal consent order. Ryan knew that, too.

'Yes, I bet your harpy of a sister enjoyed sticking her nose into my finances and making sure you get a nice chunk of my money every month, didn't she? But that figure was agreed based on my earnings being so much more than yours. With the commission I'm going to lose, I'll be earning a lot less. And you have your own business now. You can afford to take more of the financial burden. Circumstances have changed, wouldn't you say?'

The look on his face made it clear what circumstances had changed. She needed something from him. He had his power back. And he was going to make damn sure that he made the most of it. But he couldn't be saying no maintenance, or no kidney. Could he?

They were interrupted by the sound of the front door. Anna could hear her mother's voice. 'Slow down, Libby. You're going to wear yourself out. Come here and let me help you with that coat.'

Then Libby's voice. 'But that is Daddy's car. I know it is.' She raised her voice to call through to the lounge. 'Mummy! Is that Daddy's car? Is he here?'

Ryan stood up and called back. 'I certainly am, sweetheart. I've come to surprise you. Shall we go and get an ice cream somewhere?'

Libby ran into the room and straight into her father's arms. The sight of it sickened Anna. He could buy her ice cream, but he didn't want to pay for her to have a roof over her head. 'Not this afternoon. She'll be tired after her dialysis.'

Libby didn't even look at her. 'I won't. I'm not tired at all. And I want an ice cream. Can we go to that cafe? The one with the big waffles?'

'Sounds good to me. Unless Mummy says we can't go.'

'Libby, you'll get tired soon. It's not a good idea.'

Libby's face was furious when she turned around. 'I am *not* tired. I want to go with Daddy. You're being mean. Don't be mean to my daddy.'

Anna's hand flew to her chest, Libby's words like bullets. She opened her mouth to speak, but nothing came out.

Ryan turned Libby around by the shoulders to face him, his voice a thick, sickening syrup. 'It's okay, Libby. Let's not make Mummy cross or she won't let me come again. How about tomorrow?'

Not tomorrow. It was Sunday. And Sundays had become so precious: the one day of the week where there was no school and no dialysis. After being paid for this job tonight, Anna had planned to surprise Libby by saying that she would take her out wherever she wanted to go. She didn't want to say that in front of Ryan, though. He'd invite himself along. 'Tomorrow is tricky—'

The predictable flip happened. 'For God's sake, Anna, you need to make your mind up. One minute you're calling me every hour of the day and the next you're saying I can't take my own daughter out. Can you not hear yourself? How unreasonable you're being?'

Anna's mother was hovering on the threshold between the hall and the lounge and would have heard every word. Anna felt her face redden. She looked at Libby's angry face. Her daughter's body leaned in to Ryan's. His hand on her shoulder. 'Okay, yes. Fine. Tomorrow is fine.'

'Great.' Ryan reached down and hugged Libby. 'Okay, Lib. I'll come for you in the morning. How's that? Make sure you go to bed early tonight so we can have lots of fun together.'

Libby's smile filled the room and it was like the sun had come out. A sense of betrayal tightened in Anna's chest. Why was she choosing him? Why?

Anna's mother stepped forward. 'Come on, Libby. Shall I make you something to eat in the kitchen while Mummy and Daddy make the arrangements?'

As soon as they were out of the room, Ryan buttoned up his jacket. 'Think about what I've said, Anna. I'll see you tomorrow to pick up Libby.'

TWENTY-TWO

It was the first Sunday in over two years that Anna had been alone without Libby, and she didn't know what to do with herself.

The food for the party last night had been a huge success. This morning, her customer had called with effusive thanks and said that she'd given Anna's number to three of her guests who had events coming up later in the year. Before yesterday, Anna would have been really excited; now it barely took the edge off the fear that she was going to need a lot more than three customers a year to be able to keep her and Libby in the house.

She had run over it in her head so many times as she'd lain awake the night before. Had she misunderstood? Had Ryan really threatened to pull out of being a donor if she didn't let him stop paying maintenance? How could he reconcile that with this new 'Superdad' persona he was projecting onto the world?

When Ryan had collected an excited Libby at ten that morning, he hadn't mentioned the situation again. Although Libby hadn't really given him a chance to speak. Having sat with her nose millimetres from the window since she'd got up that morning, she'd had the front door open as soon as she'd seen him walking up the path. Irritated, Anna had told her off. 'You know I don't want you opening the front door without me there, Libby. It's not safe.'

Libby had rolled her eyes – a relatively new response to most things Anna said these days. 'But I knew it was Daddy. Of course, *he* is safe.'

Anna had to bite her lip.

Ryan wouldn't tell her where he was taking Libby. 'It's a surprise, Anna. Don't try and ruin it for us.'

Libby had clapped her hands. 'I love surprises.'

Anna used to love surprises as a child. As an adult? Not so much. 'I need to know where you are, Ryan. Libby, go and get a cardigan from your room so that I can talk to your dad.'

Libby groaned and dragged herself up the stairs, her heavy tread a sign of how annoyed she was.

When Anna turned back to Ryan, he had his arms crossed. 'I'm not telling you, Anna.'

'She's my daughter, Ryan. I have a right to know where she is going to be.'

'And I'm her father. It's nothing to do with you. You want me to take her out more? I'm doing it. You don't get to control where we go.'

'I don't want to control it. I just want to know where she is in case—'

She didn't finish that sentence. She was so used to worrying about Libby, making sure that there was nothing that might put her in danger. Now, as she looked at Ryan's face, she had a fluttery feeling in her stomach.

Libby was back down the stairs before Anna could say anything more, and she pulled on Ryan's hand. 'Can we go and have the surprise now?'

'Of course. We'll see you later, Anna.'

Anna couldn't help but follow them to the door. It was all she could do not to remind him to put Libby in the back of the car and make sure her seatbelt was fastened. 'What time will you be back?'

This time he didn't even turn around. 'Later.'

If she had had more notice, she could have arranged something to do today. Instead, she was wandering around the house, picking up Libby's discarded shoes, wiping the kitchen work surface, turning the TV on, then turning it off again.

In the end, she called Tina.

Tina's conversation was peppered with the crunch of biscuits. 'You've got a day to yourself? That's great. You should make the most of it. How long have you got?'

'I don't know.'

'What do you mean?'

'Ryan wouldn't tell me what time they were coming home.'

'Why not? That's ridiculous. How can you go out and do something if you don't know what time you have to be home for Libby?'

It suddenly occurred to Anna that that was exactly why he was doing it. She sighed. 'I don't mind that so much as not knowing where they are going.'

'He wouldn't tell you that either? That man is a total idiot.'

She wasn't going to get any arguments from Anna on that score. 'It gets worse.'

She explained to Tina about their conversation the night before. When she finished, there was a pause as if Tina was trying to take it all in.

'What an utter, utter—'

'Yep. I agree.'

'He can't get away with this. You need to call your sister. He has to pay maintenance. It's the law. She's his daughter.'

'I know that. And I am going to make an appointment to go through it all. But even a solicitor won't be able to force him to give her his kidney, will she?'

Tina made a growling noise at the other end of the phone. 'Let me speak to him. Shame him. Make him realise...'

'Thanks. But you can't.' Anna thought again of the doctor who had wanted to make absolutely certain that Ryan wasn't being coerced in any way. She didn't know exactly what Tina would plan to say to him, but she was pretty sure it would count.

'Oh, Anna, love. What are you going to do?'

'What can I do? I'll just have to go with it for now. Tell him he can stop the payments. Once the kidney operation is over, he won't be able to take it back, will he? I can go to my sister then. We'll get everything down properly. Legally.'

Arguing that the man who had just saved his daughter's life wasn't providing for his daughter was going to be difficult, but she just had to hope.

There was the rustle of the biscuit packet at the other end, then Tina's voice was more tentative. 'Without prying, can you afford all your bills for the next few months without Ryan's money?'

That was what she'd spent half of last night thinking about. Trying to work out where they could save money. Or how else she could earn some. If only she'd started the catering business months ago, rather than now. 'Worst-case scenario, I'd have to ask my mum if we could move in with her.'

But her mum had moved to a two-bedroom place after Anna's dad had died. She'd wanted to free up some money for holidays and to help her daughters out. 'I'd rather see you enjoy it while I'm still alive.' That was how Anna had been able to afford the key deposit and one month's rent in advance for this house in the first place. She didn't want to ask her mum for any more money.

'Is that your only option?'

'I don't know, to be honest. Maybe if I can get some more catering work? Or a part-time bar job in the evenings.'

'Are you mad, woman? Is that as well as looking after Libby and taking her to the hospital and working at the school? You do realise that there's only one of you, right? Unless you were planning on trying a cloning experiment?'

Tina was right. There were only so many hours in the day. It didn't matter how many times she looked at the problem, she couldn't see a solution. Maybe she should try to speak to Ryan about it again? Make him see the implications of what he was saying. What it would mean to Libby's life.

. . .

After procrastinating until mid-afternoon, she sat down with the intention of setting up a website for the catering business. It was something she'd been meaning to do for the last few weeks, and it would at least stop her from worrying where Libby and Ryan were and what they were doing. Halfway through a YouTube video about how to set one up, she heard the squeak of the back door opening.

For a second, she froze. The house was terraced and the only access to the back door was from their tiny garden, which backed onto an alley running the length of the houses in their block. When she heard Libby's and then Ryan's voice, she breathed out again. Although her relief was quickly replaced by irritation. What was he doing coming in the back door?

They were holding hands when they came into the living room. Ryan nodded towards her open laptop. 'Watching some crap on there, are you? It's all right for some.'

She didn't need to explain to him what she was doing; he would probably find some way to mock her about it. Instead, she focused on Libby. 'Have you had a nice time? What did you get up to? What was your surprise?'

'Wow. That's a lot of questions.' Uninvited, Ryan sat down on the armchair and winked at Libby. 'Tell her, Lib.'

Libby giggled, looked from Ryan to Anna. 'What goes on tour, stays on tour, Mummy.'

Anna looked from Libby to Ryan. 'What does that mean?'

'It means' – Ryan stretched out his arms and put them behind his head – 'that a girl and her dad can have their own secrets that have nothing to do with Mummy.'

From his light, jokey tone of voice, she could see how he had pitched this to Libby. How he had made it sound fun, a game, something between the two of them. She wasn't about to show him that she was bothered by it. She was pretty sure that Libby would tell her later, anyway. That girl couldn't keep a secret at the best of times.

She ignored him, and the lump in her throat, and smiled at Libby. 'I'm just glad you had a nice day and you're home safely.'

Libby rolled her eyes again. 'Oh, Mummy. You need to chill out.'

A chill was exactly the feeling which ran down Anna's spine. As Libby spoke, it was like listening to Ryan: the inflection, the tone, the laugh at the end. His mocking words coming from the mouth of her innocent babe. Tears sprang to her eyes and she stared hard at the wall behind Libby's head to regain control. No way was he going to see her cry. Those days were gone. 'Okay, then.' She spoke slowly to keep the tremor from her voice. 'Maybe Mummy has got some secrets of her own.'

As soon as the words were out of her mouth, she wanted to claw them back in. Ryan's eyes were full of cold mirth when he looked at her. 'But I bet Daddy knows all Mummy's secrets, doesn't he?'

TWENTY-THREE

After they'd walked home from school on Monday, stroked the ancient cat from two doors down and picked up a 'special' rock from their neat but tiny front garden, Anna told Libby she had five minutes to get changed because they were driving to a park they'd never visited before.

From under the orange woolly jumper she was pulling over her head, Libby had a thousand muffled questions. 'Where is it? Are there swings? A climbing frame? A slide?'

Anna gave the bottom of the jumper a swift tug so that Libby's blonde hair rose with static as it popped out the top. 'I'm not telling you. It's a surprise.'

Due to the chilly weather, the park was relatively empty. As soon as they arrived, Libby saw Max on the swings and gasped. 'Mum, it's Max! It's Max, over there!'

Anna smiled. 'I know. I spoke to his mum and arranged to meet them here. I told you there was a surprise.'

Last night, after Ryan had left and Libby was in bed, Anna had sent Julie a text for the first time since they'd swapped numbers to suggest meeting up today. Was it some kind of childish one-upmanship with Ryan? She didn't care. At least Libby could see that her mum could arrange fun things, too.

Libby was straining at the hand she held. 'Hurry up, Mum. Come on.'

Anna laughed at her impatience; she and Max had only seen each other two days ago at the hospital. 'You can run ahead.' She opened her hand to let her go.

But Libby kept hold of her. 'No. I'll wait for you.'

That surprised her. And when they reached the swings, Libby was even more reluctant. Standing so that she was half a pace from Anna, her body angled so that it was half-hidden behind her. Julie was sitting on the second swing and she got up for Libby. 'Hi, Anna. Hey, Libby. Max has been desperate for you to come.'

Max looked taller with his legs dangling rather than folded in front of a hospital chair. His clothes were different, too: jeans and a tracksuit top made him look older than the T-shirt and joggers he wore to dialysis. 'I told Mum to sit on the swing to save it for you. I didn't want anyone to take it.'

'Thank you.' Libby finally let go of Anna's hand and sat on the seat, moving her legs to start it swinging, still not really looking at Max.

Julie looked at Anna and raised her eyebrows, but Anna could only shrug. She had no idea why Libby was suddenly reverting to the shy girl who had met Max the first time. 'I didn't tell Libby you were going to be here, Max. I wanted to surprise her.'

Max laughed. 'I like being a surprise. You should have told me. I could have dressed up. Or I could have hidden and jumped out.' He threw his arms in the air like a jack-in-the-box and nearly fell off the swing.

Libby giggled and Max took that as an invitation to replicate the manoeuvre and stage a comedy fall. She laughed even more at that, and Anna could see her body relax. Finally, she wanted to play. 'Shall we go on the slide?'

'Yes!' Max jumped off the swing while it was still moving. Anna saw Julie start as if she was about to warn him to take care, and then put her hand over her mouth. Libby waited for her swing to slow almost to a stop before easing herself off and running after him.

For a few seconds, the two mothers stood and watched the two children, climbing the ladder, swooping to the bottom, then running around to climb up again. Something about the simple joy in their faces brought a lump to Anna's throat. 'Wow. It's good to see them so... free.'

Julie nodded. 'Yes. Not connected up to a dialysis machine. It must be strange for them, seeing each other out of context.'

That must have been what had made Libby a little shy. She was used to the Max at the hospital. Sitting down, not moving, a fellow patient. Here, he was a real boy. The two-year age difference was more apparent when they were standing up, too.

'Now they've got each other, I think we can retire to the bench.' Julie reached into her bag and brought out a flask. 'I brought coffee. It's only instant, but it's still better than that machine on the ward.'

Julie was smiling. It was strange seeing her out in the real world, too. She was an attractive woman, but there was a tiredness in her face that Anna had seen in her own mirror. It was no wonder they drank coffee like they breathed oxygen. 'Great. And I brought chocolate biscuits.'

The play area was small, so they could still hear the excited chatter of the two children from the bench. Julie nodded towards them. 'Max was so excited that we were meeting Libby today. It really gave him a lift.'

There was something in Julie's tone that made Anna look at her more closely. 'Has he been feeling down?'

The edges of Julie's smile turned downwards. 'He wanted to join a football team with his school friends. But the matches are on Saturdays, so...'

She didn't need to finish that sentence. Anna was beginning to see what this was like, having to organise your lives around the dialysis schedule. 'Poor Max.'

'Yeah. I think it's only going to get more difficult as they get older, wanting to do more, wanting to be able to do the same things as their friends.'

Watching the two of them now on the climbing wall at the

other end of the park, no one would know that they weren't two regular kids, without a care in the world. Once Libby had had the transplant, her life could be like this every day. They could go to the park, or the beach, or on holiday, whenever they chose.

Libby had frozen halfway up the wall. Anna was about to get up from her seat to help, when she saw that Max was already climbing back down to where Libby was. He was speaking to her, then he tapped the fake boulder that she should clasp next. Libby stretched out her hand and pulled herself a little higher. Anna kept watching them as she spoke to Julie. 'Max is such a lovely boy. You must be so proud of him.'

'We are.' Julie's face crumpled and she started to cry. 'I'm sorry. I don't mean to—'

'Hey, hey, don't apologise. What is it?'

'It's Max. He doesn't seem right to me. I don't know if it's just the disappointment over the football, but he's been really lethargic the last couple of days. And pale. And not interested in doing anything. This is the most he's moved since Saturday.'

Anna frowned as she looked over at Max. Maybe he did look a little paler than normal. With Libby's awkwardness when they'd first arrived, she hadn't really looked at him that closely. 'Have you spoken to the doctor?'

'Not yet. I've called and left a message. I'm waiting for a call back. I'm probably overreacting.'

'You're doing the right thing. Hopefully, it will just be disappointment making him sad. But it's best to know. He looks happy now.'

The children had moved from the playground to a nearby bush, where they were looking intently at something. Then Max held out his hand to Libby and she leaned down towards it, as if scrutinising something.

'It's probably a ladybird. He's obsessed with small creatures at the moment. Last week he wanted me to buy him a tank to keep ants in.' Julie shuddered.

'Rather you than me. Libby has got her sights set on something a little bigger. She's been asking for a kitten, but I'm not sure I've got the stomach for emptying litter trays and dead mice on the doormat.'

'Oh crikey, me neither.' Julie unscrewed the top of the flask. 'More coffee?'

Anna held out her cup. 'Always.'

They sat in a pleasant silence for the next couple of minutes, watching the two nature-lovers they had given birth to. Julie reached out and gave Anna's arm a squeeze. 'Thanks, Anna. You've made me feel a little better. Maybe seeing Libby today was the pick-up he needed. It's so hard not to worry all the time. It's good to be with someone who understands. We should do this more often. What about Sunday? If the weather's not good, we could take them to the cinema?'

Anna's heart sank. 'I'd love to. But she's supposed to be seeing her dad again. Can we make it another day?'

'Of course, no problem.'

It was a shame to miss out on a day out with them both, but at least Anna had time to plan for this coming Sunday. As much as she'd miss Libby, it would be nice to have some time to do something for herself. Maybe she'd even take Tina up on her offer to go out for lunch.

TWENTY-FOUR

The road outside was quiet the following Sunday. Libby had been sitting at the window for at least an hour, her small rucksack packed, boots on, coat within easy reach. 'What time is it, Mummy?'

'About two minutes since you last asked me. Half past ten.'

'And what time is Daddy coming?'

'He said ten o'clock, but maybe he's stuck in traffic.'

Anna was beginning to get concerned herself, but she kept her voice light. Surely Ryan would have called if he was going to be much later than this?

'Can you call him, Mummy? Can you find out where he is?'

The last thing Anna wanted to do was to call Ryan up and chase him. 'He might be driving, Lib. I'll tell you what, I'll send him a text and, if he doesn't reply, he must be in the car on the way here.'

Libby sighed and let her chin drop onto her arms. Her voice wasn't much more than a whisper: 'Come on, Daddy.'

It took Anna three attempts to word the text. She didn't want to sound judgemental. That would just start the whole day off on the wrong foot. Libby had been looking forward to this all week and she didn't want to put Ryan in a bad mood before they even left the house. Eventually, she settled for concerned.

All okay? Libby is worried about you.

The ding of the return text message came almost immediately.

Can't make it today.

Libby's head jerked up at the sound. 'What did he say? Is he nearly here?'

Anger flashed through Anna like a forest fire. He was *not* doing this. All week, Libby had been talking about the things Ryan had promised to do with her today. The zoo and ice cream and the cinema and pizza. She had told Anna at least four times that he'd said she could have the biggest tub of popcorn that had ever been made. Her hopeful face looking at Anna now for confirmation nearly broke Anna's heart in two. 'It sounds like he might have got held up. I'll just give him a call.'

She left Libby at the window and closed herself into the kitchen. The phone rang about seven times before Ryan picked it up. 'Hello?'

He would have known who it was from the caller display, so she dispensed with the niceties. 'What do you mean, you can't make it? Libby has been waiting for you.'

'Yeah, I should have called. Something came up and I need to be at work.'

Anna had worked in restaurants for enough of her life to recognise the sounds of clinking glass and chinking cutlery. 'At work?'

'Yeah. Client emergency. You know how it is. Well,' he laughed, 'you know how it is for people like me.'

Selfish pricks who let down their daughters, you mean? Anna breathed in and out three times before she replied. 'Libby is desperate to see you.'

'We'll rearrange. I could take a day off in the week?'

'She'll be at school in the week. Or at the hospital. Sundays are the best day. I explained that.'

He sounded like he was barely listening to her. 'Next Sunday, then?'

'She has been sitting at the window for an hour. Can't you rearrange your work thing instead?'

'I don't expect you to understand, Anna. But no.'

Anna was trying so hard to stay in control, but she couldn't stop herself. 'You can't let her down like this!'

There were a few moments of silence at the other end. When he spoke, Ryan's voice was clipped. 'Let her down? Really? That's what you want to say? I'm not sure the doctors I've been speaking to for the last two weeks – who want me to make sure I am prepared for a major operation – think that I am "letting her down".'

There was no point to this conversation. It would only make her angrier and risk the fragile equilibrium they were operating under. She swallowed. 'Well, can you talk to Libby, then? Explain to her that this is an emergency. If she hears how disappointed you are, she might not feel as bad.'

This was unlikely, but she wanted Ryan to hear what he was doing. But he couldn't even manage that. 'Sorry, I need to go. Just say I'll take her out next week. I'll get her double ice cream or something.'

And the line went dead.

Anna let her head fall back and closed her eyes. What the heck was she going to say to Libby?

The kitchen door opened. With her backpack and her concerned face, Libby looked like an evacuee. 'When is he coming?'

Anna crouched down so that her face was the same level as Libby's. 'Daddy is sorry, Libby. Something has happened at his work and they need him.'

Libby's face reddened and her eyes screwed up; tears fell. 'No! No! Daddy said he was coming. He promised.'

'I know, sweetheart. But sometimes—'

'Did you tell him not to come?'

Anna felt winded. Where had that come from? 'No, of course not. Why would you—'

'You don't like Daddy. And you get worried when I am not with you or Nana. Did you tell him not to come?'

'No, baby. I promise I didn't tell him not to come, but—'

Libby ripped off her backpack and threw it on the floor. 'It's not fair! He promised!'

Anna reached out and put her arms around her, squeezed her tightly as she sobbed into her shoulder. Bloody selfish stupid Ryan.

Once Libby had choked out the last of her furious sobs, Anna held her at arm's length. 'How about you and I make a cake together? That'll be fun, won't it?'

Libby shook her head. 'No. I just want to watch TV.'

She pulled away from Anna and lay down on the couch.

'Okay. Well, I'm going to make you your favourite chocolate cake and then we can eat some in front of a film.'

Libby didn't even reply. She just held out her arm and clicked on the TV with the remote.

Before she started the cake, Anna needed to call Tina. Unlike Ryan, Tina picked up after one ring. 'Hiya. I was just about to leave. Meet you there?'

Anna had been looking forward to their lunch. A rare treat. Tina was taking her to the golf course restaurant because she said their roast beef was the best in the area. 'I can't make it.'

'What do you mean? What's happened?'

'Ryan. He's let Libby down. He's not coming.'

'What? Poor Libby, is she upset?'

'Very. I'm going to give her half an hour and then start Operation Cheer Up.'

'And what about you? What about you needing cheering up? Can't your mum come over for a couple of hours so that you can still come for lunch?'

Anna really wanted to go, but how could she leave Libby when she was so upset? 'I can't, Tina. She needs me. I'm so sorry.'

Tina sighed. 'Don't apologise. It's not your fault. I get it. I'm just disappointed, that's all. Shall I come over and help? Bring some of Gracie's old dress-up clothes?'

Tina had only ever seen sunshine-Libby. Libby under a cloud was a whole other prospect. 'That's really kind of you, but I think she just needs some quiet time. Another day, she'd love it. I'd better check on her now. I'll see you at work tomorrow.'

'Okay, chick. I'm going to call Jude Law and let him know I'm free after all.'

Anna smiled. If only everyone in the world was as kind and forgiving as Tina.

Her face like thunder, Libby didn't want a strawberry milkshake or a cuddle, so Anna left her watching cartoons and started on the cake. Chocolate cake was difficult to get right; it was very easy to make it too dry or too heavy. It was just the distraction she needed.

Usually, she'd use an electric mixer, but she had pent-up rage in her shoulders that only a wooden spoon would be able to release. Beating together the eggs, flour, caster sugar and butter required sustained effort, and every turn of the spoon was her equivalent of a boxer punching at a bag.

How dare he let Libby down in this way? Months and months of not bothering to see her. Of blaming Anna for moving them away from the area. Of punishing his daughter because he hadn't been able to force Anna to live where he told her to.

And, if she hadn't sent him that message, would he even have bothered to let them know that he wasn't coming? Had he not even given it a second thought?

She didn't even believe his excuse. What kind of work emergency would he have on a Sunday? Which involved being in the restaurant that he was clearly in?

She dug the spoon so hard against the side of the bowl that she nearly pushed it out of her hands and onto the floor. Setting it to one side, she opened the cupboard door for the cocoa powder. Tipped it into a separate bowl. Years of baking this particular cake meant she didn't need to weigh and measure. She filled a small jug with tap water, then gradually added it to the cocoa, stirring it into a stiff paste. Drop after drop. Too much, and the paste would be too runny. Not enough, and there were still pockets of chalky powder. Just one splash too much, and she would have to start again.

She was used to this behaviour from Ryan. Used to being the last person he considered. Drop after drop of inconsiderate, even cruel, behaviour. She had let it go on for far too long. And now he was doing it to Libby.

The cocoa paste was sticky and thick. She scraped at the small bowl with a teaspoon to drop it into the cake mixture. It was one thing Ryan letting her down, but not Libby. Didn't she have enough to be dealing with?

Maybe this was all a terrible mistake. Letting him back into their lives. What had been the point of the moving out, of starting divorce proceedings, if it wasn't to escape from feeling like this: worthless, useless, powerless? In the last few months, she had felt like herself again. She could do and say and live however she chose. Less than four weeks of him being back in her life, and the old claustrophobia had returned.

Slowly now, she began to fold the cocoa paste into the cake mixture, the dark streaks growing wider and wider as they coloured the batter. Ryan's disappearance from their lives had actually been a relief these last few months. Now he was back, and gradually his malevolent presence was seeping into every part of her life: her house, her bedroom, her mind. Of course, she was overjoyed that he was a match for the transplant. If Ryan donated his kidney to Libby, it would change her life.

But when Ryan had saved Libby's life, Anna would owe him a debt she could never repay. Unless he was planning to take her life in return? Was saving Libby the opportunity Ryan needed to finally break her?

TWENTY-FIVE

Two nights later, Libby had been in bed for about half an hour when Anna heard the squeak of the back door opening once again. Fear squeezed at her stomach. Was she being robbed?

So, when Ryan's face appeared around the door frame, she was relieved first, and then angry.

'Thought I'd come round the back, in case you were still putting Libby to bed.'

It was bad enough when he'd brought Libby home that way. In what universe did he think it was okay to come in through the kitchen door on his own? What would he have done if she had still been upstairs? Made himself at home? Rifled through her belongings? 'I'd rather you rang the doorbell.'

'And wake her up? I'm pretty sure you'd have something to say about that. May I sit down?'

She had plenty to say about him turning up unannounced full stop, but she kept it to herself for now. 'Be my guest.'

The ease with which he slid himself onto her furniture made her even more furious. The armchair was one she'd found on a Facebook local selling page. Tina's husband, John, had picked it up for her in his van. Then the three of them – Tina had come too – had somehow wrestled it up the narrow hallway, stopping only to laugh at John's jokes. This was her armchair, her house and her new life. She didn't want him lounging all over any of it.

'Aren't you going to offer me tea? And cake? You always used to have a cake in a tin somewhere. Aren't you going to offer me anything?'

'Ryan, I'm tired. What's this all about?'

'I happened to be nearby and I thought I'd pop in. You seemed irritated on the phone on Sunday and I thought I'd better talk to you about it; nip it in the bud before you turn it into a full-blown issue.'

It took every ounce of self-control she had to stop herself rising to his bait. 'There is no issue. I just don't want you to let Libby down, that's all. She was really disappointed when you didn't turn up.'

'Yes, well, I've brought something to make it up to her. I was hoping to be here before she went to bed, but it took longer than I'd anticipated.'

'What took longer?'

'Hold on. If you're not going out to the kitchen to make me a drink, I'll have to ruin the surprise and go and get it.'

He disappeared out to the kitchen. This was just like him. He couldn't just bring a gift and give it to you. There had to be an elaborate performance: the staging, the drama, the suspense. She used to love it. Not any longer.

When he walked back into the room, he was holding a plastic box with a carry handle. It took Anna a moment to realise there were scratching noises coming from inside it.

'What the hell is that?'

He set the box down on the armchair and opened the front, reaching inside to bring out a tiny black and white kitten. 'Libby said she wanted one.'

Of all the things he could have bought her, this was the most ludicrous. 'You have got to be kidding me.'

'No. She told me, several times, that she wanted a kitten more than anything else in the world. Those were her exact words. She also said you were thinking about it, but you were taking too long. So, I've saved you a job. And it wasn't cheap.'

'Of course it wasn't cheap. And it won't be cheap to look after it, either. Why do you think I haven't got one? And it's not just the money. I'm at work all week. Or at dialysis with Libby. I just don't have the time or the capacity to care for anything else.' Looking at that kitten in his hands, Anna could have cried. What the hell was he thinking?

He held the kitten out to her. 'Come on. Take it. You'll soon change your mind.'

The kitten patted at her arm with a tiny paw. She wanted to stand firm, but he practically let it go so that she had to catch it. It was very cute. Libby would love it. And she'd love Ryan even more for buying it for her.

'You can't keep doing this, Ryan. Making decisions like this without talking to me first. Whatever has gone on between us, we have to be able to communicate. For Libby.'

Ryan was smiling. 'I was hoping you'd had time to think about it. That you'd realise that I was right. About us.'

He reached over the table to take her hand from where it rested in front of her, and she pulled it back as if she'd been burnt. Had he always been this smarmy? She couldn't believe that she'd found him charming once. Now he seemed like a cliché of himself. 'I think you've misunderstood. There is no "us". No you and me. Except when it comes to Libby.'

The smile froze on his face, but it still didn't drop. 'You don't mean that.'

She took a deep breath and launched into it: 'I've thought about your comments about the maintenance, and it's not going to work. You are Libby's father and there's a financial responsibility to being a parent. There is also a responsibility to spend time with her, to not let her down. What you're doing for her, it's immense, I'm not saying it isn't. But it's also an honour to be able to save your daughter.'

Now the smile did disappear. To be replaced with a sneer. 'That's quite a big speech. Been rehearsing that, have you?'

She wasn't going to let his mocking tone put her off. Not this time. 'And we need this sorted out, Ryan. We need to get the divorce finalised.'

He frowned. 'How can we get the divorce finalised? It hasn't been two years.'

'Adultery, Ryan. Or unreasonable behaviour. Whichever you prefer. We just need everything sorted out. For all our sakes: Libby's included.'

'Unreasonable behaviour? Yours or mine?'

Anna tried to avoid looking at him. 'Stop playing games. This doesn't have to be unpleasant: it's just paperwork.'

He moved closer towards her; his face was uncomfortably close. 'It might just be paperwork to you, but you're asking me to take the blame. We both know that you were the one who chose to leave. If anyone is being unreasonable here, it's you.'

This was how it always went. She wanted to talk about one thing and, before she knew it, they were having a whole other conversation. This time she wasn't going to let him confuse her. Though she wanted to step away from him, she wasn't going to let him intimidate her. 'We are getting divorced, Ryan. You need to be a father to Libby. I don't believe you will let her down on the transplant, because you can see how important this is. But you and me? That's over. We will be civil for our daughter, and that's it. No more.'

He slammed his hand down on the table so hard, it was like a gun going off. 'The thing is, Anna, I don't need to dance to your tune. Libby is my daughter as much as she is yours and you don't get to call the shots.'

Her heart was thumping, but she was not going to let him see how frightened she was. 'I have never, *ever*, called the shots. Can you not see it? Can you not see how you behave? You want everyone to do exactly what you want, but that's not how it works, Ryan. Yes, Libby is your daughter as much as she is mine. But she doesn't belong to you. She doesn't belong to either of us. She's not a possession.'

He flicked the back of the sofa with his hand, inches from her face. 'Now you're just being dramatic. And playing with words. You know what I mean.'

She swallowed. 'Yes, I do know what you mean, but you're wrong. Being a parent means that you give, not take. You give and give and then you give some more. If you loved Libby like I do, you'd want to do this for her, whatever was going on between us. Even if you hate me.'

Ryan leaned back against the arm of the sofa, like a predator about to spring for their prey. 'I don't hate you, Anna. I pity you. You have nothing left to throw at me, so you are using the parenting card. We all know what a great parent you are. What a martyr, sacrificing your life for your daughter. But we both know that you are enjoying it.'

'What?' She was so shocked that the word came out of her throat like a croak.

'It's easy, isn't it? When you've got a "sick daughter".' The inverted commas he made with his fingers in the air made her want to slap him. 'You can give up on your own life. No one is going to judge you for giving up your job, or staying home all the time or' – he made a motion with his hand that encompassed her from head to toes – 'letting yourself go. You can just play the sick kid card and no one can judge you.'

She knew he was nasty. Hadn't he said a thousand cruel things to her over the years? But this was scraping the barrel. 'Are you trying to say that I enjoy Libby being sick?'

He shrugged. 'Maybe *enjoy* is a little strong. But I think it's very convenient for you. Look how you were with your dad. It was all: *I have to be there, Ryan. He needs me, Ryan.* It was grotesque, the way you carried on.'

She couldn't do this anymore. She couldn't sit here and let him speak to her like this. Spouting his bile in her home. 'Get out. Get out of my house.'

A smile cracked open his face and she saw for the first time how much he was enjoying this. Goading her. Torturing her. She had walked straight into his hands. He pushed himself up out of his seat. 'I'll let myself out. Front door this time, maybe.'

She let him go. Her whole body was trembling. No one could make her feel like this except him. He knew exactly which buttons to press, which nerves to twang. How had she let him get to her like this?

She covered her face with her palms. She'd rowed with him like this before, of course she had. But this time it wasn't her who was going to suffer the consequences. What if this made him change his mind about the transplant? She wanted to think that no one was that low, but she couldn't be sure.

She'd have to call Mr Harris in the morning and see if they could put Libby on the general transplant list as a back-up option. Hopefully, it wouldn't come to that. But she couldn't be sure.

TWENTY-SIX

As they left school the next day, a thin sun had finally struggled out from behind the clouds and Libby asked if they could meet Max at the park.

However, when Anna called Julie, she said Max was really tired and was lying down in front of the TV. She sounded as if she could do with a lie down herself, but gently declined Anna's offers of help.

Libby was disappointed. 'Why can't he come? It's okay if he's tired. You could drive him in the car and then I can push him on the swing.'

'Not this time, Lib. We can always make a plan another day.'

Libby screwed up her face and jutted her hip to one side. 'I think Max would want us to go to his park anyway.'

That made Anna smile. 'Do you?'

Libby crossed her arms and gave Anna a decisive nod of the head. 'Yes. And I think we should buy him some sweets to give him tomorrow to make up for him missing it.'

It was clear where this was leading. 'And maybe some sweets for you, too?'

Libby's face was the picture of angelic innocence. 'Maybe, yes please.'

Patches had been on his own for six hours while they were at school, so they decided to take him to the park with them on the little cat lead which Ryan had left in the box. Even Anna had to admit that it was very cute, watching Libby walking him along the path to the playground: happily padding along one minute, pouncing on an unsuspecting blade of grass the next. Once they got to the swings, Anna scooped him up. 'You go and play, Libby. That was a long walk for his little legs; he needs a rest.'

Sitting on the bench with Patches in one hand, Anna checked her phone. She had also called Mr Harris today on her morning tea break. The previous evening, she had turned everything over in her mind, trying to think of who else there was in the family who might be able to donate to Libby. She had even considered Ryan's side of the family. His brother, Bradley, was a really nice guy. After any family gathering, Ryan would privately dismiss him as 'unambitious', but he'd had to eat his words when, shortly after their mum had died, Bradley and his wife, Sarah, had taken teaching jobs in New Zealand. Ryan had had more insults in his arsenal, of course. Sarah was a 'demanding shrew' who told his 'pathetically weak' brother what to do, apparently. There didn't seem much love lost the other way, either. Since they'd emigrated, the only contact had been Christmas cards. Even if Bradley had been willing to be tested, he was on the other side of the world, and if there were no other family options, the only remaining possibility was to go on the organ donation waiting list. This was what she'd wanted to speak to Mr Harris about.

'If Libby was to go on the waiting list for a donor kidney, how long might that take?'

Mr Harris had sounded surprised. 'Why would you want to do that? Is there a problem with Ryan that I should know about?'

How long have you got? she wanted to say. 'No. It's fine. I just mean, if there was suddenly a reason that he couldn't donate. How long would it take for Libby to get on the list, and how long does it usually take to get a transplant from it?'

Mr Harris's voice changed from confused to calm. 'I can

understand your concern, Anna, but everything is looking good. The multi-disciplinary team meetings have not thrown up any issues at all. There's the final MRI scan which is scheduled for' – she heard a rustle of paper which must mean he was looking at his notes – 'tomorrow, actually. And then the independent assessor who Ryan met with will sign her part off, and then the surgeon can schedule the operation. Everything is going well, really.'

It was easy for him to assume that was the case. He didn't know Ryan. 'And it's the independent assessor who makes the final decision? I'm sorry, I know you're busy, but we didn't mention that Ryan and I hadn't been in contact for a few months before he agreed to be a donor. I mean, I actually contacted him to ask him to do it. He's been seeing Libby since then, but will this independent assessor look badly on that?'

'They are not there to judge your relationship, Anna. If Ryan is keen to be Libby's donor, and it sounds as if he is, then there aren't going to be any problems.'

Watching Libby on the swing now, as she pushed her feet forwards and backwards to propel herself as high as she could, Anna wished she could have Mr Harris's calm certainty. All she could see were problems. Until the day after the kidney donation, Ryan had her in the palm of his hand, and he knew it. She wanted more than anything to find someone else – anyone else – who could take his place. But how could she have pushed this with Mr Harris? If he began to suspect that all was not well, it could bring the whole process to a halt. There was no way that she could allow that to happen before she had a backup plan in place.

Stroking Patches, who had curled up on her lap, Anna couldn't help but smile at Libby singing to herself as she swung. At times like this, she could almost forget that there was anything wrong. Her rosy cheeks and strong legs were the picture of health. Sometimes she had to kick herself out of feeling: *why her?* She knew it could be a lot worse. Libby could have an illness for which there was no cure. At least there was treatment for Libby's condition. A long-term solution. It just wasn't a solution Anna felt comfortable taking right now.

'Daddy!' Libby was looking over her shoulder now, her face lit up in excitement.

Anna turned and saw Ryan walking towards them. What was he doing here? And how the hell had he known where to find them?

He barely even looked at Anna as he approached the swings. 'Have you got a hug for your daddy, then? And how's that kitten doing?'

Libby slowed the swing to a stop by scuffing her shoes on the ground. Normally, Anna would tell her to stop that because she couldn't afford to keep replacing worn out school shoes, but she didn't want to say anything that Ryan could pick her up on. When the swing stopped, Libby fell into Ryan's arms. 'He's called Patches and he's over there with Mummy. She got really cross with him this morning because he has scratched the table leg. Have you got another present for me?'

Ryan didn't even bother to look at the kitten or Anna. He merely laughed. 'You mercenary creature. Your mother has taught you well.'

Before they'd split up, tiny barbs like this had almost lost their power to affect her, but now they scratched at her. 'You can't expect a gift every time you see Daddy, Lib.'

Predictably, Ryan flipped it back at her. 'Yes, she can. What are dads for if not to spoil their daughters?'

He reached into the inside pocket of his coat and brought out a new game for her Nintendo console. Libby squealed as she took it. 'Max and me both want this one! Mummy said I had to wait and save up my pocket money. Thank you, Daddy! Thank you!'

It wasn't Libby's fault, but her words cut through Anna, which was one of the reasons her tone ended up so accusatory. 'How did you know we were here?'

Ryan shrugged. 'Libby told me.'

'She can't have told you. We only decided to come this afternoon.'

'I mean she told me about this park. And I took a chance. Why are you acting like a police detective? Can't I come and see my daughter at the park? Anyway, I wanted to speak to her about something important. I have to go to Belgium tomorrow for a couple of nights, and wondered if there was anyone around here who might like to put in an order for some chocolates?'

Anna froze. 'Tomorrow? But you are supposed to have your MRI scan tomorrow, aren't you?'

'Actually, no. I was supposed to, but I've put it off.'

Fear crept over Anna's shoulders. 'What do you mean?'

'Just a busy week. Lots to get done. Dr Wells said it's fine.'

It might be fine for Dr Wells; he didn't know how much Anna was counting the days until this was all over with. 'It's a pretty important appointment, Ryan. The whole thing is resting on this.'

Other than the information she'd been given at the hospital, Libby had watched tons of videos on YouTube to find out about every step of the process. Not only would this MRI scan check Ryan's kidneys, it would also look at the blood vessels surrounding them. Usually, there was one artery and one vein, but there could be more. If there were too many blood vessels, it might not be possible to remove the kidney at all.

Ryan's voice was made of iron. 'I am well aware of how this all works, Anna. I am going to be incapacitated by this operation afterwards. Forgive me if I'm trying to get my work life sorted out beforehand. Let me do that, at least.'

Anna glanced at Libby; she didn't want to discuss this in front of her. Ryan was still staring at her when she looked back, so she tried to keep her voice light. 'Of course. I understand. I'm afraid Libby and I are going to have to go soon, so that she can have her dinner.'

The tone of his voice changed immediately back into fun dad. 'What about if I take you both out for pizza? My treat?'

That was the last thing Anna wanted to do. And how dare he call it his 'treat', when he didn't want to pay the maintenance which would keep Libby eating for the rest of the month? 'It's fine, thanks. We need to take the kitten home and we've got a meatloaf to finish from yesterday.'

'I hate meatloaf. Please can we go with Daddy? Please?' Libby even had her hands together as if in prayer to beg.

Anna didn't want to get into this tug-of-war again. Especially as she'd probably lose. 'Okay. I'll take Patches home and have the meatloaf. You go with Daddy for pizza. Can you make sure she's back by six thirty though, so she's got time for a bath before bed?'

The last part was directed to Ryan, but he frowned at her words. 'Actually, you're right. It's late. We'll do it another time, Libby, when it isn't so much trouble for Mummy.'

Great. So now she was the bad guy again. Libby's face had fallen in disappointment. You couldn't just make a suggestion to a child and then pull it away again like a rug from under their feet. 'It's fine, I—'

'No.' Ryan held up a hand. 'I know when I'm not wanted. I'll see you next Sunday, Libby. We can have pizza then.'

She didn't want him to have Libby again next Sunday. 'Actually, I think we're seeing her friend Max next Sunday.'

He stuck out his chin. 'It's my Sunday. You had her last Sunday, I think you'll remember.'

That was so unfair. She had been with Libby last Sunday because he'd let her down and it had been too late to arrange anything. Again, though, she didn't want to make a row in front of Libby. 'Fine. Next Sunday. And when did you say your final MRI scan is booked for?'

Ryan picked up Libby for a final hug and looked at Anna over her shoulder. 'I didn't.'

He held her gaze just long enough for the ice in it to freeze her to the spot, before winking and walking away.

Anna reached for Libby's hand, but she wouldn't give it to her; still angry she couldn't go with Ryan. Surely, he wouldn't actually pull out of this? Anna had convinced herself that he had been dragging his heels just to prove that he was the one in control:

using the donation as a weapon to punish her. Was he actually planning to go through with the transplant at all? He'd done some awful things, but that would be pure evil. There was only one person she could ask. But how was she going to speak to Nicole without Ryan being there?

TWENTY-SEVEN

When Libby was a baby, they'd used to call her Sunshine and Showers. When she was in a good mood, she was the sweetest, most affable creature in the world. When she was upset, the world knew about it. Not much had changed.

Libby had been angry with Anna since they'd left Ryan at the park. *Why didn't you let me have dinner with Daddy? Why did Daddy go home? Why don't you like Daddy?*

By the time she was getting her ready for bed, Anna had had enough of giving diplomatic answers. 'You live with me, Libby, and I have to make sure that you have your dinner on time so that you can have your bath, go to bed and get ready for school. You like school.'

'I like having dinner with Daddy, too. Why can't I do both?'

Sometimes Anna wondered if she'd spoiled Libby a little. With the upheaval of the last year – leaving her home, her school, her father – it had felt right to make sure that any part of her life that could be made easy, was. Her favourite breakfast cereal, playdates with friends, whatever she wanted to watch on the TV. It wasn't as if Anna had the money to shower her with expensive gifts, but what she could do for her, she did.

Now, though, she was feeling less generous. She was tired of being the bad guy. 'I said you could go with Daddy. He changed his mind when he realised how late he was.'

But Ryan could do no wrong at the moment, it seemed. 'No. It's your fault. Daddy wanted you to come too, and you said no.'

Occasionally Anna's mother had cautioned her: *You can't give in all the time. You are allowed a life, too.* There had been times when she'd cancelled a night out with a friend because Libby hadn't wanted her to go. Or she had changed an arrangement at the last minute because Libby wanted to come along. She knew her mother was right, that she was entitled to a life too, but her life was Libby right now. How could it be anything else?

'Libby. You're tired and you're grumpy. You need to go to sleep now and you can speak to Daddy on my phone tomorrow and make an arrangement to go out to dinner.'

Something passed over Libby's face which made Anna suspicious. Especially when coupled with the fact that Libby stopped whining abruptly and pulled the covers over her mouth. 'Night, Mummy.'

She shut her eyes tight, but Anna wasn't fooled. 'What's going on?'

When she didn't get an answer, she reached under the top of the bedclothes and tickled the bottom of Libby's neck. The spot which always made her squirm and scream and splutter with laughter. Sure enough, it had the desired response. 'I can't tell you! It's a secret!'

In the pit of Anna's stomach, a prickly, unpleasant feeling began to unfurl. She tried an old trick which had worked when Libby was small. 'What's a secret?'

'Nothing! I can't tell you. Stop tickling!'

Anna always stopped when Libby asked her to. It was important that she grew up able to stop someone from touching her if she didn't want to be touched. She tried to keep her voice light and jovial, though. 'You can't tell me? Have you lost your voice?'

'No, silly. It's a secret.' She paused. 'A Daddy secret.'

Libby's bedroom was the warmest room in the house, but a

shiver ran through Anna. 'Well, Daddy knows you can't have a secret from your mummy. He won't mind if you tell me.'

At this, Libby pulled the cover down from her mouth, her expression serious. 'He said it was just for us to know. No mummies.'

Libby's voice was more uncertain now. Anna hated making her uncomfortable, but she hated even more the idea that Ryan was telling their daughter to keep secrets from her. 'Libby. I need to know. What did Daddy say? What is the secret?'

'He bought me a present and he said that you would be cross so I mustn't tell you.'

A present didn't sound too frightening. And what could be worse than the house-destroying kitten? Anna could breathe again. 'Well, if I promise not to be cross, can you tell me?'

Libby seemed to weigh this over. Anna scrunched some of the quilt in her hand; she mustn't show her how irritated she was. Eventually, Libby came to a decision. 'I could show you. Then I wouldn't be telling you.'

On the one hand, Anna was impressed with her daughter's logic. On the other, this was a kind of sly behaviour she had never shown before. Was this a normal part of mental development, or had this come straight from Ryan? 'Good idea.'

Libby reached under her pillow. Whatever she'd hidden couldn't be large. Or alive.

In many ways, it was worse. She pulled out her hand, and with it came a brand new iPhone. She held it out to Anna, watching her, as if she wanted to be sure that Anna wouldn't break her promise not to get cross.

Anna wasn't cross: she was furious. How dare he buy a mobile phone for a seven-year-old without discussing it with her first? And – even worse – how dare he tell Libby to keep it a secret from her? When she spoke, though, there wasn't a trace of that anger. 'Wow. That's quite a gift. When did Daddy give you that?'

'A few days ago.'

'Really? And you've kept it hidden all that time? Does Daddy call you on it?'

Now it was Libby's turn to twist the quilt cover around her fingers. 'He sends me messages. And' – the next statement was more confident, as if she was offering it up as proof that her dad was looking out for her – 'he can see where I am so he knows that I'm safe.'

It took every ounce of self-control that Anna possessed not to throw the damn thing against the wall and smash it into a thousand pieces. Instead, she held it out to Libby. 'Can you show me?'

With a familiarity that made her skin crawl, Libby swiped open the screen and pressed on an app. She turned it around so that Anna could see, pointing with the forefinger of her other hand. 'Look. That's Daddy. That's Nicole. And that's me. I'm here.'

In front of Anna's eyes was a map with three thumbnail pictures of the three people Libby had just listed. She put her thumb and forefinger onto the tiny picture of Libby and enlarged the image. Sure enough, there was the name of their road on the street. Ryan could see exactly where she was.

The uneasy feeling in Anna's stomach grew into nausea. 'And do you leave the phone here, or take it out with you?'

Libby laughed. She clearly thought that the danger of getting into any kind of trouble was over. 'I take it with me. Otherwise Daddy wouldn't be able to check I was safe.'

Anna nearly gagged. These were pretty much the exact words Ryan had used on her when he had called her three, four, five times a day. *I just want to check that you're safe.* She had been as naive as a seven-year-old herself. At least Libby had the excuse that she *was* that age.

Anna held out her hand to take the phone back. 'Well, I'll take it downstairs for you now so that you can go to sleep. It's not good to have your phone in the bedroom, you know. And definitely not under your pillow.'

Libby frowned with suspicion. 'Are you going to give it back to me?'

Anna wasn't sure of that herself yet, and she didn't want to make any promises that she wouldn't keep. 'I just need to check that it's suitable for you.'

Now Libby's suspicion turned to worry. 'Are you going to tell Daddy? Are you going to tell him that I showed you?'

That one she did have an answer for. 'I'm going to tell him that I found it. That way he won't know that you said anything.'

Libby looked relieved. Maybe keeping a secret from Anna had made her more anxious than she'd realised. She lay back down in bed, suddenly looking sleepy. 'Okay. But make sure he's not cross with me.'

If anyone was going to get cross, and then some, it was Anna. She leaned down and kissed Libby on her forehead. 'I will. If he's cross with anyone, it will be me. Sleep tight, baby girl.'

When she got to the door and turned out the light, Libby whispered, 'I love you, Mummy.'

Anna smiled. 'I love you, too.'

When she got downstairs, Patches was pretending to play the piano on the arm of her chair. She picked him up and took him over to the sofa with her. 'We've got some detective work to do, Mr Patches.'

She swiped open the screen of Libby's phone. There, again, was the tracking app. A tiny smug Ryan next to tiny smiling Nicole. She wanted to swipe them both away, and not just from the phone screen. This was how he had known where they were at the park. It hadn't been a lucky guess at all. He had been using this phone – using Libby – to track their movements.

The kitten began to pat the screen with his tiny paw. 'Yes, look what the horrible man has done, Patches. Well, two can play at that game.' Ryan's icon would be moving miles away on his business trip tomorrow, but she would be able to see exactly where Nicole was. Which meant that she'd be able to find her and speak to her while he was miles away and out of range.

She brought Patches up to her face until they were nose to nose. 'Let's see what she has to say for herself, shall we?'

TWENTY-EIGHT

This East London park was essentially a large field, ringed by trees. As well as runners, there was a small group working out with a personal trainer, and a handful of dog walkers.

Anna checked Libby's phone again. Nicole was definitely here somewhere. She sat on a bench near the exit to the car park and scanned the field. It took her five minutes before she saw her, on the opposite corner of the field. Purple leggings and a long black T-shirt. Hair pulled back into a ponytail. She watched her purposeful, confident strides as she covered the length of the field, turned the bottom corner and ran in Anna's direction.

As Nicole came closer, Anna could see the focus in her face. The only time she moved her eyes from looking ahead, she was glancing at her wrist. Maybe she was timing herself. Even when she was almost level with Anna, she showed no sign of realising it was her sitting on the bench.

'Hi, Nicole.'

Nicole's head whipped around and she almost tripped in surprise. 'What are you doing here?'

'I came to speak to you. Have you got a minute?'

Although she'd stopped running, Nicole was jogging from one foot to another. 'Not really. I have a couple more miles to do.'

Anna nodded to the other end of the bench. 'I won't keep you long. Sit down.'

Nicole glanced at her watch again, then seemed to make a decision. She stopped running on the spot and perched on the edge of the seat. It was as if she was trying to keep her clothes clean. Or be ready to fly off at one wrong word from Anna. She looked into the middle distance, rather than at Anna. 'What do you want?'

'Is Ryan away?'

Nicole's face flicked around to face Anna. 'I don't see what that's got to do with you. How did you know I was here, anyway?'

Anna brought Libby's mobile out of her pocket and waved it. 'The same way Ryan knew that Libby and I were at the park. There's an app, apparently.'

Nicole glanced at her watch. At close range, Anna could see that it was an Apple watch. Maybe the icon on the phone was tracking that.

'As I said, I haven't got long. What do you want to talk to me about?'

She might as well get straight to it. 'I was wondering whether you could help me?'

Nicole frowned. 'Help you?'

They had been best friends once. Had lived together for years, spent time together watching terrible TV shows, and laughing and shopping and drinking and joking. And they had talked, really talked, about their lives and their ambitions. They had even told each other their dating and relationship horror stories. Nicole's blind date with a man whose head had been level with her breasts and he'd insisted on saying he was 'the perfect height for a great view'. Anna's short-lived relationship with a guy at catering college who kept a notebook on every girl he'd ever slept with. When it came to talking about Ryan, though, it had taken longer for her to open up. Nicole had been Ryan's friend first. Even now, she needed to take tiny steps.

'The thing is, Ryan is trying to change our arrangements for Libby. I know that he wants to be more... involved in her life, which is great. But he is making some quite unreasonable demands.'

She paused to gauge Nicole's reaction.

Nicole laughed. 'So one minute you're saying he doesn't do enough for Libby, and now you are saying it's too much? He's so right about you. He can't win, can he?'

Anna pressed her lips together. She needed to stay calm. 'I'm not talking about access arrangements. Libby loves to see her dad. I mean the conditions he is trying to impose. With maintenance, for example.'

Nicole clearly had no idea what she was talking about. 'He pays his maintenance. I know he does.'

'Yes, he does. At the moment. But he wants to reduce it.' Anna took a deep breath. She was just going to have to go for it. 'He basically said that, if I don't accept no maintenance payments, it'll be no divorce and no kidney.'

Nicole stared at her. 'He said those exact words?'

'Well, not those exact words, but—'

Again, she interrupted with a laugh. 'So you're twisting his words again? Do you never get tired of this? I understand that you're bitter, but you need to let this go, Anna. For all of our sakes. For Libby's sake.'

Hearing Libby's name on Nicole's lips took the top off Anna's patience. 'I'm doing this for Libby's sake. She needs that kidney. But she will also need food and clothes and a roof over her head. If Ryan stops that maintenance, I have absolutely no idea how I'm going to provide that.'

Nicole's phone rang. The strange ring tone must have been personalised to that caller because the speed with which she ripped open the Velcro on the pouch on her arm which held it, made it clear that she knew who was calling. She stood up and walked a few steps away, turning her back to Anna. Her voice became smooth and calm. 'Hi, honey... Yes, I'm at the park... Just me... No, no one else... No, of course he's not with me, I told you, he's just someone from the running club... I know you do... Yes, I love you too... Okay, see you Saturday.'

The ease with which Nicole lied suggested that she was used to it. Keeping secrets. Keeping safe. Had Ryan noticed yet that she had deleted the tracking app from Libby's phone?

Nicole slotted her phone back into the pouch and sat back down, looking even more uneasy than she had at the start.

Anna tilted her head. 'Ryan?'

'Not that it's your business, but yes.' Nicole brushed imaginary dust from the front of her T-shirt, composing herself.

'How many times a day does he call you?'

'A few. He likes to talk to me during the day. Actually, the girls at work are jealous of how attentive he is.'

'Are they?' Anna remembered how the other women at the cafe she worked in had remarked on how attentive Ryan was. Always popping in on a Saturday to see her. Sometimes more than once. Or calling to speak to her, two, three times a day. Until they'd begun to think it was weird. One of the older women had actually gone as far as to ask Anna if everything was okay at home. She had reacted in pretty much the same way as Nicole was now. 'It's not normal behaviour, Nicole. He's controlling.'

'He just worries about me, that's all. After you left and took Libby away, he lost all his confidence.'

'I left because I found out he was sleeping with someone else.'

'Ryan says you made that up. To have an excuse. To tell your lawyer.'

'Well, I didn't make it up, but I do wonder if I should look her up and thank her, because she did me a big favour.'

Nicole folded her arms. 'I've had enough of this. I'm not here to talk about my relationship with Ryan, Anna. And, to be honest, I don't know what you expect me to do. It's his kidney; I can't tell him what to do with it.'

'It's not that. I'm pretty sure he's made up his mind to do it. It's the other stuff. The maintenance. Letting Libby down. Giving her a mobile phone and telling her to keep it a secret. Come on, Nic, you must admit that none of that is fair.'

Nicole held up her hands. 'None of that is anything to do with me. You've driven him to this, Anna. If you hadn't stopped him from seeing Libby—'

'I never stopped him from seeing Libby!' Frustration made Anna more vehement than she'd intended, and a man passing with a Labrador a few feet away turned to look at them both. She lowered her voice. 'I never stopped him, Nicole. I just told him to stop messing her around. Letting her down. And now he wants to see her on a Sunday, which is the only full day we have together.'

'Which was your choice. Why would you schedule the dialysis for a weekend, when that is the only time Ryan can see his daughter?'

Her choice? None of this was her choice. 'She has to have dialysis three times a week. She already misses the end of two days of school because of it. Sunday is the only day when she has no school and no dialysis. It's the one day we can do something together. I suggested Ryan and I alternate it.' That had been difficult enough to offer. Sundays were so precious. Which had made her even more upset about the Sunday they'd wasted at home waiting for a man who didn't come at all.

'You need to listen to yourself, Anna. You want everything your way, on your terms.'

The absolute injustice of this burned inside Anna. This clearly wasn't getting her anywhere. 'How often do you get your own way with Ryan, huh?'

'I told you, this is not about—'

'Who chooses the clothes you wear when you go out? Who picks the restaurant?'

She could tell by the way Nicole twitched that she'd hit a nerve. 'Ryan has good taste, he—'

'And how often does he get cross with you over dinner because you smiled at the waiter, or you're not showing enough interest in his terminally boring work stories, or because he's noticed that you've bitten your nails?'

Nicole paled. 'I don't think—'

'And then you have to make it up to him, right? What do you do? Cancel a lunch with your friend the next day? Give up an exercise class which he says is taking up too much of your time? Change jobs because he has a problem with one of your colleagues?'

'He doesn't—'

'It's not normal, Nicole. I know how he makes you believe that it shows that he loves you, but it isn't true. It's controlling and unhealthy.'

'No one is perfect, Anna. Even you. Ryan is funny and romantic and he loves me. That's what this is all about, isn't it? You're jealous that we're together.'

She had been angry at Nicole, but now Anna just felt sorry for her. 'Of course, he is funny and romantic. And he can be generous and thoughtful and charming. Why else would you – and I – put up with all the rest of it? But you have to ask yourself, is it worth it? Is it worth walking on eggshells, letting him make the decisions, cutting yourself off from your friends and maybe even family?'

The last one had been a shot in the dark, but the way Nicole flinched made it clear that Anna had hit the target. Then her phone rang again. This time she didn't get up.

'Hi, Ryan... Sorry... Yes, sorry... Sorry... Yes, I'm about to leave for home... No, I'm fine, just a bit out of breath... Yes, I know but I was running some hill sprints... Of course, yes... I'll call you later... I love you too.'

When she put the phone back in her bag, Anna could see that she was trembling. 'I have to go. You need to work this out with Ryan. Please don't corner me like this again.'

Anna watched her walk away, and she could hear one of her mother's favourite sayings: *There but for the grace of God, go I.*

She could only hope that Nicole wouldn't tell Ryan about their meeting. They were already on rocky ground, and she needed to keep him on side until she had found an alternative solution for Libby.

She said a quick prayer of thanks that at least Libby's dialysis was keeping her well. They had time to work this out.

TWENTY-NINE

'What the actual eff—'

'I know, I know.' Anna put up a hand to interrupt Tina. 'Your face right now is pretty much how I must have looked on Wednesday night.'

Tina hadn't been in work yesterday, so their coffee this morning was the first chance that Anna had had to update her on Ryan's latest 'surprise'. 'I just can't believe it. Who does that? And asks a little girl to lie to her mother, too. I mean, that's not normal.'

Tina was right. It wasn't normal. And yet, after her initial anger had worn off, Anna couldn't honestly say that she was shocked he had done it. 'It's what he's like. What he's always been like.'

Tina shook her head. 'I still can't believe that someone like you was with someone like him. I mean, no disrespect to other women or anything, but I just can't understand it. You're not some little mouse who lets someone walk all over her.'

It was an understandable comment. Who wouldn't assume that you needed to be weak to put up with a man controlling you, telling you what to do? 'It's difficult to explain.'

Tina glanced up at the clock on the wall. 'Well, we've got five minutes until everyone starts arriving. Talk fast.'

Five minutes was not enough time to explain something which

she didn't understand herself. How she had gradually given Ryan more and more control over what she did and said and wore.

'I'm more concerned about what to do now,' Anna said. 'If I don't give in to what he wants, I'm worried that he's going to change his mind about donating his kidney. But if I do give in, I have no idea how Libby and I are going to live.'

Tina was nodding along, but she didn't look as if she was listening. Anna paused to see if she was going to reply and was surprised to see a smile appear on her face. 'I've got it.'

'Got what?'

'What is it that Ryan has been most interested in during this whole thing? Since you first asked him about the kidney transplant?'

'I don't know. Getting back together, maybe?'

Tina shook her head. 'Other than that. What else is he getting out of it?' She didn't wait for Anna to answer. 'Attention. Being a hero. Everyone thinking how wonderful he is. Classic narcissist.'

She folded her arms as if Anna should now know exactly what to do. Except she didn't. 'Okay. But how does this help me?'

'Fill the kettle up again and I'll tell you.'

Dialysis on a Saturday was always worse because they knew that everyone else was either relaxing at home or out having a good time. Anna hadn't been sure whether Ryan would take her up on her invitation to join them at the dialysis ward, especially as he'd only flown home from Belgium that morning.

'I must say I'm surprised you asked me to come here. You seemed to want me to stay away last time.'

She was glad that he couldn't read her mind right now and see why she'd actually suggested it. 'I was wrong. I think it's important for you to see everything that Libby needs to do. Let me introduce you to the team.'

He looked pleased with that. She remembered Tina's words yesterday. *Flatter him. Fool him.*

The nurses on the ward were so familiar that they were becoming more like friends, or family. In the last few weeks, Anna and Libby had actually spent more time with them than they had with their extended family. More than once, they had propped Anna up when she had cried with exhaustion or worry. One of them would keep an eye on Libby while another took Anna aside and let her burble on about whatever thoughts – logical or improbable – were weighing her down. As well as being nurses, they were cheerleaders, therapists, angels in comfortable shoes. Anna wouldn't have got through the last few weeks without them.

There were three nurses on the ward that day, but Anna picked the youngest and prettiest first. Jane couldn't have been much more than twenty-three, but she had the presence and calm of someone much older. 'Hi, Jane. This is Libby's dad. You might see him around a bit more, so I wanted to introduce you.'

Jane held out her hand and shook Ryan's. 'Libby has told us a lot about you recently.'

Ryan smiled. 'All good, I hope?'

Fran, an older nurse with the patience of a saint, came up behind Jane and chuckled. 'Oh yes. I think you're a bit of a hero round here. She tells us all the time that you are going to donate your kidney.'

It was almost pathetic, the way Ryan was lapping this up. This was exactly what Anna wanted, though. 'It's going to change Libby's life.'

'Yes, it's brilliant. It really is. Libby is such a sweetheart.'

As usual, Ryan turned the conversation back to himself. 'Well, I'm just glad that I can do this for my little girl. It's an honour, being able to do this for her.'

Anna hadn't expected him to use the very words she had thrown at him on Tuesday. Maybe he had been listening after all? 'Still, we're grateful to you.'

'Please.' Ryan held up his hand. 'You're embarrassing me.'

The nurses didn't have the time to stand and chat for too long, so Anna led Ryan over to where Libby was absorbed in a film on

Max's iPad. They had to stand there for almost a minute before she looked up and realised that they were there.

Immediately, her face lit up. 'Daddy!'

She was so excited to see him, so happy. If only he deserved the adoration she gave him without any expectation of anything in return. 'Hey, Libby. I thought I'd surprise you.'

It hadn't been his thought at all, but that was beside the point. Anna just needed to keep up the narrative. 'Daddy wants to find out more about your dialysis, Libby.'

Libby shrugged. It shocked Anna, how much she looked like Ryan in the way she tipped her shoulders. 'It's okay. Just boring. Apart from Max, of course.'

Max smiled, but when Anna looked at him, there was something not quite right. He was even more pale than usual, and the energy that always glowed from him just wasn't there. Julie was sitting next to him and Anna tried to catch her eye, but she was staring at him, too. 'Max, are you feeling okay?'

All of a sudden, Max's eyes rolled back in his head and his body started to fit. From everywhere, people appeared. They lowered his chair back so that he was lying flat and checked him over. Seconds later, they were pushing him out of the ward, with Julie following behind.

'Mummy, what is happening to Max? Is Max okay? Mummy, what is happening?' Libby's voice got louder as she became more and more panicked. Anna sat in the chair which Max's mum had just left and took Libby's hand, tried not let her own panic taint her voice. 'I don't know, sweetheart, but the doctors will take care of him. I'm sure he'll be okay.'

She wasn't sure of anything of the sort, but she wasn't about to frighten Libby any further. Especially as Libby started to cry. 'I'm scared. I'm scared, Mummy. Where are they taking Max?'

Jane was straight over with her usual calm confidence. 'Max is with the doctors, Libby. Your mum is right; they'll look after him. Now, weren't you about to tell me about your new *Minecraft* village?'

Somehow, Jane managed to take Libby's mind off Max for a few minutes. When Anna turned towards Ryan, she could see how white he was. 'Is that kid going to be okay?'

Anna hoped with every ounce of her that he was going to be fine. But if this experience had frightened Ryan, this was too good an opportunity to pass up. She lowered her voice so that Libby couldn't hear her. 'I hope so. But this is why I'm so pleased that you are donating a kidney to Libby. Once the operation is over and she has recovered, she'll never need dialysis again.'

Ryan nodded slowly, looked again at the tubes going in and out of Libby's arm. If Max being okay was top of Anna's silent prayers right now, Ryan going through with the transplant was a very close second. Was it too soon to nudge him in the right direction? 'Have you called to reschedule your MRI scan? If not, we could do it now.'

As luck would have it, Jane overheard. 'I can sit with Libby for a bit if you want to go and call from here? If you don't have the number, they'll have it on the desk.'

True to form, Ryan wasn't going to make an excuse in front of Jane. If anything, he stood taller, as if to rise to the occasion. Anna could practically see his chest puffing out. 'Good idea. I'll call now.'

Inside the pocket of her trousers, Anna crossed her fingers. She just hoped that this was enough.

She tried not to hover as Ryan made the call to his doctor's office. When he came back to the ward, she made sure she was standing near to the nurses when she asked him, 'What did they say?'

'They have a free appointment on Monday. It'll mean I have to juggle some important clients, but I just want to get this moving as quickly as possible. The less time Libby has to be on dialysis, the better.'

This speech was for the benefit of the nurses who were standing nearby, but Anna didn't care. Two more days and they would be a step closer to the transplant. She was going to buy Tina the biggest fresh cream slice that she could find on Monday. 'That's great news.'

Ryan puffed out his chest. 'Yes. I'll go and tell Libby. That'll cheer her up.'

Anna didn't think talk of scans and operations was going to cheer her up after watching her much-loved friend being wheeled away. Maybe it would make Ryan more likely to go through with it, though? Once they knew that Max was okay, Anna could start to prepare Libby for her own procedure. Then maybe, one day soon, the two of them would be healthy and happy, and would be able to have much more fun together than an afternoon in the park. Did she dare to dream that day might come?

THIRTY

Although they needed warm coats, the next day was bright for February, so Anna had picked up her mum and driven the three of them to Chalkwell Beach. She bought a coffee, a tea and a hot chocolate from the Saltwater Cafe and they sat on the wall, looking out to sea. Libby hadn't stopped asking about Max all morning.

'Does he have to stay in hospital or is he at home now? Can I go and see him?'

Anna wanted to tell her that everything was okay. That Max was going to be fine and she didn't need to worry. But if she said that and – God forbid – he wasn't, Libby would never forgive her. 'I don't know, Libby. I'm sure his mummy will let us know when she has time.'

These days, calling someone unexpectedly felt like an intrusion, especially when you didn't know what was happening in their life. Anna had left it until this morning to even text Julie.

How's Max? Let me know if you need anything.

As always, Anna's mum was able to come up with something to distract Libby. 'Why don't you collect some nice shells for him, Libby? We could make something with them when we get home.'

Libby was all over an art project. She slipped from the wall onto the beach and was soon lost in a hunt for shells in the pebbles and silt.

When she was out of earshot, Anna's mum turned to her. 'And how are you? It must have been frightening at the hospital yesterday.'

Anna smiled. With everything going on for everybody else, her mum still wanted to check how it was affecting her. Once a mother, always a mother. 'Yeah. It was scary. I can't imagine how it must have been for his mum.'

Julie hadn't even glanced in Anna's direction, but Anna had seen the terror in her eyes. As soon as they'd moved Max, she had been behind the gurney, reassuring him. *It's all going to be okay, Maxie. Mummy's here. I'm coming with you. It's all going to be okay.* She'd left everything behind on her seat: the book she was reading, her scarf, even her purse. The nurses had collected it together for her after she'd gone, but her focus had been fully on Max and nothing else.

Anna's mum nodded. 'I miss your dad, of course I do, but the thought of something happening to you or your sister, or any of the little ones' – she nodded in Libby's direction – 'it would kill me, I think.'

Anna pushed her hands deeper into the pockets of her coat; they were cold now that she was no longer holding onto her hot coffee. She should have brought gloves. Sometimes she was so focused on making sure that Libby was wrapped up, she forgot about her own clothing. 'I know, Mum. Me too.'

For a few moments, they watched Libby as she wandered further away. The beach was almost empty apart from a couple of runners and an older man walking a West Highland terrier. Libby had always loved water: splashing in the bath, the swimming pool, the sea. After she had her transplant, Anna was going to save enough money to take the three of them away somewhere warm, where she could swim every day. They could start to live again.

Her mobile started to ring in her pocket. It was Julie.

'Hi. How's Max?'

Julie sounded exhausted. 'He's stable. The doctors are running tests to see what happened. Thanks for your text. Sorry it took so long to reply. I know Libby must be worried.'

How kind of her to think of Libby right now. 'Don't apologise. She knew you were busy looking after Max. So, he's going to be okay?'

There was a pause at the other end. 'No one is saying either way. It's the usual, *we're doing everything we can to find out what it is.* They're keeping him in until they're confident he won't fit again. Which worries me that they think he will.'

Anna knew about doctor-speak. They couldn't make promises when they didn't know for sure what would happen. As a parent, you wanted certainty. To be told, *do this and everything will be fine.* Waiting, not knowing, was excruciating. 'It's good that he's in their hands, though. They have the best doctors there. I'm sure they'll get to the bottom of it and he'll be back to normal as soon as they do.'

She could have kicked herself. *Back to normal.* What did that even mean? Nothing was normal for their kids, was it? But Julie clearly knew what she meant. 'I hope you're right. It's awful seeing him just lying there. He doesn't want to do anything except watch those stupid YouTube videos they love so much. He can't even summon up the energy to play with his Nintendo.'

Anna couldn't imagine Max being anything other than chatty and active. Even sitting down at dialysis, his face would move through a thousand expressions as he gave detailed explanations of the characters or buildings he was creating in his *Minecraft* village. 'Would you like me to bring Libby in for a visit?'

'That's kind, but he's only allowed close family at the moment. He's napping again now, which is why I had a chance to call you. Maybe they can do a FaceTime call later?'

'Definitely. And is there anything you need? Anything I can drop to the hospital?'

'A fully functioning magic wand if you've got one? No, I'm fine. Tell Libby that Max will call her soon.'

'I will. Take care.'

When she ended the call, Anna joined her mother where she'd moved to keep a closer eye on Libby. As she walked nearer to the sea, Anna could see her feet sinking into the wet sand. She put her hands either side of her mouth to shout. 'Not so far, Libby. Come back this way a bit.'

Libby moved about one step in their direction and then bent to pick up more treasure from the beach. Anna tried not to think how filthy she was getting. Her mum kept her eyes on Libby as she spoke. 'How's Libby's friend?'

'I don't know, really. His mum sounded pretty worried.' It had been more than that. As well as worry and exhaustion, there had been something else in Julie's voice. Something Anna didn't even want to name.

'Well, at least he's in the best place.' Although this was a platitude, it was true. The centre was the best in the country. And what did anyone have in circumstances like this, except platitudes? *He's in the best place. The doctors know what they're doing. No news is good news.*

'I'm scared, Mum.'

'I know, darling, but I'm sure he'll be fine. Little ones are so resilient.'

Anna was ashamed to admit it, but that wasn't quite what she meant. 'Not just about Max. I'm scared about Libby. I don't know if I'm more scared about her having the transplant or that it won't even happen.'

Her mum frowned. 'What do you mean? I thought Ryan's tests all looked positive?'

'So far they do, but he has MRI scan to go yet.' This wasn't exactly what she meant either. After years of hiding the reality of Ryan from her family, it was difficult to say it out loud. 'But I'm also frightened Ryan will pull out. That he'll change his mind and not go through with it.'

Her mum looked shocked at the very thought. 'He's her *father*, Anna. He won't do that. Whatever else he's said and done

– or not done – he would have to be a monster to let her down over this.'

Anna bit her lip. One day she would tell her mother what life had been like with him, but she didn't have the energy for that conversation right now. 'I hope you're right, Mum. I really do.'

A breeze was coming off the sea and she shivered. Her mum nodded towards the sky. 'It looks like we might get some rain soon, and I'm pretty sure that Patches will be shredding the bottoms of your curtains as we speak. Shall I go and call Libby?'

Anna held out her hands for the empty cups her mother was holding. 'Yes, please. I'll go and drop our rubbish in the bin.'

The bin was just behind the wall. After dropping the cups inside, Anna turned and watched the two of them coming back up the beach together, hand in hand. Libby was chattering away and holding out her palm to show her grandma the shells that she'd chosen for the friend she loved.

Anna closed her eyes for a second. *Please, God, let Max be okay.*

THIRTY-ONE

All day Monday, thoughts of Max had been driven from Anna's mind. All she could think about was the MRI scan that Ryan was having that day.

Although she was grateful that he was no longer demanding that she attend his medical appointments, it was driving her crazy that she didn't even know what time he was due to be there. The test was a scan, so the results would be available for his doctor to look at almost immediately. How long would it take for them to make a judgement on whether it was viable for transplant? Mr Harris had assured her that they would be able to move as quickly as possible. But was their quickly as fast as hers?

She'd been useless at work all morning. In the end, Tina had physically pushed her into the small office. 'Go in there and find something to keep you occupied that doesn't involve you trying to mix gravy granules into the chocolate custard.'

The way her mind was all over the place, Anna didn't even trust herself to place any food orders, so she focused on tidying away the invoices into their rudimentary filing system. She was trying to refill the ancient stapler when her mobile buzzed in her pocket: a rare message from her sister, asking her to call as soon as possible.

. . .

Catherine's law firm's office was only about twenty minutes away from the school, but Anna had never actually visited her there before. In their brief telephone conversation earlier, Catherine hadn't given much away, apart from to say that Ryan's lawyer had been in touch with her. She'd suggested Anna ask their mum to take Libby after school so that they could discuss the details at her office, but Tina had offered to have her – and Patches – over to play. Catherine hadn't even intimated whether the news she had was good or bad.

As one of the partners, Catherine had her own office. It was small, but comfortable. She sat behind a large desk, looking every inch the successful lawyer. Anna was proud of her. 'This is nice.'

'Thanks. Can I get you a coffee or anything?'

Anna laughed. 'Crikey. Am I getting the full client treatment?' She screwed up her eyes. 'How much is this costing me?'

'Very funny. Shut the door and sit down. I need to talk to you about something.'

As soon as she sat down, Catherine pushed a piece of paper in her direction. 'I've been emailing Ryan's solicitor for an update on the divorce and not been getting any joy. But this morning, out of the blue, I got this.'

Anna scanned the printout of the email, which was headed: 'Residency'. Most of it was in legal speak. She looked up at Catherine for an explanation. 'What does joint residency mean? That he can have her to stay at his place?'

Catherine shook her head. 'More than that, I'm afraid. It means that Libby would live half the time with you and half the time with Ryan.'

'But that doesn't make sense. It can take up to an hour to drive to him when the traffic is heavy. How would he get her to school on time?'

'Have you not read that far? He is suggesting that you made the choice to change her school without consulting him. He wants her to go to a private prep school which is equidistant between the two of you. He is even offering to pay the fees in their entirety.'

Anna wasn't stupid, but the formality of her sister's speech was making her head spin. 'Slow down. He wants her to change schools again? And live with him half the time?'

'Yes. And the biggest issue for us is that he says you didn't consult him before changing her school. Is that true?'

Anna could barely remember. It had been such an awful time. 'I don't know. I mean, he knew I was moving out of the house. And I couldn't drive her all the way back to her old school every day. It was obvious that she would have to transfer somewhere more local.'

'So you didn't?' Catherine sighed and rubbed the back of her neck. 'Oh, Anna. I told you that you needed to keep him informed of everything. I knew something like this was going to come back and bite you.'

The injustice of all of this made Anna's voice louder than she intended. 'You're saying this is my fault? I'm the one to blame?'

Catherine shook her head. 'No, no, of course not, I'm sorry. I'm just so angry that he's doing this to you. To Libby.'

The sympathy in her sister's voice defused Anna's anger and she sat back in her chair, trying to wrap her head around Ryan's argument for Libby not living with her. It didn't make sense. 'But what about her dialysis? How is he going to get her to and from hospital?'

Even as she said the words, the cogs were moving in her brain. She was almost there when her sister filled in the gaps. 'She won't be going to dialysis after the transplant.'

Anna's head started to swim. She felt sick. And hot. And dizzy. How could he do this? How could he offer the greatest gift with one hand and then demand she pay for it with the other?

At the same time, it made perfect sense. Wasn't this what he had always done? Whatever he had given her – holidays, clothes, jewellery – she had been made to feel like she owed him. But this? This was an act of such cruelty that she could barely breathe.

'I can't believe... But why... I mean, how is this good for Libby? I know he wants to see her – and she wants to see him – but how can it be good for her to be shunted back and forth between two houses?'

'I don't think he is thinking about what's best for Libby, Anna. But if we pursue the point that she will be unhappy living in two different places, he could petition for full residency. Which means she would live with him and you would have access visits.'

Her sister was staring at her, her eyes loaded with unspoken bullets of truth. 'He's punishing me.' Still Catherine continued to look at her, as if waiting for her come to a realisation. 'Can he do this? Can he make the court do this?'

'He can try. It is very unlikely that he'll get anywhere with a judge. They will want to reduce disruption or change for the child and will always choose the set-up that is most stable. Taking Libby out of a school and a home where she is happy and has been resident for six months with her full-time parent just for more time with an absentee father would clearly be mad. But do you really want to go to court? I just want you to know what could happen here.'

It was all very well Catherine telling her that it was 'unlikely' that Ryan would get anywhere, but she didn't know Ryan. She hadn't seen the way that Libby was gravitating towards him, pushing Anna away. Was this all part of his plan? 'But what if he holds us to ransom? What if he says that he won't go ahead with being a living donor if he doesn't get custody?'

Catherine shook her head. 'Don't worry about that. The law moves slowly; we can keep this all waiting until after the transplant has gone ahead.'

Desperation clawed at Anna's throat; the email crumpled in her hand as she leaned towards the desk. 'Please, Catherine. You have to help me. I can't lose her. I can't lose Libby.'

Catherine pushed away her chair and came around to sit on the chair next to Anna's. 'You won't lose her, Anna. We've got this. I promise you.'

She could barely breathe. 'But you don't know what he's like.'

Catherine took Anna's face in her hands. Looked her in the

eye. 'Anna. I'm a family lawyer. I've met hundreds of Ryans in my time. I've seen the way he is with you. I've seen your reactions. The flinching. The fake smiles. The tremble in your hand. I understand why you've kept it to yourself, but I think it's time you told me everything.'

Anna's eyes blurred; her heart was galloping. 'I don't know where to start.'

Catherine leaned backwards and picked up a notepad and pen. 'Start at the beginning and then go forwards.'

A tear dripped from the end of her nose. 'I don't even know when it began.'

Catherine reached out and squeezed her hand. Her voice was gentle. 'Don't worry about what happened when. Just tell me what comes to your mind first.'

THIRTY-TWO

What came to her mind first?

No. Not that. Not yet.

'He always needed to know where I was. So, if I was out with a friend and they suggested going on somewhere else, I would have to call him or text him before we went.'

Catherine was taking notes. 'To ask permission?'

He hadn't made it sound like that. At least not at the beginning. 'Not exactly. I mean, he mostly didn't mind, but sometimes he would say that he missed me and wanted me to come back.'

'So, then you'd go home?'

Anna shuffled in her seat. She'd known it wasn't going to be easy, but this was the more straightforward stuff. 'I know it sounds pathetic, but to start with, I liked the fact that he wanted to be with me all the time.'

Catherine didn't look surprised. 'And later?'

Anna pictured the friends she'd had to let down, their complaints as they'd begged her to stay, or worse, their shrugs as if they'd expected it. 'I'd want to stay out a bit longer and it was annoying to have to leave.'

'But you still did?'

'It was just easier.' How could she explain to Catherine, whose husband, Vikram, was the kindest, most easy-going man on the planet, how Ryan would behave if she stayed out longer than she'd said she would? 'He would just sulk all evening if I didn't. Sometimes for days after. I would have to win him back by making a really nice dinner, or cancelling other plans which hadn't included him. It was unbearable otherwise.'

'Unbearable how?'

There was no way to do this calmly and slowly. She'd only just begun to peel the lid off it all and memories were flying at her like bees from a disturbed hive. 'Once, he told me that I had twenty minutes to get home or he would cut up my favourite red dress. Another time, he...' Her hand flew to her mouth to stop her lips from wobbling. Could she tell Catherine this?

'What is it?'

She had to keep going. Ryan wanted to take Libby. She needed to focus on that. 'Do you remember the jewellery box Dad brought me back from that work trip he had to go on? When I was about Libby's age? The one with the little ballerina in it? That played a tune?'

Catherine smiled. 'Of course I remember. He brought me back a big stationery set because he thought I was too old for ballerinas, but I was dead jealous of it. He and Mum had to buy me one the following Christmas.'

'Well, once I took longer to get home than I'd said. There was traffic. The taxi couldn't go the usual way. I was frantic. I knew he'd be sat at home, stewing on me getting there. I'd had the jewellery box out to clean it up to give it to Libby and he knew how much it meant to me. He called me and played the tune before throwing it from the bedroom window so that it smashed on the ground.'

Catherine looked up at her. 'Oh, Anna.'

She shook her head fiercely. If Catherine started showing her sympathy, she'd never have the courage to get it all out. 'There's worse than that. The week that Dad died, and Mum called me to say it was close and I might want to come home?'

Catherine froze as if she knew what was coming. 'Yes, Mum spoke to Ryan and he said he would tell you.'

Back then, Anna's mum had always called the landline rather than their mobiles. She used to say she was worried they'd be driving. Anna had been in the shower when Ryan had taken the call. 'He didn't tell me.'

Catherine actually gasped; her hands flew to her face. 'Oh, Anna. So, when I called you a couple of days later...'

Anna nodded. 'And thought that I hadn't even bothered to call Mum back? Yep, I didn't know anything about it.'

'But I was so angry with you. Why didn't you tell me?'

'And admit what he'd done? You would have hated him. I would have had to show you what he was really like.'

'Anna, we're your family. You could have told us.'

It sounded so simple. She *could* have told them. So why hadn't she? Shame? Guilt? 'That's why I didn't get to say goodbye to Dad. That day you called, I got straight on to Ryan at work, asked him to come home so that he could collect Libby from school and I could come home to you all. She was only four, had only started school two months before, if you remember. I didn't know anyone else who could collect her.'

'And he didn't answer his phone?'

It was worse than that; he had answered his phone. 'He refused to come home.'

She had been beside herself. Not knowing what to do for the best. Begging him to come home and then trying to think of any other solution that didn't involve taking her four-year-old daughter to her grandfather's deathbed. Eventually, she'd called the school and taken her out and just driven towards home, hoping that there would be someone there who could watch Libby – a neighbour, a friend of her mother's. But she had wasted too much precious time.

Catherine didn't normally cry. She was the strong one. The pragmatic one. But now the tears rolled down her cheeks. 'And Dad slipped away that afternoon, with me and Mum either side.'

The pain of that image, and her missing from it, almost made Anna howl with rage and grief. She hadn't been there to say goodbye. She would never get that back. Never. 'I know you were angry with me. I'm so sorry, Catherine.'

Catherine leaned towards her and pulled her into her arms, crying into her hair. 'Don't you dare apologise. I am sorry. I am sorry that we didn't know how bad it was. I am sorry that we didn't help you more. Oh, Anna, I am so sorry.'

Anna pulled away. Before she could accept her sister's love and sympathy, there was one more thing she had to tell her. 'I did something really awful.'

'It wasn't your fault, Anna. He—'

'No.' Anna cut her off. 'Not about Dad. Something else.'

Catherine still had her hands on Anna's forearms. 'What is it? You can tell me anything.'

Anna had to hope that that was true. 'I was pregnant.'

'With Libby?'

She shook her head. 'After Libby. Just after. When I realised I was pregnant, she was only nine weeks old.'

When Catherine frowned, she'd developed the exact same crease at the top of her nose as their mother had. 'Is that even possible?'

Anna had been as bewildered as Catherine now looked. 'Apparently, yes. You can get pregnant as early as three weeks after birth. I had gone back on the pill and I thought it'd be okay, but maybe we didn't leave it the full seven days before having sex or maybe it was an upset stomach. I don't know. Those first few weeks with Libby were such a blur.'

Constantly tired and emotional, she had been distraught at the thought of being pregnant again so soon. Those early weeks with Libby had been so difficult that she hadn't even been sure that she wanted another child. At no point, however, had she considered terminating the pregnancy.

But it had turned out that termination was what he wanted.

'Ryan said that he didn't want another child. That Libby was "more than enough". He was sick, he said, of having to put up with me giving her so much attention.'

Catherine practically spat the words out: 'The selfish bastard.'

She was right. But wasn't Anna just as bad? 'I begged him. I said that I would get some childcare, spend more time with him, make sure I looked better.'

Anna could still feel Ryan's spit on her face as he'd told her how 'disgusting' she looked since having a baby. More than once she'd turned away, using her body to shelter Libby's tiny ears from his poisonous words.

Catherine didn't interrupt her this time. Instead, she stroked her arm with her thumb, just like their mother used to do when they were small and upset. Like Anna did to Libby now. 'I lasted out three weeks. Three weeks of his threatening to leave. To never have anything to do with Libby. I was still so fragile after Libby's birth. He wore me down. I let him book the termination. I let him drive me to the clinic. I let him drive me home again afterwards and tell me never to speak about it again. He wanted me to get rid of our baby, but I was the one who did it.'

Catherine's face was full of sympathy and love. 'Women have abortions, Anna. You know that. You wouldn't judge them for it, would you?'

'Of course not. Women have the right to make a choice for themselves. But it wasn't my choice, was it? It was *his* choice. And I let him do it. I let him do it.'

This time she did let Catherine surround her with her arms and they sobbed together until Anna had exhausted her tears. She blew her nose and drank the glass of water Catherine poured for her. She felt lighter somehow. She had given voice to the darkest part of herself and Catherine was still here. Still loving her. She wanted to get this finished now and get home to Libby.

'I'm fine. Keep going. Ask me something else.'

Catherine understood. She picked up her notepad. 'Okay. And how did he behave towards you in front of your friends? Was it different to how he was at home?'

Anna's bitter laugh made her sister glance up in surprise. 'He could be like two different people. With friends, he was so funny and generous. He was always the one commenting on someone's new haircut, or remembering their birthday. He was quite flirty with my friends.'

She cringed inside at the memory of him at a party just before they'd separated. He had been in the kitchen for ages, talking to one of the mums from Libby's preschool. She must have been at least ten years younger than him, but he had clearly loved her rapt attention to the stories that Anna had heard a thousand times before. Anna had been left in the front room talking to an older couple, feeling like a complete and utter idiot. Maybe she shouldn't have been surprised to find out that he and Nicole were together. They'd always been friends and, if Ryan had turned up the charm, Anna could imagine how easy it had been for them to slip into a relationship.

'And we know, of course, that he was unfaithful. Even though his lawyer won't admit it.'

Other than her own first-hand account of catching them in bed, Anna had no evidence that he had slept with that woman. But now he was with Nicole, while they were still married, surely that was admissible? 'He's with Nicole now. I'm not certain they're living together, but he's definitely in a relationship with her. Won't that count?'

Catherine looked up. 'Will she sign something to that effect?'

Anna slumped back down in her chair. 'I doubt it.'

'That brings us back to unreasonable behaviour. Was he ever aggressive towards you? Verbal threats? Physical violence?'

'He got very angry when he was jealous. If I spent too much time speaking to another man, he would—' she stopped. Talking about it like this was bringing it all back. All the things she had tried not to think about for months.

Catherine was gentle. 'He would what?'

'He would say really nasty things. I was a slut. A whore. Who did I think I was kidding anyway? As if any man would want to sleep with me. I just made him look ridiculous, putting myself about like that.' As she said the words, she could taste his voice and it made her want to spit them out before they poisoned her.

Unlike the other revelations, Catherine didn't seem surprised. 'I'm so sorry to make you talk about this, Anna. But it will really help to build the case. Are you okay to carry on?'

Now they had started, she wanted to get it over with. 'Yes. I'm fine, honestly.'

Catherine nodded. 'Did he ever hit you? Or do anything physical?'

Anna closed her eyes. She could almost hear his hand slamming down on the table, feel his breath on her cheek as he leaned in close to her face. But he had never actually touched her in anger. 'No. No. He wasn't abusive.'

Catherine stopped writing and looked up at her. Amazement on her face. 'He might not have hit you, Anna, but Ryan was abusive. Make no mistake. You have been a victim of his emotional abuse for years.'

Anna felt sick. There was something about those words. *Victim. Abuse.* They sounded so serious. So awful.

But it had been serious. And it had been awful. Worse than awful. The control. The manipulation. The insults. How had she stayed there for so long? 'Catherine, you must think I'm such a fool.'

Catherine shook her head. 'No. I've had professional women in here who manage huge teams of people and make million-pound decisions who let their husbands choose their clothes and what they eat. These men are masters at what they do, Anna. And they are often attracted to women who are strong and confident and outgoing. And then they bring them down.'

Anna held a hand to her throat: it ached with holding her emotions. She'd thought she had no more tears left, but here they came. 'I don't want to be a victim.'

Catherine shook her head. 'You are not a victim, my darling sister. You are a survivor.'

THIRTY-THREE

Catherine offered to follow Anna home and carry on the conversation there, but Anna didn't want any of these stories from the past to exist in the air of her new home. She and Libby were safe there; it had never been Ryan's and he had no power over her there. That's what she kept telling herself, over and over.

A quick call to Tina confirmed that she was more than happy to give Libby some dinner and keep her and Patches there for another hour until Anna got home. Apparently, the kitten was keeping them all entertained, hunting a ball of wool around the kitchen. She could hear Libby's excited yelps in the background, her infectious giggles a salve for Anna's bruised heart.

The worst of the revelations were over now and, hard though it had been, Anna felt better for sharing the truth with her sister. After she'd filled Catherine in on the events that had unfolded since she'd called Ryan to first tell him about Libby's diagnosis, her sister had put her solicitor hat back on and gave her a list of instructions which included keeping records of any text messages and voicemails – and making sure she locked her back door.

When Anna picked Libby up from Tina's, she was already looking sleepy, so they didn't hang around. Patches had been a hit, apparently, so Tina was pretty reluctant to hand him over. 'It was nice having him. It's the first time my two have been in the same room together without World War Three starting. If he's too much for you to deal with right now, he can stay.'

Sleepy from his afternoon of wool-chasing, Patches had settled into the crook of Anna's arm. He was still so tiny she could barely feel his weight, but he was warm and soft and, actually, quite comforting. 'I think we'll keep him for now.'

Tina smiled a knowing smile. 'Okay, chick. See you in the morning.'

On Tuesday morning, there were two deliveries first thing and then they were rushed off their feet, so Anna didn't have a chance to tell Tina about everything that had happened in her meeting with her sister. If she had been a liability yesterday, today she was a downright danger to herself. One of the girls only just stopped her grabbing the hot lasagne tray with her bare hands.

In the end, Tina got exasperated with her. 'You're going to kill one of us in a minute. What's got into you?'

Anna rubbed at her temples. Either the emotional release of yesterday, or the pent-up stress of waiting for a phone call from Ryan had given her a headache from hell. 'I'm sorry. Ryan had his MRI scan yesterday. I still haven't heard anything. I can't think about anything else.'

Tina hit her own head with the heel of her flour-covered hand. 'Of course. Sorry, I wasn't thinking. I'm sure it will be okay. This is the final test, isn't it? And then it's full steam ahead?'

'Yeah. It is.' Yesterday, she had been so desperate to hear that it was okay, that Ryan would get the final decision that he would be able to donate his kidney to Libby. But now? Now, she was terrified what that would mean for them both in the long term. Either way, this waiting for news was like balancing on a knife edge.

When she and Libby got to the dialysis ward that afternoon, Anna *still* hadn't heard from him. The suspense was eating her up, but she knew that that was a part of his plan. After speaking to Catherine, the final scales had dropped from her eyes. None of this was about Libby, for Ryan. It was all another way in which he got to play puppet master. He was already holding enough strings; Anna didn't need to hand him any more. Instead, she called Mr Harris's office and left a message with his secretary, asking him to let her know as soon as the results came through. Until then, she would just have to put up with this unsettled feeling of not knowing.

It was odd, being there without Julie and Max. Libby felt it too. It wasn't just the empty seat next to her. Max was a force of nature and they felt his absence like a vacuum.

The nurses couldn't tell her anything about him. 'We don't know anything.' Jane looked up at Anna from where she was hooking Libby up. 'And even if we did, we couldn't say anything.'

'Of course.' Anna knew as much, but she had been hoping that Max would be there today. Smiling and telling Libby all the gory details of his stay on the ward. She wanted to see Julie, too. She'd brought cookies to ease the taste of the awful coffee.

Libby had been half-heartedly flicking bricks into place on the castle she was building in *Minecraft*. 'I miss Max. When is he coming back?'

'I don't know, sweetheart. Why don't we think up some fun things to do when he gets back? We could plan another trip to the park, maybe? Or a picnic?'

Libby perked up a little. 'Can we go to the swimming pool? The one with the slide in it that Auntie Catherine took me to last year?'

Would she be able to swim with the AV graft? 'We'll check with Mr Harris. If he says it's okay, as soon as Max is up to it, we'll ask his mum if we can go to the pool. What about you try and get that castle finished before we see him, too? I bet he'll be impressed.'

Libby resumed her brickwork with renewed enthusiasm. Anna leaned towards the screen, trying to be interested. There was an extra section to the side of the castle which didn't look like the rest. She pointed at it. 'What's that?'

'That's the dialysis room. I'm building it for me and Max. It's a magical one where you only have to go inside for ten minutes and then you're all done and you can go back to the castle.'

It made Anna want to cry. Even in a fantasy world that she was building herself, this damn disease was still there for Libby. Ryan *had* to go through with this transplant. Their daughter deserved to be rid of this part of her life.

Her phone beeped in her pocket and her stomach clenched. Was that him, now? What was the result? Was this all going ahead? She took a deep breath and held it.

But the message wasn't from Ryan. It was Julie. Max's mum. She sent up a silent prayer before she opened it. *Please let him be okay.*

It was obvious that it was a generic message which must have been sent to more people than just her. Just three devastating sentences:

We're heartbroken to tell you that our beautiful boy passed away in the early hours of this morning. We will be in touch with you all individually when we can. Hold your babies tight tonight x

THIRTY-FOUR

Anna waited until they had eaten – macaroni cheese, Libby's favourite – and were on the sofa together before she started to talk to Libby about Max.

For the first time, she was thankful for Patches. He might have wrecked the bottom of her armchair, but he was making up for it now by sleeping on Libby's lap as she stroked his soft fur. Anna moved up a little on the sofa and put an arm across Libby's shoulders.

'Libby, I need to talk to you about something that is very sad.'

She felt Libby stiffen against her. 'Is it Max? Is he not getting better?'

There was no way to soften the initial blow; dragging it out would only make it worse. 'It is Max, sweetheart. He was very poorly and his condition got worse. He died this morning.'

To begin with, Libby didn't move. It was a lot to take in. When she spoke again, her voice trembled. 'Did it hurt? Was he in pain?'

Anna stroked the top of her head. 'I don't think so. He was in hospital, so the doctors would have been able to give him some-thing so he wasn't in pain, and his mum and dad were there too, so...'

Libby turned her head into Anna's armpit, her body convulsing with sobs. Anna picked up Patches and laid him on the other side of the sofa, then she pulled Libby into her body, almost on her lap, and held her close. 'It's okay, baby. I'm here. It's okay.'

Her words were instinctive, but it wasn't okay. It was anything but okay. That wonderful little boy, full of fun and friendship, the one who had reached out to Libby and helped her so much – he was gone. Nine years was not long enough for a life. Especially a life which had been curtailed by hospital appointments and operations and an inability to do all the things he dreamed of.

Libby pulled herself away and looked at Anna. Her face was swollen, red and wet. 'It's not fair. Max was my friend. He was so nice. Why can't it just be the horrible people who die?'

If only there was an answer to that question. How did you explain the injustice and random nature of life and death to a seven-year-old? 'I know, it isn't fair, is it? It's okay to be angry about it, Lib. It's okay to be cross and sad and anything else you feel right now. Max was your friend and we are going to miss him very much.'

Libby started to cry again and Anna pulled her onto her lap. Libby's head was on her chest and Anna rested her chin on the top of it. She was so big now, her legs so long, but in many ways she was still just a baby. Her baby. How must Max's mum be feeling right now? Her lap empty. Her boy gone. Anna was fighting back tears herself.

Gradually, Libby's sobs shallowed and became more like hiccups. Anna gave her a tissue to blow her nose and used another to dry her face. She kissed her still damp cheek. 'Are you tired, sweetheart? Shall we go up to bed?'

Libby nodded. Her face still looked as if it could crumple back into tears at any moment.

After teeth cleaning and pyjamas, Anna usually read to Libby. Libby loved the *Treehouse* books and had told Anna recently that she and Max would build a treehouse one day. It was probably best to pick something different for bedtime tonight. Anna looked on the small bookshelf in Libby's room for something that was light enough to be soothing. While her back was turned, a voice came from the bed. 'Am I going to die, too, Mummy?'

In all the treatment, all the appointments, all the decisions they'd had to make, Libby had never asked that question. As far as Anna knew, she had never considered it before. Children were invincible in their own eyes: it was so bloody unfair that Libby had to find out like this that they weren't.

Anna sat down on the bed and looked her in the eye. 'Max was very sick, Libby. The doctors had been trying for a long time to make him better. But, in the end, his body couldn't fight it any longer.'

Libby's eyes were wide with fear. 'Is that what will happen to me?'

'No, my darling. Because you're going to have a transplant soon. Daddy is going to give you a wonderful healthy kidney and you are going to feel – and be – so much better. I promise.'

'But Max had a transplant and it didn't work. He just got sick again.'

How did she know that? Anna hadn't ever spoken about it with her or in front of her. Max must have told her himself, in one of their many conversations. 'I know. But that isn't going to happen with you. Daddy is a really good match. And Mr Harris is really confident it's all going to go perfectly. We trust Mr Harris, don't we?'

Libby nodded, but she didn't look certain. 'What happens when you die?'

Another million-dollar question. How should she navigate this one? The websites she'd looked at before broaching this tonight had all said the same thing: be honest. 'No one knows for certain, but lots of people have their own opinion. Some people believe in heaven.'

'What do you believe?'

Right now, Anna wanted to believe more than anything that Max was playing football on a heavenly pitch, running and laughing and free from pain. 'I think that Max is up there telling God all about *Minecraft*.'

Libby smiled. 'I think Max is in heaven too. With Grandpa.'

Anna's heart ached at that. Libby had been four when Anna's dad died, and he'd been very poorly for a while before that. She wouldn't have remembered much about him. Her notions of him were framed from the memories of others.

'Can we go to see Max's mum? And his sister? They are going to be so sad.'

This girl had such a huge heart. 'Yes, of course. Maybe not just yet, because they might want it just to be them and their family right now. But we can make them a card and send it. Let them know how much we loved Max, too.'

This time she couldn't stop the tears leaking from her eyes. She couldn't even begin to imagine how Max's family were feeling right now. The utter sense of loss must be overwhelming. She lay down next to Libby, who shuffled over in bed to make room, then reached out and stroked Anna's hair, something she used to do as a baby. 'Do you want to stay with me in my bed tonight, Mummy? I can cuddle you and make you feel better?'

'Yes. I would like that very much.'

The effects of the dialysis plus the emotion of the last hour must have exhausted Libby, because she fell asleep in a couple of minutes. There wasn't really enough room for Anna beside her in bed, but she couldn't leave. She told herself it was because she didn't want Libby to wake and find her gone, but the truth was that she couldn't bear to be away from her. Her precious, precious girl.

The next morning, Anna woke up still beside Libby, her body twisted around her. Libby had tangled her fingers into Anna's hair and she had to extricate them before uncurling herself from the bed. It took her a moment before she realised that she'd been woken by her mobile phone ringing downstairs.

In the events of the evening, she'd forgotten to shut Patches into the kitchen last night. He was sitting on the sofa, prodding at the buzzing mobile with his paw. She dreaded to think what mischief he'd got up to in the night. She scooped him up with one hand and the phone with the other. The number that came up on the screen was from the hospital. 'Hello?'

Normally, it would be Mr Harris's secretary who called her to arrange appointments or let her know about test results, so she was surprised to hear the man himself at the other end. 'Hi, this is Mr Harris. Is that Anna?'

'Yes, it's me. Is everything okay?'

Mr Harris coughed. 'I was wondering if you had any time to come in and speak to me today. I have some bad news, I'm afraid.'

Anna rubbed at her forehead with her thumb and forefinger. 'I know. We heard about Max. Libby is really upset. But it's kind of you to call.'

Mr Harris paused. 'No. It's not about Max. It's about Libby. About the transplant.'

THIRTY-FIVE

Tina offered to take Libby home with her after school again so that Anna could leave for her appointment as soon as the lunches had been served and cleared away.

Mr Harris had wanted to wait until she came in to explain everything, but she hadn't been able to wait that long. 'Please can you tell me what it's about now? Otherwise, I'll be worried all day until I can come in.'

Eventually, he had given in. 'Unfortunately, it seems that Ryan is not a viable donor.'

She'd sunk down onto the sofa then, unsure whether she could trust her legs to keep her upright. 'I don't understand.'

'I'm afraid I'm not allowed to go into detail because of patient confidentiality. But I had an email from his doctor this morning to confirm it. Ryan cannot be Libby's donor.'

The back of Anna's neck had got very hot. It was difficult to breathe. 'But he was a good match. Everyone said he was a good match. What happened at the MRI scan? What did they find?'

Mr Harris's voice was calm and measured; this couldn't have been the first time he'd had to deliver bad news. 'This is a lot to take in, Anna. Can you come in and see me today? We can go through the next steps, look at Libby's options?'

When Anna had dropped Libby off at her classroom, she'd

taken Paul to one side and told him about Max. She knew that Libby was likely to be more sensitive today, and even get upset, so it was better that her teacher was prepared. As usual, Paul had been thoughtful and caring. 'Poor Libby, I'll definitely keep an extra eye on her today. And how are you?'

'Me?'

'Yes. It must have been hard for you to explain it all to her. It's a lot more difficult when the person you've lost hasn't had a long and happy life.'

That was exactly it. What did you say in those circumstances? 'It was pretty tough. And he was a lovely kid. But it's Libby I'm worried about, not me.'

'Of course.' He glanced back into the classroom. The learning support assistant had the class under control, completing their early morning work of corrections from the day before. 'I was thinking. If you fancy an evening out sometime to get a break, I can do pretty much any night. Dinner, a glass of wine, or even just a coffee. No strings, just a friendly ear.'

He was so kind, and she had really liked speaking to him at the Christmas party and the PTA. It would be nice to have an evening out, but she couldn't make any plans further than a day ahead right now. 'That would be nice. Can I let you know when things have calmed down a bit?'

He held up his hands. 'Of course, no pressure. It's an open offer.'

After that, it had been a busy morning at work with deliveries and then an oven that had gone on the blink, meaning that three trays of sausage rolls were still raw. Somehow, they'd managed to juggle everything around so that every child got their chosen meal option, but Anna hadn't had much time to think. Instead, she'd just carried around a feeling of impending doom like a rucksack on her back. As soon as the last lunch sitting had been in and out of the hall, Tina gave her a nudge. 'We can finish up here. Why don't you get going? If you give me your key, I can collect Patches again. It will be nice for Libby to have him with her.'

Tina's eagerness suggested it would be nice for her, too. Anna grabbed her coat. 'Thanks.'

The waiting room was empty, apart from a cleaner who was slowly pushing his floor polishing machine up the corridor. The monotonous buzz echoed the noise in Anna's brain as she ran everything over in her mind. It had all looked so positive. Blood group, tissue types – all were a very good match. And Ryan was healthy: annoyingly so, since he and Nicole had taken up their triathlons. He didn't smoke, had never been a big drinker or over-weight. What had they found that had made him ineligible to donate a kidney to his daughter? What had those YouTube videos said?

The cleaner clicked off the machine and took up a cloth to wipe a smudge from the wall. In the silence, something occurred to Anna. The more she thought about it, the more the idea grew and grew, until she was almost certain that she was correct. It had to be that. She tapped her foot on the floor. She knew she was early, but she was desperate to see Mr Harris. He might not be able to tell her verbally whether she was right, but his reaction might give it away.

After another agonising ten minutes, Mr Harris came out of his office into the waiting room to collect her. 'Anna. Thanks for coming in so quickly. Can I get you a coffee? Tea?'

'I'm fine, thanks.'

Before she told Mr Harris about her epiphany, she let him explain the email he'd received from Dr Wells, Ryan's consultant. 'As I said on the telephone, I don't have the details as to why Mr Ferguson is no longer a viable donor. But I think you're aware of the kinds of issues that an MRI scan might throw up. Though it's not common, it can be that there are too many blood vessels connected to the kidney which make it too difficult, and potentially dangerous, to remove.'

Anna couldn't wait any longer. 'I don't believe him.'

Mr Harris paused. 'Dr Wells is a very experienced consultant. If he says that Mr Ferguson is not viable—'

'I'm not saying that he got it wrong. I mean, I think that the reason Ryan is no longer viable has got nothing to do with the MRI scan.'

In the first weeks after Libby's diagnosis, Anna had researched kidney donation extensively, watching video after video online where people talked about their experiences. One of the things that had struck her was how well the donors described their treatment, and how important their own health and wellbeing had been to the doctors. One of them had said something which had come to her in the waiting room. A donor who was providing a kidney for his sister had been told by his consultant time and time again that he could change his mind at any time. Which was exactly what Ryan had been told. The donor on the video had explained how his doctor had said that, if he felt he wanted to pull out, but was worried how it would affect his relationship with his sister, they would tell her that his kidney wasn't viable. That way, no one would blame him in any way. Was that what was happening here?

Mr Harris looked uncomfortable. 'I can't discuss Mr Ferguson with you, Anna. You'll have to speak to him yourself. I can only tell you what I've been told: the donation is no longer viable. We need to discuss what you and Libby want to do next. I strongly advise we get her name on the transplant list straight away.'

There was something in his tone which made her uneasy. 'Is it more urgent than it was before? Is there something else I need to be concerned about?'

Mr Harris shook his head. 'Not at the moment, no. But we know that things can change quickly. Kidney disease is an unpredictable animal.'

For a moment, he looked sad. Anna knew from Julie that Mr Harris had been Max's doctor, too. How did doctors feel when they lost a patient? Particularly a patient as young as Max. 'Of course, please put her on the transplant list. How long is it likely to take?

Mr Harris held out his hands. 'It's difficult to say. The average wait time is two and a half to three years. Unfortunately, the demand for donations is much greater than the supply. Although children are given priority, so it could be sooner.'

Three years? Libby could be nearly ten before she got a transplant? Of course, Anna would put her on the transplant list, but she wasn't going to leave it at that. She was convinced that the reason the donation wasn't going ahead wasn't medical. That Ryan had changed his mind and it was nothing to do with the MRI scan or anything else.

If that was the case, she still had a fighting chance to change his mind back again. And she was willing to do anything – anything – to make that happen.

THIRTY-SIX

As soon as she left Mr Harris's office, Anna called Tina and asked if she could keep Libby for a few more hours. At home, she took a shower, blow-dried her hair, put on make-up. If she was going to do this, she had to give it her best shot.

By the time she left home, it was the middle of rush hour and, even though most people were commuting out of London at this time of day, the traffic going in was still torturously slow. Cars crowded together, both lines bumper to bumper. A driver a few cars back pressed their horn, and Anna's hand hovered over her own, wanting to second it. *Move out of my way.*

She wasn't expecting to see Ryan's car outside his house. He rented a garage two streets away, in which to keep it safe from opportunistic thieves or jealous key scrapes. It had always been her car that used to sit outside on the street. She'd only bought a car of her own once she was pregnant with Libby, not wanting to struggle on and off public transport with a pram. It only seemed like moments ago that she would look in the rear-view mirror at the baby seat behind. Checking that Libby was awake, asleep, alive.

It had been a few months since she'd had to park on a busy London street and she'd lost the knack of reverse parking between two other cars with a whisper of space in front and behind. Right now, she was too agitated to even try.

But this, at least, went her way. At the end of the road, four doors from Ryan's, there was a space which she could drive straight into. She turned off the ignition and sat still for a few moments. Letting go of her grip on the steering wheel, trying to slow the thump of her heart. Then she grabbed her bag from the passenger seat and got out.

It took three rings of the doorbell before she heard movement in the hallway behind. The doorbell was new: it looked like one of those modern Ring doorbells where you could see a video of whoever was at your front door. She recognised it because Catherine had bought one for their mum a few months ago for added security. Was Ryan watching her? Making her wait? *Come on, come on.*

Even the opening of the door was slow. It was all Anna could do not to step forwards and slam it all the way open herself.

Ryan rubbed at his eyes, as if he'd been staring at a computer screen. 'Anna? What are you doing here?'

'I need to say something. Can I come in?'

He shrugged, stood back. 'If you must.'

The hallway hadn't changed much since she had lived there, apart from the absence of the family photographs she'd taken with her, but the lounge looked very different. New dark red sofa, rectangular glass coffee table, low mahogany cabinet running along the far wall. For a moment, she wondered where the old furniture had gone. Despite the fact it had technically belonged to both of them, it certainly hadn't been offered to her and Libby. She wasn't about to fight that battle right now, though. *Stay focused.*

Ryan didn't offer her a seat, but she took one anyway. The new sofa was firm, resistant, nothing like the comfortable three-seater that had been there before. 'Why have you changed your mind?'

With no sense of urgency whatsoever, Ryan sat down on a chrome-legged chair opposite. His legs apart, eyebrow raised. 'Weren't you told? My kidney wasn't viable. Sad, but true.'

His eyes were full of cold mirth. Anna dug her fingernails into her palms. 'It's not true, though. Is it? That's just what a doctor says when someone backs out of a donation.'

Ryan leaned back in his chair and appraised her like a used car. 'Veritable Miss Marple, aren't you?'

She had to say everything she'd come to say before she lost her nerve. 'And my sister told me about your solicitor's letter, too.' She took a deep breath. 'I'll do anything, Ryan. Anything you want. The maintenance, custody arrangements, my share in the house. Take it all. Whatever I need to do to make sure that this happens, I'll do it.' She looked him straight in the eye, needing him to understand what she was saying. 'Anything.'

The slight curve of his mouth was a giveaway that he understood completely what she was offering. 'What's brought this on? This sudden generosity?'

Maybe if she told him why she was so frightened, it would help. 'Max. Libby's friend. He died.'

Saying it out loud didn't make it any more real. Despite Max's ongoing treatment, he'd been so full of life. Full of character. Funny, bright, caring: how were his parents ever going to be able to go on without him?

Ryan merely nodded, as if she'd given him a logical explanation. 'And it's made you worry about Libby?'

Did he need it spelling out? 'It's made me realise that this disease is unpredictable. She might be okay right now, but things can change. Quickly. And it is better for her to go through the operation when she is in good health than wait until it's urgent.'

'Better for her. But what about me?'

What about me? How the hell could he sit there and say that? Being a parent was about putting someone else before yourself. Anna would give anything, *anything*, to make Libby well. Which was why she was here. 'I know it's a big thing to do. But you will be fine. Once it's over, you'll have no long-lasting effects.'

'Oh, you're a medical professional too, now, are you? Is that something you do in-between spooning mashed potato and baked beans onto the plates of five-year-olds?'

She wasn't going to rise to it. 'No, of course not. But I have done a lot of research, Ryan.'

'Oh, *research*.' His mocking tone crept over her and made her skin crawl. 'But there's a lot of difference between research and actually being the one to go under the knife, wouldn't you agree?'

She couldn't stop herself. 'Are you scared?'

His eyes flashed at that. 'Scared? You want to take a look in the mirror. You're the one who looks scared.'

She didn't need to look in the mirror to see that. She knew what it would reflect. White face, strained expression, absolute terror. 'I'm not ashamed to admit it.' She'd gone too far, she could tell that by the set of his mouth; the old fear crept over her. She needed to pull this back. 'I mean what I'm saying, Ryan. I'll do whatever you want. I'll come back. Or I'll sleep with you. Or... anything.'

He glanced in the direction of the door. Was he not alone? Was Nicole here, too? 'What makes you think that I want you?'

'You said. That night at my house.'

'Said what? That I wanted to be with you? I don't think so.'

He had said that, hadn't he? Made it clear that he wanted to be back together with her? Had she misread the situation? Her face started to heat up. 'You talked about us being a family again.'

Ryan waved a hand of dismissal. 'You've always had your own version of events. Why would I want to be with you? Look at you. A school dinner lady. You dress like your mother. And you're such a doormat. You've really let yourself go, Anna. There's nothing for me here.'

This time, he used his hand to sweep the length of her in negative appraisal. It was humiliating.

But this wasn't about her. 'What can I do, then? Get your solicitor to write up the divorce papers the way you want them. I'll sign anything. Please, just don't let Libby down.'

Ryan leaned forwards, making a steeple of his hands, his elbows on his knees. 'Beg.'

She thought she must have misheard. 'Pardon?'

'If you want it so badly, get down on your knees and beg me.' He nodded towards the floor in front of him.

Surely he must be joking? He sounded like a clichéd bad guy from a B-movie. 'Seriously, Ryan, I—'

'Seriously.' There was an iron glint in his eye that she'd seen before, and it made her stomach tighten. 'If you mean it, you'll beg for it.'

Still, she thought he was going to laugh, mock her, tell her that she was pathetic if she thought he meant what he said. Even pretend it was one of his 'jokes'. But he didn't. He just stared at her and pointed at the floor.

During their marriage, there had been many instances which Anna had found humiliating. The way he'd spoken about her to others, in front of her. The way he'd left her waiting like a naughty child if she'd done something he didn't like. But this? This was a whole new level. Her throat was dry and she found it difficult to speak. 'Ryan, surely this is—'

'Beg.' Now his face was flushed, but this wasn't embarrassment. It was power. Control.

She wanted to slap him. To walk away and never come back. To take their daughter far away from him and never, ever let him into their lives again.

But she couldn't. Libby needed his kidney. And Anna knew it. If this was what she had to do, then so be it.

Without taking her eyes off him, she lowered herself to a kneeling position and clasped her hands together. 'Ryan, please give Libby your kidney.'

'You didn't say "beg".'

She squeezed her hands together so tightly that her knuckles stung with the pressure. 'Ryan, I am begging you. Please give Libby your kidney.'

He shook his head from side to side as if he couldn't believe what he was seeing. 'God, you really are pathetic. How did I not see it before?' He walked past her towards the lounge door. 'I'm afraid the answer is no.'

Anna froze. 'What do you mean?'

'What I mean is, I'm not going to do it. I know you're trying to guilt me into this by telling me about her little friend dying. But we both know that Libby is fine on dialysis. She's well. She can wait for a donor to come up on the list.'

Anna was still kneeling. She couldn't move. 'She's okay right now. But that could change any time, Ryan. That's what I'm trying to say.'

'So you can come back to me then, and I might reconsider.'

Anna stumbled to her feet. She was going to be sick; she needed to get out. But not before she'd given it one more try. 'Ryan, please, please reconsider.'

He looked irritated now. 'You need to leave, Anna. And don't tell Libby about this yet. I want to tell her myself. I don't want you twisting it.'

'Twisting it?' She practically spat at him. 'How the hell can I twist it? How the hell are *you* going to twist it in a way that makes this sound okay? It is not okay.'

'Stop shouting, Anna. You're just making a fool of yourself.'

She needed to get out of the door before she started to cry. She wasn't giving him the satisfaction of seeing that, too.

The ten paces towards her car became more and more blurry, until she practically fell into the driver's seat. Then she gave in to it. Covering her face with her hands, she sobbed and sobbed. All the tension, all the worry, all the fear of what she was going to have to do, plus the absolute fury that he could stand there and tell her that he wasn't going to do this for his own daughter. It all came out in lumpy, jagged sobs. She was crying so hard that she barely heard the knock on her window.

When she looked up, there was Nicole's pale face looking back at her.

THIRTY-SEVEN

Nicole made a motion with her hand to ask if she could open the door and Anna nodded. What did she want? Because if she was going to warn Anna off again, she wouldn't be held responsible for her response.

But once she was sitting down on the passenger seat and looking at her, Anna saw that Nicole's face was white, her eyes round and wide. When she spoke, her voice was gentle. 'Are you okay?'

If she hadn't felt so wretched, Anna might have laughed. Her make-up was halfway down her face, her nose was running and she probably had a red mark on her head from leaning against the steering wheel. Did she look like she was okay? 'How much did you hear?'

Nicole faced away from her and looked out of the windscreen. 'All of it.'

For the next few seconds, they sat in silence. Anna replayed her conversation with Ryan in her head: it couldn't have been easy for Nicole to hear.

Nicole twisted back in the passenger seat and faced her. 'I can't believe that he's just done that to you. The way he spoke. And then, making you... Oh, Anna, I feel sick. It was just so... so horrible.'

Nicole reached out a trembling hand as she spoke, then retracted it. Even though she was upset, and clearly shocked, Anna saw a glimpse of the Nicole she'd known. Although that Nicole hadn't been quite so naïve. 'Really? You can't believe it? I'm surprised.'

Nicole wiped at her eyes with the heel of her hand. 'I know he can be... cutting. But that... it was just so cruel, so...'

'Evil?' Now that her first wave of grief had subsided, Anna's fear was turning colder, harder.

Nicole pressed her lips together. Her eyes filled again. And she nodded.

Anna turned away. She had no room right now for someone else's grief or disappointment. Nicole didn't deserve her sympathy.

Nicole's voice was barely a whisper. 'Is what you said in there true?'

Anna kept staring out of the window. The small garden in front of her was neat and pretty. A nice family probably lived there. 'Which part?'

She heard Nicole take a deep breath. 'Did Ryan actually ask you to go back to him? Did he want you to come home?'

Anna was beyond caring about anyone else except herself and Libby. She was also beyond telling anything but the truth. She turned back to Nicole and looked her straight in the eye. 'Yes. He did.'

Nicole chewed at her lip; she looked as if she was fighting to stay in control. 'I see.'

Despite everything that had happened, Anna couldn't help but feel a little sorry for her. 'I tried to warn you about him, Nic. He is not a good man.'

Nicole twisted her hands in her lap. 'And I don't suppose I am a very good woman, either.'

What could she reply to that? *No, you weren't. You were my friend and I loved you and you let me down.* What was the point? 'I know how persuasive he can be.'

Nicole was still chewing at her lip. She didn't used to do that. 'I didn't take him away from you, Anna. I hold my hands up and admit I have not been a good friend to you, but I didn't do that.'

Anna didn't speak. Nicole seemed to take that as permission to keep going. 'When you left, he came to me. He was in pieces, Anna. I've known him since we were at school together and I've never seen him like that. I was scared he might do something stupid to himself; that's how awful he looked.'

'The something stupid had come beforehand – you know that. When I found out that he was sleeping with someone from work. I walked in on them, Nicole, remember? I was supposed to be staying with my mum, but I'd forgotten Libby's toy. I came back to get it. I told you all this at the time. And yet you still wanted to be with him?'

At least Nicole had the decency to blush. 'When he told me about it, he was so remorseful. Said that he'd been a complete fool. That it was all the stress of... well, he said you didn't want to be with him anymore, that he'd needed someone to...' She trailed off at the look on Anna's face.

'Sounds pathetic when you actually say it aloud, doesn't it?'

Nicole chewed at her lip again. 'Yes.'

'How long before you were in his bed?'

Nicole coughed. 'It wasn't like that. I was your friend, but I'd known him forever. I had to be there for him.'

'How long?'

'We just talked. Spent time together. He really opened up about a lot of things.'

'How long?'

'Absolutely nothing happened before I was sure that it was definitely over between the two of you. You were the one who told me you were never going back.'

Anna could remember that phone call. From her mother's tiny guest room. Curled up on the bed like a child. Back when she'd thought that Nicole was still her friend. 'So, about a month?'

'It just happened. He was really upset; I came over and... it just happened.'

When Anna had overheard Ryan and Nicole's phone conversation in the hospital, she'd felt so betrayed. Her mind had been busily unpicking the past, trying to work out if there had been something between them before she and Ryan had split up. 'Have you always had a thing for him?'

Nicole started to shake her head and then stopped. 'I suppose I was attracted to him when I first knew him. But then it turned into friendship, and I didn't think of him like that anymore.' Her head jerked up. 'I don't want you to think that I was coveting him all the time you were together. It really wasn't like that.'

Anna barely had the energy to shrug. 'It doesn't matter.'

They both sat and watched the rain, which had begun to spit on the windscreen. Anna knew she should go home to collect Libby from Tina. She checked her phone. Knowing how she worried about her daughter, Tina had sent her a couple of photos of Libby with Tina's daughter, Gracie. Gracie was putting make up on Libby and it looked like she'd also done something stylish with her hair. Libby would be having a great time.

Now Nicole was nodding her head, as if she was agreeing with some kind of internal monologue. 'I think he only got together with me to take me away from you.'

'Surely not?' The reply was instinctive, but as soon as it was out of Anna's mouth, she realised how easily it could be true. Even if it wasn't, the fact that they both thought it could be spoke volumes about Ryan. Nicole and she had been close. What better way for Ryan to end Anna's closest friendship than to sleep with her friend? Still, it didn't excuse Nicole's behaviour one bit. 'You were my friend, Nicole.'

Her voice was barely audible. 'I know. And I'm so sorry.'

The rain got heavier, rattling against the windscreen. It was odd, sitting so close to Nicole, and yet it wasn't. How many times had the two of them been next to each other in the car like this, on their way to a shopping trip or a restaurant? Memories of singing along to George Michael, or laughing at something that had happened to one of them at work floated to the forefront of Anna's mind. The problem was that those memories were now sullied by what had happened next. Why had Nicole done it?

Anna tried not to sound accusatory, but it was difficult. 'Do you know what I really don't understand? You knew what he was like. I'd tried to tell you often enough. You'd seen how he was. And yet you still started a relationship with him.'

Nicole shook her head, her eyes full of sadness. 'No, I didn't know what he was like, not really. I knew he was jealous. A little overprotective. That he could be moody. But I had no idea how far it went. I didn't know how he really was until—'

'Until it was too late? Until you were in love with him? Until he made you feel as though you were the unreasonable one, every time you questioned something he did?'

Nicole looked up sharply. 'He isn't all bad.'

'Oh, I know that.' Of course, he wasn't. Because if he was, Anna wouldn't have stayed so long, would she? Whether it was instinct or judgement, Ryan seemed to know the exact balance of how far he could push her before reverting to being charming and generous.

Nicole seemed to deflate a little in her seat. 'I just don't know where I am anymore.'

Anna turned and looked at her. 'Or who you are?'

Nicole pressed her lips together. When she opened them, Anna couldn't have been more surprised by what she said.

'I want to be tested. To see if I'm a match. I want to donate a kidney to Libby, if I can.'

THIRTY-EIGHT

Three weeks later, Anna was in the hospital with Nicole, waiting for her blood test results.

They were both relieved that Nicole had a different doctor to Ryan's. Dr Fields was young and enthusiastic and had agreed to get Nicole through the first stages of the process as quickly as possible. She'd arranged for Nicole to have the initial blood tests on the same day they first met.

Between the two of them, there was a quiet truce. Anna would never be able to forget that Nicole had betrayed her, but how could she be cold towards the woman who was offering to try to save her daughter?

A few seats along from where they sat, a young mother was feeding her baby, balancing him on her knee and helping him to feed himself from a small yogurt pot. Every time he managed to get more in his mouth than down his top, she praised him for being a clever boy. Watching them together, Anna felt an emptiness inside her that she might never fill. Was it nostalgia for Libby's baby days or a yearning for that child she might have had?

Nicole sighed. 'I would have liked one of those.'

That was surprising. Nicole had never seemed particularly bothered about children. 'Really?'

'Ryan always said he doesn't want any more children.' Nicole

blushed as she spoke, so Anna assumed he'd actually said a lot
more about what he thought about being a father. *Selfish prick.*

One day, she might tell Nicole the price she'd paid for Ryan's
reluctance to have another child. But not today. 'Well, you're free
to meet someone else now. Someone who *does* want children.'

Nicole shook her head. 'I don't know. What are the chances of
meeting a man who I like, who likes me, who wants kids before I'm
too old to have any? Time is ticking.'

The way she listed it off like that, Anna could see where she
was coming from, but that was far from the complete truth. 'You'll
easily meet someone else, Nicole. You're beautiful. And funny and
clever.' She wanted to add, *and you were wasted on Ryan*, but she
thought better of it.

'Maybe it would have been easy once, but I'm not sure that's
still the case. Men our age are all going for younger girls now. I
think I've missed the boat.'

'Not all men are like Ryan, you know.' As she said it, Anna felt
the truth of it. She thought of Paul Benham: his kindness, his
patience, his honest blue eyes.

A door opened and a nurse called out Nicole's name. She
smiled at Anna. 'Wish me luck.'

'Good luck.' Anna watched her go. It was only a few weeks ago
that she'd sat here and waited for Ryan. This was a complete long
shot – Nicole wasn't a relative – but there was still a chance and
Anna had got to try anything.

Hopefully, Nicole wouldn't be in there too long. She hated
leaving Libby alone on the dialysis ward: especially now she didn't
have Max for company. She missed him so much, everyone did. It
was a much quieter place without him.

But she'd felt as if she had to be here with Nicole. The night
they'd sat in the car together, Nicole had made up her mind to
leave Ryan. Finding out about his proposition to Anna had been
the final straw. However grateful she was to Nicole for offering to
be a living donor, Anna had asked her several times to reassure her
that she wasn't doing this as some kind of penance. Once she knew

the connection between the two of them, even Dr Fields had stipulated that Nicole have additional sessions with a counsellor on site to make sure that she was making this decision for the right reasons.

Would they be able to rebuild any kind of friendship? Having spoken to Nicole a few times on the phone this week, Anna had realised how much she had missed her. Initially tentative, their conversations had become more relaxed; they'd even shared memories of some of the fun they'd had together. Could Anna ever get past the fact that Nicole had chosen Ryan over her?

The clock on Anna's mobile showed that Nicole had only been in with the doctor for five minutes, but it felt more like fifty. How long did it take to say yes or no? Mr Harris had put Libby on the transplant list at her last meeting with him and she'd stay on it unless Nicole was confirmed as a viable donor.

There were unread text messages from Ryan on Anna's mobile, too. She didn't read them these days, they were vile and accusatory, but Catherine had told her not to delete them. She might need them as evidence.

Ryan hadn't seen Libby since Nicole had left him, either. There had been one awful phone call where he had told Libby his version of events – that he was heartbroken that the doctors wouldn't let him donate his kidney – and then nothing. Anna had been forced to go along with his lies. Libby's world had already been rocked by losing Max; there was no way Anna was going to tell her that her father had let her down, too. As Catherine had suggested, Anna had sent Ryan an email asking him when he would like to spend time with his daughter, but he hadn't even replied to it.

Of course, there was little she could do to protect Libby from Ryan's lack of contact. It was painful listening to her ask Anna if she had upset him. Had she done something wrong? Anna had tried to pass it off as Ryan having a lot to do at work, but she wasn't sure how much longer that excuse was going to hold out. Libby was a bright kid, soon she was going to work it out for herself.

Dr Fields' door clicked open further along the corridor and everything in Anna tightened in response. Nicole stepped out sideways, so she had her back to Anna, shaking the doctor's hand. Dr Fields was speaking to Nicole, but her face was a blank sheet of professionalism. What was she saying?

When Nicole turned in Anna's direction, her face was ashen; she looked as if she might have been crying. Anna stood, but she didn't walk towards her. As Nicole got closer, she looked Anna in the eye, and slowly shook her head.

THIRTY-NINE

Anna tried to console Nicole, but her heart was heavy and she needed to get back up to the dialysis ward. She promised she would call her later that evening.

When she got back to the ward, there was someone talking to Libby. Until she turned around, Anna didn't recognise that it was Julie, Max's mum.

Julie smiled as Anna approached. The lines around her eyes were deep and fresh; she looked tired. No, not tired: defeated. Anna wanted to open her arms and hug her, but they didn't know each other well enough for that to feel natural. Instead, she made do with rubbing her arm. 'It's lovely to see you. How are you doing?'

That was stupid question. How did she think she was doing, after losing her son?

Julie shrugged. 'We're taking it one day at a time.'

'Of course. Look, I was just about to get myself a cup of diluted battery acid from the drinks machine. Can I interest you in a cup?'

Another weak smile. 'I was only popping in to bring some chocolates and flowers for the nurses. But how can I resist one for the road?'

Libby was already sneaking her headphones back on to carry on watching her iPad, so Anna didn't feel bad about leaving her for another ten minutes or so. The hard, plastic-covered sofas by the coffee machine were empty, so they wouldn't be overheard. 'I'm so sorry, Julie. I wish I could say something comforting, but I have no idea what.'

Julie held her paper cup in both hands. It was warm in there, but she shivered. 'There's nothing you can say. I appreciate it, though. Some people get so tied up in what the right thing is that they don't say anything at all. It's hard for everyone. It was nice to talk to Libby about him. She was honest and real. Kids don't have a filter, do they?'

Anna winced. She knew how blunt Libby could be. 'Oh, crikey. That doesn't sound good.'

Julie's smile was genuine. 'No, it *was* good. She just said that she misses him every day and she has got a new high score on *Subway Surfers* and she wanted to tell him and then she got sad because she couldn't.'

Her voice wobbled over the last words and a tear dropped from the end of her chin. Anna reached across and squeezed her hand. 'I'm so sorry if she upset you. She wouldn't have meant to.'

Julie waved her away. 'Really, Anna, don't apologise. It's not possible to upset me more; I'm already there all the time. When she said she missed him, it made me glad that he had had her as his friend. Glad to know how much he was loved.'

It was difficult for Anna to speak, because she was pushing down her own rising sadness. 'He was very loved. Such a wonderful little boy. I keep thinking of his little face on Libby's first day at dialysis. She was so scared and anxious about what was going to happen. His being here was a gift to us, it really was.'

Julie nodded, her eyes bright and full. 'That's how I feel about him. He was a gift. His way of looking at the world, the way he rolled back from every setback, saw the best in every situation. He taught us so much. I am trying to be happy that I had the gift of him as my son, and not be so angry that I didn't get to keep him.'

Her tears were flowing freely now and it was impossible for Anna not to cry, too. She moved onto the opposite sofa so that she could sit next to Julie. 'It's okay to be angry. It isn't fair that you didn't get to keep him.'

Julie fumbled for a packet of tissues in her bag. 'It's not right, you know? Your child going before you. It's not the way it's supposed to be. I lost my dad a couple of years ago and it was awful. But this? This is absolutely unbearable. I don't know how I'm going to get through it.'

Anna took the packet of tissues from her, opened it and gave her one. 'You don't have to think about that now. Don't think too far ahead. Like you say, a day at a time.'

'I don't know what to do with myself. Tim has had to go back to work and Luna is at school. All day long, I can't settle to anything. I find myself wandering the house, picking things up, putting them down again. When you have a child who is sick, your whole life revolves around them. Your weeks, your days, your hours: they are all planned out with where you need to be and what you need to do and what medication you need to administer. And now? Now I don't know what I'm supposed to do. Do I get a job? Do I volunteer somewhere? I'm just lost.'

'These are such big decisions. Right now, you need to just be.'

Julie shook her head. 'I can't. Because if I sit still, the weight of it just overwhelms me. It's like the grief is this huge heavy stone and I need to keep pushing it around, because if I don't, it will roll over and crush me.'

'Oh, Julie, I am so, so sorry.'

Julie put her elbows onto her knees and rested her face in her hands, her shoulders shuddering with her sobs. Anna shifted closer and put her arm across her back. As Julie cried, her voice was muffled, 'I just miss him so much. It hurts. It really hurts.'

Anna kept her arm around Julie while she cried. When she raised her head again, she pulled out another tissue and passed it to her.

Julie looked a little embarrassed. 'I'm sorry. We don't even know each other that well. Sometimes it knocks me over. And you're so kind.'

'Please. Don't apologise.'

After wiping her face and blowing her nose, Julie reached for her cup. 'This stuff truly is vile. I've been researching coffee vending machines, you know? Tim and I were discussing buying something for the ward. To make life a little easier for everyone here. But they are really expensive. We thought maybe a more comfortable sofa. I just want to do something. Make a difference. Make his time here mean something. Does that sound stupid?'

'Not at all. It's a lovely idea. And you are good people, to be thinking of others when you are going through all of this.'

Julie knocked at her forehead with the heel of her hand. 'Sorry, I haven't asked you how you are. It sounds as if you've been through it yourself in the last few days, too. Libby tells me that her dad isn't going to be a donor anymore?'

'That's right. We did have another possibility, but we've just found out that she's not able to be a donor, either.' This wasn't the time to go into detail about everything that had happened. It didn't feel right to roll out her disappointment in front of Julie. Not when Anna's daughter was still here, still doing okay. It was hard not to show it, though, when it was still so fresh.

Julie put her hands up to her cheeks. 'Oh, Anna. I'm so sorry. What a worry for you. And I can imagine that this happening to Max has made it worse.'

It was true, but Anna didn't want to say that out loud. 'She's on the waiting list now. Blood group O or B. We just have to hope that she gets a match soon.' She didn't end that sentence, except in her own head: *Before her condition worsens.*

Julie put her hands into her lap and stared at Anna. For a second, Anna worried that she actually had said those words out loud. Then she spoke. 'What about me? I'm B positive. I could be tested. I might be able to be a donor.'

Anna started. She hadn't been expecting that. Surely Julie didn't think that was what she'd been hinting at? 'No, it's good of you, but, no, it's too much.'

Julie was barely listening to her. 'I want to do something to help. I want to make someone's life better. What better way to do that? I mean, I know it's still a long shot that I will be a match, but – what if I am?'

One of the key points made about living donors was that they didn't feel obliged or coerced into the donation. They had to make their decision of their own free will. Anna clearly hadn't asked Julie to make this offer, but she felt like she would be taking advantage of someone at the most vulnerable time in their life. 'Julie, no. I am so grateful for your offer, but you need to focus on your family. On yourself.'

Julie grabbed hold of her arm. 'Don't you see? If I can save Max's friend, it would bring me so much comfort. I'd be doing this for me as much as for Libby. And I'd be doing it for Max. Please, Anna, please let me do this. Please let me at least try.'

Could she accept Julie's offer? After all, the transplant team would insist she spoke to a therapist to ensure that she was mentally prepared. Scheduling the tests would take time, which would give Julie space to think about whether she really wanted to do this. All of these questions might be redundant anyway, if they found that she wasn't a match.

There was a spark in Julie's eye that hadn't been there ten minutes ago. This wasn't Anna's decision to make.

This time, she did open her arms and take Julie into them, and they sobbed on each other's shoulders while the thin black coffee got cold.

FORTY

As Anna had predicted, the medical team had been concerned that Julie was in the right place mentally to be a living donor. Even after all the tests had come back – miraculously – positive for her being a match for Libby, they had insisted that she attend several counselling sessions to ensure that this was something she was doing for the right reasons.

Even Julie's husband, Tim, had been dubious at the beginning. The mere thought of another member of his family on the operating table had been too much for him to contemplate. Julie had kept on explaining it to him, though, and she told Anna that eventually he had understood. Hadn't he been a living donor himself? The date of the operation was set for the end of June.

That morning was bright and warm. Libby knew that she couldn't eat anything before she went into hospital. They had to be in early, despite the operation not taking place until later that afternoon. There would be a host of last-minute checks and tests. One of the first things Anna had done was to check her phone to see if there was any kind of message from Ryan for Libby. There was nothing. In the three months since Julie had offered to become a donor for Libby, he had only been to see Libby twice. He was sulking like a spoiled child. The limelight was not on him and he didn't like it.

Anna was still nervous about the custody issue. Catherine had reassured her that there were no grounds for Ryan to be given sole custody. Nevertheless, she needed to keep him informed on absolutely everything to do with Libby, whether he replied or not. That was why she had sent him both an email and a text that Libby's operation was today.

Anna had made a 'hospital bag of treats' for Libby to take in with her, and had wrapped it up for her to open. New pens, colouring sheets, a book, a glittery hairbrush, some accessories and small bags of sweets to have after the operation was over. Libby squealed when she found all the hair clips and a bottle of longed-for nail polish. 'Thank you, Mummy.'

'You are welcome. The nail polish is for when you come home. I don't know if you're allowed it in hospital. Would you like me to plait your hair and put the clips in?'

Libby turned around and passed the new hairbrush to Anna. 'Can you do two plaits, please?'

'Your wish is my command.' Brushing through her hair, Anna realised how long it had got. She still hadn't got used to the fact that Libby was seven now. What was that quote? *Give me a child until he is seven and I will show you the man.* What about the girl at seven? How much of the adult Libby was already formed by now? What traits and thoughts and ideas about herself and the world would she take through with her for the rest of her life? Her genes were half Ryan's and half Anna's. What did that mean for the woman she would one day become?

While Anna brushed her hair, Libby threw rolled-up wrapping paper for Patches to pounce on. It made the job much slower, but Anna wasn't about to deny her the giggles it was giving her. Hopefully it would also tire Patches out before she dropped him off at Tina's on their way to the hospital. Tina had kindly offered to keep him until Libby came home.

Once Libby's hair was finally brushed free of tangles, Anna parted it down the middle and started to plait one side. 'How are you feeling this morning?'

'A little bit scared.'

If only Anna could have the operation in her place. 'Well, that's completely normal, Libs. But after today, everything will be much easier. No more dialysis.'

She'd said it to make her feel more positive. But the dialysis would always make them both think about Max. And about Julie.

'Will I see Max's mum today?'

'I don't think so, but I'm not sure. Would you like to?'

Libby thought about it for a few moments, clipping and unclipping the hair accessory in her hands. 'Yes. I think I would.'

It was actually more straightforward than Anna had thought it would be to see Julie, because they all turned up at the hospital at the same time. Watching her walk across the car park, Tim holding her hand, it struck Anna again what a huge thing Julie was doing for them. It brought tears to her eyes.

Julie's smile was wide enough to hide her nerves from Libby, if not Anna. 'Hey, Libby. How are you feeling today?'

Her kindness knew no bounds. Libby's voice was small. 'A little bit scared.'

Julie nodded. 'Me, too. Shall we sit on the bench for two minutes?'

She glanced up at Anna as if to check that this was okay, so Anna nodded. As if she would refuse this woman anything for the rest of her life. Libby sat down on the bench next to Julie. 'Are you scared it's going to hurt, too?'

Julie tilted her head to the side so that Libby could see she was taking her question seriously. 'Maybe a little bit, but I know that the doctors will be able to give me medicine to stop it from hurting, so that will be okay.'

'Was Max scared when he had his operation?'

Anna didn't want Julie to be upset by talking about Max, but she remembered Julie's words on the dialysis ward: *It was nice to talk to Libby about him.*

'He was the same as you, I think. A bit scared that it was going to hurt. But he was brave like you, too.'

'Max's didn't work. He told me. What happens if this doesn't work? Will you be cross with me?'

Anna was surprised. They had talked about Max's transplant and she had done her best to reassure Libby that it was very unlikely that this would happen to her. But she had never said she was worried about Julie being cross.

Julie looked startled, too. 'Oh, sweetheart, why would I be cross with you?'

Libby looked down at her lap where her hands were twisting at the fabric of her summer dress. 'Because you are having a big operation and giving me your kidney and if it doesn't work, you can't have it back.'

Julie reached out and took Libby's hand. 'I wouldn't want it back. I want to give you this kidney like a present. You don't give presents back, do you?'

Libby shook her head, but she didn't look very certain. 'But sometimes you give them to the Oxfam shop so that another little boy or girl can play with them.'

Julie's eyes were full and Anna could see that she was battling to keep her voice calm and her face happy. 'When Max had his operation, I really, really wanted to give him my kidney. Just like your mummy wanted to give you her kidney.' Julie looked up at Anna and her face made Anna's heart ache. 'But, like your mummy, I couldn't do it. This time I can, and it makes me so happy, Libby. You make me so happy, that you are going to have this operation and I can help you to be well. It's like I wanted to give Max a present and I couldn't, so I'm giving it to you instead.'

Libby looked up from her hands. 'Like when you gave me all Max's Nintendo games to play?'

Julie bit her lip, taking a moment to calm herself. 'Yes. Like that. One day you won't want those games anymore because you've played them until the end. One day the kidney I'm giving you might not work anymore and you'll need another one. That doesn't mean I won't be glad I gave it to you. I'll never stop being happy about that.'

Libby smiled at Julie, then she reached over and gave her a huge hug. 'Thank you for all my presents. The games and the kidney.'

Julie's eyes were closed as she hugged Libby tightly, her cheek resting on the top of her head. 'Thank you, Libby. For being such a lovely friend.'

Once they were in the hospital, they had to go their separate ways. Anna promised to come and visit Julie as soon as the operation was over. There was so much that she wanted to say to her, but now didn't seem the right time. She watched Julie and Tim walk down the corridor away from them and pause for a moment. Tim turned Julie in to his chest and wrapped his arms around her as her shoulders shook. Anna turned away: it was too private and painful to watch. 'Let's go and find your bed, Libby. And we'll ask the nurses if we're allowed to paint your nails.'

It didn't take long to get Libby settled into her bed with her colouring books and pens around her. All of the nurses were cheerful and kind as they did all the observations they needed. The worst part was having the cannula put into her little hand, but the 'magic cream' did its job and Libby barely flinched.

Libby had just decided to get her Nintendo console from her case when Anna's phone beeped with a message. She was expecting it to be her mum or sister, wishing Libby luck. But it was Nicole.

Ryan is on his way to the hospital. He wants to stop the transplant.

FORTY-ONE

There was only one entrance to the hospital from the car park, and Anna was waiting there for Ryan when he arrived. He spotted her straight away and marched over to where she stood with her arms folded.

'I want this operation stopped.'

'What are you talking about? Don't be ridiculous.'

This seemed to inflame him even more. 'I have changed my mind. I want to donate my kidney. Not some stranger.'

'Everything is ready to go, Ryan. We don't need you.'

She hadn't meant to make that sound so bitter, but she could hear that she had. He picked up on that straight away. 'So now, who is the one who is putting themselves before Libby's health? Just because you don't want me to be the one to donate a kidney, you are going to—'

'Enough!' Anna hadn't intended to raise her voice, but she couldn't bear to listen to him for another second. She lowered it straight away. 'You know that you are lying. We both know that you would end up backing out again.'

Ryan seemed to be enjoying the fact that there were people looking over from where they were sitting on nearby benches. 'I see how it is. It's always me who is the villain, isn't it?'

The attention of strangers was excruciating. What must they

be thinking of her? 'Ryan. You need to leave. I will call you when Libby is out of surgery. Then you can come and visit her.'

'It's always on your terms, isn't it? When you say I can see her. When you decide to call me. Where you decide to live. It's always the same with you, Anna.'

He was right about one thing: it had always been the same with her. Putting up with his judgement, his control, his lies. But not today. 'I won't have you making me feel guilty any longer, Ryan. You made me feel like I was nothing. That I couldn't make a decision on my own without checking it with you. But that's changed. Libby is your daughter and, as long as she wants you in her life, I will support that. But you need to watch out, Ryan, because that little girl is growing up and she is going to realise who you are. Do you want to go in there and tell her that you are stopping this transplant from going ahead? That you are the reason she has to go back to dialysis?'

She stepped forwards, pushing her face close to his. Her heart was thumping, whether with fear or adrenaline, she wasn't sure. He looked uncertain, like she'd rattled him. 'If it's not—'

'Not what? You and I both know the truth, Ryan. That you were too scared or too selfish to donate your own kidney. Right now, Libby doesn't know that. As far as I am concerned, she doesn't ever need to know that, because it would hurt her more than I'm willing to allow. But if you do anything to stop this transplant today, I will make sure that everyone in your life knows. Your friends, your family, even the damn CEO of your company.'

She'd never seen Ryan look so uncertain. Was he trying to work out if she was bluffing? His face twitched as his mind clearly clutched at ways to wrestle this situation back under his control. 'You think you're so clever, don't you? Well, she can have this transplant. Because once she no longer needs dialysis, there will be no reason she has to live here, close to the hospital. Maybe I'll apply for full custody. After all, my solicitor has enough evidence of the times you haven't kept me in the loop with Libby's life. How would you like that?'

Anna had no idea if he was telling the truth, but she had to trust that the legal system would never take a child away from a mother who had done nothing but put her first. 'I'm glad you mentioned your solicitor, Ryan. She'll be getting a letter this week, listing your unreasonable behaviour.'

Ryan laughed. 'Unreasonable? Not giving up my kidney is unreasonable?'

'Not that. The way you've acted for years. The threats. The vile remarks. The nasty behaviour.'

He laughed again. 'You are a piece of work. That's all in your head. How are you going to prove that?'

There was no need to answer his questions any longer. 'And there is also the adultery, of course.'

Even that didn't wipe the smile from his face. 'What adultery? There is no evidence that I have been anything other than a doting husband and father.'

Nicole stepped out from behind him and came to stand by Anna. Anna hadn't even seen her arrive. 'Yes, there is.'

Ryan's lip curled into a snarl. How had Anna ever found him attractive? He looked from one of them to the other. 'Oh, I see how it is. All girls together, eh? Sisters forever?'

His poisonous laugh made Anna shudder. 'Just leave, Ryan.'

He turned his attention to Nicole. 'This might explain why the sex wasn't great, eh?'

He took a step forward. Anna felt Nicole flinch beside her. She put a hand on her arm.

Someone must have called for a security guard because a man in uniform appeared, holding the radio on his belt like a gun on a holster. 'Is everything okay here? Is this man bothering you, ladies?'

Anna shook a smile at him, then squeezed Nicole's arm and looked Ryan straight in the eye. 'No. He's not. Not any longer.'

FORTY-TWO

Signing the consent form for Libby's transplant was a tough thing to do. Ticking a box to show that she understood that there was a chance – however small – that Libby wouldn't make it through the operation, was terrifying. They had been through so much in the last few months to get to this point, and she'd spent so much time reassuring Libby, that she hadn't had time to really think about the operation itself.

Libby looked so tiny on the bed in her hospital gown. Anna was glad that she'd brought her lots of things to do. She seemed quite content to rotate between her colouring and the console and her reading book. For Anna, the wait was torturous. Julie's operation would happen first, during which the first team would retrieve the organ, then there was another team who would test it to ensure it was suitable and then, finally, Libby would be taken into surgery by a third team. She was grateful for each and every one of them.

Anna's mum had wanted to come to the hospital with them this morning, but they'd agreed that it would be calmer and quieter for Libby if it was just Anna. As soon as Libby was wheeled into surgery, though, Anna called her mum. The phone barely rang once before she answered. 'Hello? Anna?'

'She's gone down, Mum.'

'I'm on my way.'

. . .

Anna leaned against the wall behind her, breathing slowly to control the somersault of emotions in her belly.

One of the nurses touched her gently on the arm. 'It's half-price muffins day in the canteen. It'd be a shame to miss it.'

Anna had been holding in the tears for Libby's sake, but this kindness made a few of them escape. She wiped them away with her finger. 'Thank you. I won't.'

It was mid-afternoon and halfway between lunch and dinner, so the canteen was quiet. Anna wasn't hungry, but the coffee smelled good and it would give her something to do other than swipe mindlessly through her phone and imagine the worst. There was only one other person in the queue, but it wasn't until he'd paid and turned around that she realised who it was.

'Tim? Hi.'

Tim looked startled, as if he'd been somewhere else entirely. 'Oh, hi, Anna, sorry, I was... Did Libby get down to theatre okay?'

How were this family so selfless that, with his own wife having just gone through surgery, his first thought was to ask after her daughter? 'Yes. All good. I'm a nervous wreck, obviously, but she's a superhero.'

Tim smiled; it cracked something in Anna's chest to see how much of him had been in Max. 'Yes, I remember that feeling. Well, actually, I don't know exactly, because I was still jacked up on an anaesthetic and morphine cocktail when Max was...' His voice wobbled and shut down his attempt to make a joke.

They had moved away from the coffee counter to talk, but Anna didn't feel as if she could hug him as she would have done Julie. This was a good man. A kind, good, loving man. This was what a dad should be. 'How's Julie? The nurse told us it had all gone well?'

'Yes. She's a superhero, too. She's still in recovery, but she's come through it all perfectly. The surgeon says it was textbook. She'll be pleased with that. She's always been an A-grade student.'

Making light of the situation was all well and good, but Anna had to say something. 'Tim, I just want you to know—'

He held up a hand to stop her. 'There's no need to say anything, Anna. I know there's nothing you can say which explains how you feel, and I also know what it means to you and Libby. You don't need to say a thing.'

'But Julie—'

This time he shook his head. 'Has done exactly what she wanted to do. I know she must have told you that I was scared about this, but she had made up her mind. And I understand, I do. So do you.'

Anna's throat was so tight she could only nod. She did understand. The need to give. The need to make things better.

Tim waved a paper bag in the air. 'She'll be out of recovery soon, so I'm going to get back with these muffins. I doubt she'll be allowed any for a while, but I'm not brave enough to take the chance.'

Anna couldn't just let him go like that. 'Can I give you a hug to pass on to your wonderful wife?'

'Of course.' Tim held out his arms and, as she squeezed him tight, she felt him gulp back a solitary sob. As they came apart, his eyes were full. 'You take care of that gorgeous girl of yours.'

She could barely whisper a response. 'I will.'

She was so busy blowing her nose that it wasn't until she'd picked up her coffee and looked around for a clear table, that she noticed a familiar face in the corner.

Nicole gave her a little wave as she walked towards her. 'Hi. How's Libby?'

'She's in surgery now. They've promised to call me if there's any news. I'm just waiting for my mum to arrive. How come you're still here?'

Nicole shrugged. 'I don't know, really. Ryan left and I just felt a bit wobbly. At first I thought I'd grab a drink before getting back into my car, but I haven't been able to move. I've been going back and forth about texting you to say I am here if you need me. I even wrote and deleted a message a couple of times.' She held up a take-away cup. 'This is my third cup of tea.'

Anna pulled out a chair and sat opposite her. I'm glad you're here.' As she said it, she realised she meant it. She'd missed her friend.

'Really?' The look of hope on Nicole's face was almost child-like. 'Oh, Anna. I've made such a mess. I felt like, these last couple of months, you and I were starting to get close again and then, Ryan being here today. It was my fault. I completely forgot that he had access to the calendar on my phone. I put the date of the Libby's transplant in there. He called me today to ask how I knew when it was, we got into a huge fight and he said...' She tailed off. Shook her head. 'Sorry. I'm sure you don't want to hear about all the things he said today.'

Taking Tim's lead, Anna almost wanted to joke about when would be a good time to talk to your ex-best friend about her ex-relationship with your ex-husband. Instead, she sipped at her coffee. 'To be honest, this is probably the perfect time. Right now, I don't care about anything except Libby coming out of that opera-tion. Ryan? Your relationship? None of it matters.'

Nicole chewed at her lip. The old Nicole would have made a dark joke, pulled a face, brazened it out. This anxious woman in front of her was a shadow of the woman she'd once been. Nicole lowered her eyes. 'I know we've already talked about this, but I am so, so sorry, Anna. I don't even know how I let it happen.'

Anna remembered saying those exact words to Catherine only a few weeks ago, felt the familiar twinge of guilt that came with the memory of what she'd let happen. But then she remembered Catherine's words, too. She reached out and laid her hand over Nicole's. 'I know better than anyone how persuasive that man can be. How he can turn your own logic on its head and make it sound okay. Let it go.'

One day she might tell Nicole just how far her blind trust in Ryan had taken her. But today was not a day for thinking about that. Today was about Libby. Whether or not she and Nicole could rebuild their friendship was a topic for another time.

Nicole seemed to understand that. She placed her other hand over the top of Anna's. 'Can I stay with you until your mum comes?'

Anna smiled. 'Yes. That would be nice.'

Anna was hovering outside recovery within two minutes of getting the call that Libby was out of theatre. The clock on the wall seemed to go backwards as she waited for someone to appear at the door and let her in. Finally, the door opened and she was greeted by another smiling nurse. 'She's all ready to see her mum.'

If Anna could have flown to her side, she would have done. There were a scary number of tubes and drains coming from Libby's little body. Mr Harris had told her what to expect, but it was still a shock. Libby's eyes were closed, but they fluttered open when Anna bent down to kiss her cheek. 'Hey, baby girl, you're all done.'

Libby nodded, still half under the anaesthetic. 'Can we go home?'

'Not just yet. But soon.'

Her eyes started to close again. 'Okay.'

Anna pressed her nose gently into Libby's soft warm cheek. It was okay. Libby was okay. It was all going to be okay.

EPILOGUE

Anna had finished her shift in the school kitchen, popped home to check on Patches, and was back in the playground in time to see Libby run out of her classroom. She looked so happy and healthy: pink-cheeked and breathless from running.

'It's half-term, Mummy! Time for our holiday!'

Last October, Libby had been able to go back to school, and the last three months had felt like being released from a hostage situation. Libby could go to sleepovers with friends on a Friday night and there was no rush to pick her up for dialysis the next morning. No fear that she was going to get sick.

It was strange, too. Longer periods of time when Anna didn't see her. A month ago, Libby had stayed Friday night with her friend Karis and they'd been having so much fun that Libby had called from Karis's mum's mobile to ask if she could please stay another night. Anna had cheerfully agreed, but she had missed her like a limb.

On a couple of those sleepover evenings, she had gone out with Julie. First for a drink and then for dinner. Julie had recovered quickly after the operation and had started a part-time job at the local library. She couldn't bear being at home alone during the day, she said, but wanted to be around to collect her daughter from school. Anna had to practically arm wrestle her to allow Anna to pay for dinner. The irony wasn't lost on either of them. How do you ever repay someone who has given your child a physical part of themselves? In three lifetimes, Anna wouldn't know how.

Ryan had been in and out of Libby's life. Big extravagant gifts and promises one minute, followed by weeks of little contact the next. He frequently tried to change arrangements, asking Anna to swap one weekend for another. Catherine, with her solicitor's hat on, told Anna to be firm. But if they had no plans, Anna let him do it. Not if it meant changing their own plans – hers or Libby's – though. Her days of organising her life around his were over.

Libby still idolised her dad. The weeks of little contact were quickly forgiven. This worried Anna sometimes, but as Tina reassured her, Libby would learn. As she got older and more knowing, she'd get the measure of him. The best thing that Anna could do was surround her with people who did act like decent human beings. People like Paul Benham.

Their relationship had stayed a friendship all the while Libby had been recuperating. Even after that, Anna hadn't been sure that she would ever want to date someone again. It didn't matter that her mother kept telling her that not every man was like Ryan; she barely trusted herself to choose wisely. On top of that, Libby had had enough change in her little life this last year; Anna didn't want to do anything to jeopardise their positive new chapter. Even when it was clear that their feelings for each other were not just platonic, she had been reluctant to start anything with Libby's teacher.

But now he wasn't Libby's teacher anymore. He had a new job, and from last September had been Deputy Head of a one-form-entry primary school in Chelmsford. Her last objection, he had gently pointed out last summer, was no longer true. That night, he had kissed her for the first time. And the part of Anna that had been catatonic for so long had begun to unfurl and wake up.

Paul was coming with them on this February half-term holiday. It was actually his friend's place they were staying at in Tenerife. It had been all Libby had been able to talk about for the last month.

The beach she was going to build castles on, the swimming pool she planned to swim in, the ice creams she was going to eat.

She wasn't the only one building castles. For the first time in a really long while, Anna knew that they were looking forward to the future. She had no idea how things would work out with Paul, but it was more than that. She and Libby could do whatever they wanted from this point on: they were the ones in control.

A LETTER FROM EMMA

I want to say a huge thank you for choosing to read *To Save My Child*. If you did enjoy it and want to keep up to date with all my latest releases, just sign up at

www.bookouture.com/emma-robinson

Your email address will never be shared and you can unsubscribe at any time.

The beginnings of the plot of this story came on a writing retreat when we were discussing family relationships. The thriller writer, and my friend, Sue Watson, brought up the idea that, whatever the cost to yourself, if your child needed a kidney you would ask absolutely anyone for their help. That got me thinking – who would be the person a mother would least want to ask?

It wasn't until I started to research coercive control, however, that I realised how many people have been affected by a relationship like this. I was very fortunate to have several people share their experiences with me. I am no expert on this subject, but if anything in Ryan's behaviour has resonated for you, or someone you care about, please do reach out for help and support.

I hope you loved *To Save My Child* and if you did, I would be very grateful if you would write a review. I'd love to hear what you think, and it makes such a difference helping new readers to discover one of my books for the first time.

I love hearing from my readers – you can get in touch on my Facebook page, through Twitter, Goodreads or my website.

Thanks,

Emma

www.motherhoodforslackers.com

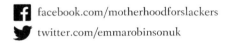 facebook.com/motherhoodforslackers
twitter.com/emmarobinsonuk

ACKNOWLEDGEMENTS

Grateful thanks, as always, to my brilliant editor Isobel Akenhead. Isobel, this one is for you: for picking *The Undercover Mother* from the submissions pile, for encouraging me to change genres and for pushing me (gently!) to go deeper and braver. I hope we write lots more books together.

The whole team at Bookouture are wonderful and supportive and I would thank them by name if I wasn't terrified that I'd forget someone! I must give a big thank you to my pal and PR Queen Kim Nash for all her help and to Noelle Holten and Sarah Hardy for their support. Thank you to Gabbie Chant for copy-editing and Laura Gerrard for proofreading, as well as Alice Moore for the cover design – you all do such a fabulous job.

The more books I write, the more I have to rely on the generosity of other people sharing their life experiences with me. This time, I have so many people to thank for helping me out with my questions on a variety of topics: from catering to coercive control to kidney transplants! Thank you so much, Sarah Buckwell, Tracy Halverson, Clare Noon, Emma Reed, Sanjay Mistry and Kerry Enever. Your help was invaluable. Any mistakes are mine. And, on the subject of mistakes, a huge thank you to my eagle-eyed friend Carrie Harvey for spotting all of mine when I can no longer see them. You're amazing.

My friends and family deserve to be thanked after every book, as I couldn't do it without their faith and encouragement and I wouldn't have space and time to write anything without my husband and my mum. (I could probably write a lot more without the kids and the dog, but I love them anyway.)

Lastly, to everyone who has bought, read and reviewed one of my books, I am truly grateful. I hope you enjoy this one too.

Printed in Great Britain
by Amazon

22672755R00152